The Confession

Also by Janet Bettle

Unnatural Causes

The Confession

Janet Bettle

PIATKUS

This is a work of fiction. In a work of this type, it is inevitable that there will be characters who are immoral, grasping and deeply unpleasant. All the characters in this book are products of my imagination. Reference to political offices and their occupants are made merely to provide a realistic setting for this novel. Names, characters, places and incidents are either the product of my imagination or used fictitiously. Should it transpire that despite my checking there are persons with similar or identical names or other characteristics to characters in this novel it must be emphasised that such resemblance is entirely coincidental and unintended.

For more information on other books published by Piatkus, visit our website at www.piatkus.co.uk

First published in Great Britain in 2000 by
Judy Piatkus (Publishers) Ltd of
5 Windmill Street, London W1P 1HF
email:info@piatkus.co.uk

The moral right of the author has been asserted

A catalogue record for this book is available from the British Library

ISBN 0 7499 0542 5

Set in Times by
Action Publishing Technology Ltd, Gloucester

Printed and bound in Great Britain by
Biddles Ltd, www.biddles.co.uk

Author's Note

I first saw the wreck of the *Richard Montgomery* ten years ago. It was one of those leaden-skied days with a lumpy, choppy sea to navigate – the sort of weather which always seems to exist whenever I've sailed in the Thames estuary. As we lurched our way onwards, out of the sea appeared a set of masts, reaching over at a crazy angle. It looked for all the world like the type of ship that transported tea around the globe centuries ago, living on in bizarre and muddy splendour off Sheerness.

As we drew closer I realised that I wasn't looking at a sailing ship at all. It was the wreck of the *Richard Montgomery* – an American liberty ship, built during the war, which had gone aground on a sandbank in 1944. What I had thought were sails was actually seaweed flapping from the masts which still stand.

It was downright creepy. And worse was to follow. As we sailed on by, I was told that the ship had gone down loaded with thousands of tons of explosives. The men had been evacuated safely, but it had been too dangerous to lift the bombs off. So there they have remained, to this very day. In time, they'll become inert. Maybe they already are. Nobody wants to risk finding out for sure.

So there we have it – a potentially lethal relic of the Second World War, sitting in the middle of one of Europe's busiest waterways. I couldn't believe it, and became fascinated by the wreck. What has happened there? What stories lie untold?

The wreck is real. There is a helpful factual account of what happened and what remains in *The Wreck of the USS* Richard Montgomery – *The Thames Estuary Timebomb* by FR Turner. My story, though, is fiction. But as ever, a story needs its roots in specialist knowledge and experience and I am indebted to others for help. Vernon, my husband, showed me the wreck in the first place and unwittingly started off this chain of events. He read the manuscript and his comments were invaluable. My parents-in-law, Daphne and Frank, are a constant source of support. The members and clerks of East Anglian Chambers have been incredibly kind and understanding towards my writing efforts – it really is a pleasure to work with you all, chaps and chappesses; and last but not least, my friends – particularly the gang at the school gate – thanks, girls, for the help and support you give on a daily basis.

Finally, I dedicate this book to my parents. My father, the late Captain Fred Wilkins, late of West Tilbury and Cornwall, was a voracious reader, a wonderful jazz pianist, and the sort of parent who encouraged me to dream. My mother, Charlotte Wilkins, late of Morriston and Cornwall, brought up four children in locations all over the world and held it all together for us. I don't know if they have books in heaven, but if they do, I hope they enjoy this one.

Janet Bettle

Prologue

August 1944, Thames Estuary

The crack as the hull split could be heard a mile away.

'Christ Almighty! She's going down!'

'Abandon ship!'

Officers raced along the decks, checking that the men were in position. The sirens rang out, their deafening notes sounding deep into the bowels of the *Richard Montgomery*. Already, the sea was flooding in. Metal started to shudder.

Then came the sound which would remain with the American crew for the rest of their lives. A high creak at first, it reached upwards to a point where the crew felt pain, followed by a shattering, plunging descent as the ship entered its death throes. It was like an animal *in extremis* – a low, scraping whine which was less heard than felt; a visceral tearing which pulled at every tissue in the body.

The men were quickly into the lifeboats, desperate to escape the spectacle. They wouldn't die . . . well, not from drowning at any rate. They were within sight of land with a port authority only too well aware of what was going on. No, they were more worried about the cargo.

Crazy really. They'd successfully steamed across thousands of miles of Atlantic with their lethal load, with God only knew how many U-boats out there – all of that just to break up on a sandbank in the Thames Estuary.

1

One rating hesitated. An officer took him by the shoulder.

'Come on. Time to go.'

The man turned towards him, his eyes calm.

'We can't . . . what about . . .'

Roughly, the officer pushed him towards the boat.

'Let the port authority worry about that. It's their problem.'

'But there's three thousand tons of explosive sitting in the holds – surely we've got to do something about it?'

The officer pulled rank.

'This is an order, sonny. Don't play fucking heroes or you'll blow us all up.'

'But sir . . . If that lot goes up, this part of England is going to be blown to kingdom come.'

'For chrissake, just get into the lifeboat. The port authority got us into this mess, they can bloody well get the cargo off . . . there's bugger all you or I can do about it at the moment. What you gonna do? Lift it all out and row it ashore?'

There was a shout from the lifeboat.

'Just get in, Frank. Do you want to kill us all?'

The rating shrugged his shoulders. Orders were orders after all. And the Brits would sort it out somehow. Sure, there was a war on, but one day they'd get there. Nobody would leave thousands of tons of live explosive sitting in the middle of its most important river estuary. Not there, not like that.

Quickly, he climbed into the lifeboat.

Chapter One

May 2000, The Old Bailey

She was about to lose her virginity.

That's what they called it . . . the first time on her feet in court, asking questions, making points. Running a case.

In this instance, only a small part of a case, but no matter. Abby Penhaligon had trained for precisely four and a half years for this moment.

'My Lord, my junior, Miss Penhaligon, will conclude the cross-examination of this witness.'

The judge, Mr Justice Dightfort, stared at her expectantly. The court was silent as she rose to her feet.

There was no going back now. This might be her first and last time, probably the shortest known career at the Bar. Better make it memorable.

In front of her were the two senior barristers who had spent the last two weeks locking horns: Waters and Ditchcombe. Their final battle. After this, things would never be the same again.

Daniel Ditchcombe desperately wanted to win his last case. Seb Waters QC wanted to stop him. It had been one hell of a struggle.

The charge was murder. Ryan Harrison, 18 years old, had been stabbed to death near a Basildon nightclub. The police knew who'd done it. Kieran Cragg. With a fistful of

3

previous convictions for some very nasty GBHs, and two spells inside, he had been involved in a long running feud with Harrison over some girl. He'd been in the vicinity when Ryan was killed. He'd done it all right, they just had to prove it.

Which was where things became difficult. Kieran Cragg knew the score only too well. A jury, blissfully unaware of his past ... Yes, he'd known Ryan. Didn't see much of him, now you mention it. That night? Yes, he'd gone out, but it was a Saturday night and everyone in Basildon went to that nightclub. He'd left and gone off home in the opposite direction to where Ryan had been found.

Daniel Ditchcombe had tried every trick in the book, but he was pitched against a witness who was exceeding all expectations. Polite, small, young; the jury were looking at him sympathetically. Daniel knew only too well that they did that when they were going to acquit.

Seb Waters, on the other hand, was feeling good. He and Daniel went back a long way. Best mates at Cambridge, they had received the two top scholarships to the Bar nearly twenty years ago. They'd done battle in court many times before. Seb had taken silk, getting the coveted title of QC, but Daniel had overtaken him now. In a week's time, he would be His Honour Judge Ditchcombe, one of the youngest judges ever appointed. Seb had never sought judicial advancement, he had found his niche and he knew it. But he wanted to win this one last time against Daniel.

And the prospects were looking good. He had to admit it, the client was playing a blinder. Lots of experience, of course. Kieran Cragg knew just what the jury wanted. Clean, well scrubbed and polite, he'd anticipated the hostile questions and deflected them with ease.

Of course Cragg had done it. Seb had seen the list of previous convictions and knew all about the feud with Harrison. But the lad had not admitted anything. His defence was that he had gone quietly home and there was

4

not enough evidence to prove anything else. So that was the line Seb had to take. He'd stopped thinking about the morality of it all long ago. The morality, he told those who took the trouble to ask, was in giving the defendant a chance to put his case. He had to have that right. It wasn't for the barrister to judge whether the man was telling the truth or not – that duty lay firmly with the jury.

Seb knew it was going well. If there was any doubt, he had only to look at Daniel Ditchcombe, who had become increasingly frustrated at his inability to make any headway. He was running over the same ground, and the jury knew it. They had started looking away, coughing discreetly, anything to relieve the boredom. Daniel knew he was up against an expert in Kieran Cragg, but he desperately wanted to go out on a high. Win your first case and your last and you'll be a happy barrister, because those are the ones you'll never forget.

And now he had handed over to his pupil, qualified only this day to get up on her feet and make her mark in the court. Seb had noticed her on the first day of the hearing: tall, curvy, blonde. There seemed something vaguely familiar about her. Probably seen her around the Temple somewhere. Still, lucky Daniel, spending the last six months in her company.

She looked a little nervous though, the girl. Understandable, if this was her first stab at cross-examination. For all that, the jury were looking at her, paying attention once again to the prosecution case.

'Miss Penhaligon?'

The judge was trying to prod her into saying something. Poor girl, it was always bloody awful the first time. Cragg waited patiently in the witness box. He would have noticed that the girl was nervous too, but had the sense not to smirk. If Seb had liked his client even the tiniest bit, he would have felt almost proud of him.

She spoke, her voice low and controlled.

'Mr Cragg . . . what happened to your leg?'

5

'Sorry?' He looked surprised for a moment.

'You seemed to have difficulty with the steps to the witness box.'

Her voice was a little shaky. Perhaps she was just trying to think of something sensible to ask. She'd regret that one.

Kieran Cragg collected his thoughts.

'I had a road accident a few years back . . . makes it difficult for me to get around sometimes.'

'Why didn't you mention it before?'

Oh dear, thought Seb. She's playing into his hands now. I could confidently put money on his reply.

'I don't like to complain – and I get a bit embarrassed about it. I can't run properly . . .'

Just as expected. This man was a real pro. Plant the idea ever so gently in the jury's mind without being too explicit. How could a man with a crippled leg carry out a murder?

She didn't flinch. Good for her.

'You find it difficult to walk up steps, then?'

'Yes. I avoid them, to tell the truth.'

She nodded, looking slightly embarrassed. Daniel Ditchcombe stared ahead of him, impassive.

'You've already told us that you were on your way home that night from the club.'

'Yes.'

'And home is at Alwyne Grove?'

'Yes.'

'Which we've seen on a map.'

The jury shuffled through their papers. They'd been handed a map at the start of proceedings. The nightclub was in a shopping precinct and they could see that Alwyne Grove was off to the east. Harrison's body had been found in the opposite direction.

'Can you just remind us which way you went home?'

Cragg allowed himself a smile. The silk had given up. It was downhill all the way now. This girl was a rookie, getting a bit of practice in.

6

'Sure. This is the precinct, there's my road. I simply went off down that side, and you can see the path towards Alwyne Grove.'

Perfectly straightforward, thought Seb. This Penhaligon girl was either very clever, or pretty dim.

'You can't do that without going up steps.'

Shit!

The heads of the jury members bobbed up almost in unison. Maybe she *was* very clever. Very clever indeed.

''Scuse me?'

'You have to go up 47 steps to get out of the precinct that way.'

Cragg was starting to go a little pink.

'Escalator. There's an escalator.'

She had him now.

'Only working when the shops are open.'

'No, I definitely went up it . . .'

The judge was smiling at her. He wanted a conviction, too.

'Miss Penhaligon, is this a matter which you have checked?'

'My Lord, I don't want to give evidence, but I am from the town in question. If Mr Cragg is not prepared to concede the point, Your Lordship might care to consider a site visit, and perhaps evidence from the precinct manager about the escalator operating hours . . .'

'Very well. Now Mr Cragg, what do you say?'

Cragg was clutching the front of the witness box.

Abby was on a roll now.

'Mr Cragg, do you accept that there was no way you could have taken the route you described without climbing those steps? Or do you want the judge and jury to take a trip to Basildon to see for themselves?'

This was extraordinary. She had changed her accent. Gone were the Cambridge tones. Now she was talking only to him, Essex to Essex. Just get it over with, Kieran, you know I've got you . . .

7

He shrugged.

'OK. I did go up the stairs.'

'Why deny it then?'

She was quick, giving him no chance to worm a way out. Seb sat back. The jury were loving it, watching her carefully along with everyone else in court.

She had it, he knew. That quality which meant that all eyes would turn to her in court. It was not just good looks, but something more. Some sort of presence. And she had it in spades.

'There is also a level way out, isn't there, Mr Cragg?'

He was on the defensive now. Gone was the polite expression. He was starting to look very pissed off indeed.

'I don't know what you mean.'

'Course you do, you've lived there all your life, haven't you? Let me show you.'

Maps out again, all eyes down.

'You go west out of the door, and do a square right round to the connecting road. Right past where they found Harrison.'

'That's a route home, certainly, but not the one I took.'

'Why did you lie about the steps, then?'

Wonderful, thought Seb. Daniel was right. We need her. We've got to have her.

The two men retreated to the café to drink their last coffee as equals.

'I'm going to miss this, Seb.'

'Oh, there'll be compensations . . . regular hours, decent pay. Don't break your heart, Danny boy.'

'Oh sure. Don't get me wrong, I'm glad I got it. But I'll miss the fights – especially with you.'

Seb grinned. 'Bet you say that to all your opponents.'

Daniel smiled. 'Glad I won the last one, though . . .'

Seb gritted his teeth.

'You can't take any of the credit for that, sunshine. If it hadn't been for your pupil . . . I shall rue the day I

8

persuaded you to let her get on her feet.'

'What did you think of her?'

Seb paused. 'I agree with everything you said. She's got it – you can tell, can't you?'

Daniel nodded. 'She really needs a chance, Seb. Brought up on a council estate, scholarship to Cambridge. She had her next pupillage lined up at 40 Crown Office Row, but they've had a bust up and gone their separate ways. I think she's going to do very well. Bit chippy, at times, mind you.'

'What about your Chambers? I don't want to tread on toes.'

'You won't be. She wants to do crime and family – some social commitment thing. I think she's mad with her brains, but there it is. She needs a generalist set like yours.'

Seb frowned. 'If I manage to keep it that way.'

'Is there a problem?'

'Only the usual – we've got a few who want to concentrate on the commercial crime stuff. I need to pack the benches with some more generalists to make sure they don't get their way.'

'Then you need some good pupils who want that sort of work.'

Seb nodded, his mind made up. In fact, he'd decided the moment she started to lay into his appalling client. There was something about her. It was difficult to describe but it was there, somehow.

'I think she'd be brilliant. I'll offer her a working pupillage with us as soon as I can. Can you put in a good word for me? I'll write to her tonight.'

Daniel grinned back. 'Thanks Seb. Probably best not to tell her I approached you – she's a bit sensitive about using contacts.'

The tannoy crackled into life. 'Those in the case of R v Cragg back into Court Two please. Verdict.'

Seb looked at his watch. 'Two hours and twenty minutes.'

9

'Twenty quid on a conviction?' asked Daniel.

Seb shook his head. 'No way. I don't want to end my career losing a bet to you as well as a verdict.'

Chapter Two

'Come and do your second six months training here.'

Abby took her time over her response. She had to jump the right way. Her whole career would depend on the decision she made right now.

She'd received the letter at Chambers and taken it straight to Daniel. He'd seemed very positive about it. It was a good set, there would be a lot of paying work for her to do. No, he hadn't known anything about it, but Seb had been very impressed with her performance in court.

She liked Seb. There was something about him that felt familiar, comfortable. Interviews were usually painful for all involved: tense, staged exchanges of pre-determined questions and meaningless answers.

Not this time, though.

She had stood on the threshold of 29 Pump Court for a while, early for the appointment. Painted on the white board outside were the names of the tenants of the Chambers of Sebastian Waters, QC. Hers could be there too, in six months time.

A short, fat man came out. Loud grey check trousers over white slip-ons. A creased white shirt, the sleeves rolled up chaotically. Shirt tail not entirely within the trouser band.

11

''Scuse me . . .'

The man paused a moment.

'Can I help you?'

'I'm due to see Mr Waters.'

He looked at her quizzically.

'I'm Abby Penhaligon.'

He smiled in welcome, a broad grin, and held out a rather pudgy hand. The nails, she noticed, were bitten down to the quick.

'Miss Penhaligon . . . Mr Waters is seeing you today, he did mention it. I'll just take you into the waiting room. I'm Ron Falconer, by the way, senior clerk.'

He showed her into a large room at the front of the building, complete with Georgian sash window, powder blue wallpaper and carpet thick enough to swim in. Someone had hung the most ridiculous curtain arrangement – bright yellow, swagged and tailed to within an inch of its life. A reproduction mirror hung over a rather good fireplace. There were some squashy sofas around three corners, and a large cherry table in the middle.

Abby checked her reflection in the mirror. Hair still tidy. Lipstick needed touching up but it would do.

She stood beside the table and looked through the pile of magazines stacked neatly on the top. Sixteen interviews she'd had in as many Chambers and they all had the same bloody titles. *Tatler*, without fail, *Homes and Gardens*, and inevitably . . . yes, there it was, *Country Life*. Girls in pearls and country estates for sale. What was it about barristers? Why did they play the country gentleman? It was patently ludicrous, here in the heart of the City, but they all did it.

Seb Waters was waiting for her answer. He was watching her intently, his eyes assessing, questioning.

Abby wasn't perturbed. She looked right back at him. He was stockily built, solid without being fat. He'd obviously been blond once, but it had faded with the years to a speckled grey. His suit was dark, beautifully cut. He held her gaze as she thought through her reply.

Abby kept her voice low and collected, sounding as though she had all the time in the world in which to balance competing offers. She prayed that he didn't know the truth. Privately, she suspected that he did.

'What are the chances of a tenancy?'

She had to get a permanent place, and quickly at that. A pupillage carried no commitment; unless Chambers decided to offer you a tenancy at the end of it, you were out. Thank you and better luck elsewhere. Her overdraft was up to twenty thousand now. There had been the fees and living expenses through Bar school, then pupillage. The best she could do on her current earnings would be to meet the interest on her debt. If she was going to make inroads into it she would have to get a permanent place pretty bloody quickly. If not, she may as well let the bank pull the plug now and put her out of her misery.

'I want to expand these Chambers,' Seb responded. 'We've lost three tenants recently – two high court judges appointed and one circuit judge. There could well be a tenancy going at the end of pupillage.'

Abby paused for a moment. She desperately needed to know how much money she was going to make over the next six months. She had to stave off the bank with something. But it was unthinkable to' ask. In a profession which was obsessed with money, it was the last great taboo. Yet she'd have to make an oblique enquiry at the very least.

'How much work is available?'

Seb paused. He knew what she was really asking. He'd been there himself once.

'Lots. Family and crime. We'll get you into court quickly. The family work won't pay for a while, but the criminal stuff will. You should receive around eight thousand pounds for the six months.'

She smiled at him and it was all he could do not to grin back like an idiot. This was the first time he'd felt any sort

13

of stirring for the opposite sex since his wife had left. Well, since a long time before that, now he thought of it. Pull yourself together, man. She's twenty years younger than you.

Clarrie had left him six months ago for another silk. It had been rather a relief. Now he could just get on with his work, rather than be forced to trail around the county social scene trying to make sensible conversation with women whose IQs were smaller than their hip measurements; the sort of women who viewed Alice bands as the height of style.

There was just him and Dad now.

Abby Penhaligon started to smile again slowly. She looked him in the eye and nodded firmly.

'It's a yes.'

Seb breathed out. Reel her in, he thought.

'Tomorrow early enough?' he asked.

'Tomorrow's just fine by me.'

'Rita!'

Damn! He had shouted. Just as he'd promised himself he would never do. Once he started doing that, he'd call out her name when he was with his wife. And the Honourable Lucinda, with her silly voice and rock hard eyes, would make mincemeat of him.

Oh shit. 'Rita!'

He couldn't help himself. She was appalling, ugly, loud, brash. But she was in bed with him and was giving him the time of his life. As she moved her hips one last time he gave in. Totally, completely, absurdly.

Afterwards they lay back on her bed. A gentle breeze wafted across the South Kensington rooftops. It came in through the open window, gently ruffling the thin muslin curtains. The bed, by now thoroughly untidy, had become too hot and they both lay still, satiated. After a few minutes, she spoke.

'That was pretty good for a first time.'

'Thanks'

He fumbled for his jacket and found it, flung carelessly onto the floor in his haste to reach the bed. Embarrassed now, he took his cigarettes from the inner pocket and lit up. For once in his rather comfortable life, Alexander Golightly had no idea what to do or what to say. Should he make small talk with his mistress? Protestations of love? Or should he just go now and hope like hell there would be a second time?

Rita Dengie looked across at him. Surprisingly reasonable lay, she thought to herself. Mind you, he'd been building up to it for months. Hints in Chambers, regular visits to her room, meal at Le Caprice. Today had been the inevitable result. A quiet day, a good lunch and a suggestion that they stop at her flat to pick up some papers on the way back to work. Like giving sweets to a kid, really.

As he lit up, she smiled gently at him. He had no idea what to do next, she knew. He was presumably shitting himself about his wife. They all did.

Well, he'd get over it.

Chapter Three

'Dorothy, let's find you a table.'

Marcus Kirkwall took the arm of the elderly lady and steered her gently across the crowded room. He found a threesome looking for a fourth, wished them a good game and left them to it. He negotiated his way back across the church hall, wondering if it was time to get the coffee going.

He had his dog collar on – he'd tried not to wear it in the past but had tired of explaining to people that no, he'd not forgotten or lost it or left it on the tube, he just didn't want to walk around being a vicar all the time. People saw a man in a dog collar as a vicar and nothing more. It defined him and he hated being defined by a small black and white collar. Besides it was bloody uncomfortable. But trying to explain his feelings on the topic was worse. The elderly in his Archway parish in North London expected a dog collar, so that was what they got.

And, by and large, Marcus liked his parishioners. If they wanted him to wear the collar, he doubted that, all things considered, he had the right to refuse. They had fought wars, paid taxes, worked hard. He respected them and was there to care for them. It seemed rather a small matter to be concerned about.

He looked out of the window as he negotiated a path through the tables. It was amazing that anyone had bothered

16

to put a window in. The gap between the church hall and the funeral parlour next door was no more than half a metre. Any light that miraculously found its way between the two buildings was lost amongst the filth on the outside pane. Window cleaners were a rare enough commodity, and it would take an obsessive anorexic to be able to clean the glass just there.

Magnus thought back to his interview earlier that day. About a month, the bishop had said. But it's a sideways step, out of the ordinary . . .

He had known what he was being told. Go for it, by all means, but it won't take you anywhere. No promotion prospects in drug projects in Edinburgh, Marcus. And somebody like you might have wanted a bit more of a career, instead of throwing your energies away on a bunch of no-hopers.

He'd worked that one out for himself the moment he saw the advert. But then he'd always known that he'd never hack it on the Church of England promotion ladder. Teamwork and diplomacy had never been his forte – truth told, he was bloody awful at both. All those meetings in bishop's palaces, committees about things that mattered bugger all to anyone, fat women in hats with accents: he'd never stay the course. No, giving that up would be easy.

Leaving his parish would be more difficult. But he had to go to Edinburgh. It was the only way he could try to make amends for his own failings all those years ago. Stop the dreams, the ceaseless self-criticism. Finally move on.

Marcus walked towards the side room, planning to switch the urn on. Marie was helping him in the kitchen, but he was on his own out front, running the whist drive, as his usual lay assistant was off with the flu. It was no great problem. It just meant that he would have to get on with organising the practical side of the afternoon rather than talking to his parishioners. He enjoyed chatting with them – their experiences of life were so different to his own. He'd read history at university, and his own family home was

17

furnished with portraits of long dead Kirkwalls who had served in famous battles.

The history he got from his parishioners was very different – tales of the poor bloody infantry; of the campaigns in the trenches; of life during the Blitz; of making ends meet in the depressions of the seventies and late eighties. The tales were by and large those of survival against the odds, and Marcus had become increasingly aware that this was an experience which was alien to him.

He'd been up most of the night, sitting with a lady who was dying. She hadn't wanted to go alone, and it was clear that the nurses at the hospital were too busy to spend time with her. So he had sat, holding her hand, until the night was almost gone. She had slipped away quietly in the end. On to better things, he hoped.

He was still in his clothes from yesterday – his jeans, scuffed around the knees, a crumpled shirt and the blasted collar. He'd not had time to shave and his thick dark hair needed a cut. People rarely noticed these shortcomings, though. His face was dominated by the brightest blue eyes people could ever recall seeing; Marcus's parishioners often said it was like having someone look right into your own conscience.

As he turned towards the kitchen, the swing door to the hall crashed open. He turned round quickly. There had been a bit of trouble with some skinheads a few weeks ago and he was ready to chuck them out again. The last time, they'd been a little surprised at their confrontation with Marcus. A public school education with compulsory boxing and seven years in the navy had made him well able to lay one of them out cold.

This time, though, the entrant was an elderly man. He must have been at least in his mid-eighties, by the look of him. His hair was straggling around his shoulders and he had a scrub of light beard. He was wearing a long, filthy raincoat, buttoned up even in this late spring weather. His shoes were gaping at the front and he carried an ancient

18

looking Sainsbury's bag. The weight of it seemed to pull one side of his thin body downwards.

The room became silent as the whist players turned to face him.

'I want the priest.' He spoke softly.

Marcus hurried over to him.

'I'm the vicar.' He held out his hand and touched the older man gently on the shoulder. Never, ever, turn someone away without listening to him first, he'd been told. Judge ye not on appearances.

'I have to make a confession.'

Marcus realised the problem immediately.

'I'm afraid that I'm a Church of England vicar. I can find a priest to take your confession – there's a Catholic church nearby . . .'

The man shook his head.

'No time. I must confess now. There's no more time, you see.'

As he spoke, Marcus smelt the alcohol on his breath. Combined with the body odour, it formed a heady mixture. Wonderful, he thought, a drunk with a confession on a Monday afternoon.

'Come this way.'

He showed the man into a side room, in which chairs and tables were stored. The heating had been left off and it was freezing. At least it might hurry him up a little. Marcus found two chairs and set them facing each other before sitting down. The older man sank into the nearest one, placing the plastic bag carefully beside him.

'Forgive me Father, for I have sinned.'

Marcus wondered whether to explain again that he was not a Catholic, but there was no time. The man was into the next part of what sounded like a prepared speech.

'I have murdered another man.'

Marcus sat up straight.

'You've what?'

He had no practice at all in taking confessions. He could

19

– indeed, he had to – listen and give absolution if needed, but he'd never had to do it before. He wondered how often this sort of thing happened to Catholic priests.

'I have murdered another man.'

'Tell me about it.'

The older man drew in a breath and paused for a moment.

'Yes, I will. God has told me to, you see. I have a radio and when I switch it on he talks to me through it. This morning, he said to confess before I died.'

Wonderful, thought Marcus. An alcoholic with a psychosis. Care in the community can work so well these days.

'Tell me what happened.'

This, he knew, was the way to play it. There was no point in trying to impose reality on someone in this state. Listen to what he had to say, give absolution and let the man be on his way.

There was a pause as the old man gathered his thoughts.

'It was 1945, you see. My name is Henry Jenkins. Then, I was a copper in Southend. Detective Inspector. Anyhow, I'd been up to no good and was about to get found out by a newspaperman. Denny Jacobs, his name was. And – God rest my soul – I killed Denny and framed one of his staff for it. It was VE night and I just dragged his body into the bloke's room – he was called Abraham James.'

Jenkins looked directly at Marcus as he spoke. Marcus felt a chill run down his spine.

'I investigated the murder and got Abraham to plead guilty to it. He'd been so drunk at the time he had no idea what he'd done and he was terrified he'd get the death penalty. So I offered him a deal and he took it. Guilty to manslaughter and a nice long spell away rather than the noose.'

Marcus sat quietly, letting the man continue. He paused again, and Marcus saw tears start to roll from his eyes.

'I'm going to die today, Father. I don't want to go to

hell . . .' He started to cry properly, spitting out his words through his sobs. 'I must be forgiven if I am to avoid damnation.'

Marcus spoke gently.

'If you truly repent of your sins, God will forgive you.'

'He won't. He has told me that I must do something first.'

'What must you do?'

The man picked up the Sainsbury's bag from its place beside his chair.

'Take this.'

He handed it to Marcus, who glanced inside. It was stuffed with £50 notes, neatly wrapped in bundles. There were dozens of them. No wonder the bag was so heavy.

'What the . . .?'

'Take it and use it to find Abraham James. God told me he is still alive. He'll have come out of prison in the Sixties, I reckon. Just find him, spend what you want from this, and then use it to pay for an appeal so that the truth can come out. You have my confession that I murdered Jacobs and framed Abraham James. Use it, or else I shall go to hell.'

'But why did you do it?'

'I can't tell.'

Marcus touched the man's hand lightly and looked into his eyes.

'Tell me – what you say to me will not be passed on unless you ask me to.'

The old man had stopped crying. He grabbed Marcus's hand. His fingers were sinewy, almost claw-like, and he clung on desperately.

'Yes, I must tell you. God told me that you should know whatever you asked. But I beg of you, never tell a soul what I am about to say now. And the money must be used to put things right.'

'I promise.'

'Very well. In 1944, a ship was wrecked off Southend

21

where I was working. It was an American liberty ship called the *Richard Montgomery* and it had come from America with a load of explosives on board. It went aground on a sandbank and broke its back, just sitting there in the middle of the Thames Estuary. It's still there now, in fact. Well, there was another cargo on board, apart from the explosives – it was all a bit hush hush, you see . . .'

The man continued his story as Marcus listened, unsure as to whether there was any truth in it. Still, sworn to secrecy on this part, at least, it would make no difference what the man said to him.

'. . . And I must seek absolution. What I did was a mortal sin.'

Marcus spoke slowly and clearly. 'I absolve you of your sins.'

There was silence for several seconds and he listened to the other man's laboured breathing.

'Shall we pray together a moment?' Marcus lowered his head.

When he opened his eyes, the man was gone, marching quickly through the hall towards the exit. Marcus ran after him, cursing inwardly at the tables which stood in his way. The whist players looked up, startled.

When Marcus reached the door, the man was on the pavement, walking amongst the throng moving towards the tube station. Marcus went to run after him but stopped himself. What could he say, after all? He had provided what the man seemed to be seeking, so there was no point in chasing him any further. He was clearly mad, anyhow. Lot of it about these days.

Marcus walked slowly back into the church hall. The tables were being packed up by the players as he re-entered. It was four o'clock – time he was getting along. They hadn't had their afternoon tea after all, although no-one seemed to be complaining.

Later, he helped with the washing up, but couldn't stop thinking about Henry Jenkins. The man had to be mentally

22

ill, you didn't need to be a shrink to work that one out. But what if he had been telling the truth?

It was unlikely, he knew. But then, never write anyone off, he always told his parishioners. Just because a man's ill, it doesn't mean you ignore what he says. Mind you, how on earth would you check a story like that? Marcus had enough on his plate at the moment, without spending days unearthing some long forgotten trial.

But if it was true . . . just thinking about it made him shiver and drop a cup on the floor. It shattered instantly. Quickly, Marcus found a dustpan and brush to clear up the mess. Some of the china had got as far as the plastic bag, still propped against the old man's chair.

The money. He had to do something about it. He was sitting in a church hall in North London with thousands of pounds in £50 notes. He had to move quickly, get it to the safety of a bank.

'Marie, could you close up and pop the key back to the vicarage?'

'Sure.'

Hurriedly carrying the bag in one hand, Marcus left the hall. He smiled goodbyes to his parishioners, anxious to be on his way. He tried to look nonchalant as he walked up the high street. If people knew what was in that Sainsbury's bag, he'd never get within a mile of a bank. Relax, he thought. The old man had got safely through the streets. There was no reason why he couldn't do the same.

At last, he was there. The bank was almost empty. Thank heavens the opening hours were longer these days.

He swung the bag onto the counter. As it landed, some of the bundles of notes started to spill out of the top. The cashier peered through the glass at him, astonished.

'Can you help me?' he asked.

Marcus had just counted the money, opened an account and paid it all in when he heard the sirens. He looked up through the window in time to see the ambulance race by, its noise deafening as it passed him.

23

Instinctively, he knew the sirens were ringing for Henry Jenkins.

'*I'm going to die today, Father.*'

The words echoed around his head. My God.

He hurried out into the street. There was an ambulance outside the tube station, its blue light flashing as it waited on the pavement. A police car was behind it, an officer remaining in the vehicle on the radio to control. There was already a gathering outside the entrance to the station, everyone complaining that the doors had been shut and they were going to be late. The crowd seemed to divide as he sprinted towards it, and the policeman looked up momentarily from his radio. He climbed out of the car quickly and walked towards Marcus.

'Just what we need right now. Will you come with me, sir?'

Marcus paused.

'There's a man screaming blue murder about God and sin – he's jumped in front of a train. They're doing what they can but you may be able to help.'

'Of course.'

Marcus took a deep breath.

The officer stopped. 'I've got to warn you, it's not a pretty sight.'

Marcus rode the escalator down to the tube line, the officer behind him. It seemed unworldly to be standing with one other person in a deserted tube station at this time of the day.

They walked swiftly towards the platform. The stopped train was blocking the view, just waiting, its passengers unloaded and ushered out of the way to a nearby platform. As they got closer, Marcus heard the screaming.

'Forgive me Father, please ... please. God – God in heaven ...'

There were murmurings and calls for saline, morphine, from the ambulance men.

Marcus reached the front of the train. Two men in

24

fluorescent yellow coats were straddling the central rail. One held a drip and was bending over to find a vein.

Marcus steeled himself and looked down.

It was Henry. He was lying across the rail. His face was intact and his eyes open. He screamed once more.

'It's OK,' called Marcus, keeping his eyes on the man's face. It was contorted in pure, indescribable agony.

'Don't let me go to hell . . .' pleaded the man.

Marcus stood at the edge of the platform. He willed himself to look away from the face.

Jenkins's legs had been completely severed from his body. They were lying over the electric rail, metres away. The train had cut them off just above the knees. Blood was pouring from the stumps, forming a puddle underneath the rail. He hadn't hit the live rail himself and had escaped electrocution. But this was far, far worse. The man was raving, in appalling agony, twisting and writhing as the ambulanceman tried to give him fluids.

Suddenly, Jenkins went stiff, and let out another scream. He struggled a moment, and then fell back, his eyes closed.

'Cardiac arrest, Bob.'

'OK, let's get him up. Lift together.'

The two ambulancemen lifted Jenkins onto the platform and laid him down gently. One started resuscitation, massaging his heart and putting an oxygen mask over the face. Marcus could only stand and watch, helpless.

'No good. Let's try defibrillation.'

The other man brought out the electrical pads and applied them.

'Stand back.'

The thud of electricity was felt by all of them.

'Nothing. Try again.'

Marcus watched. There was nothing he could do now, he knew.

'I'm going to die today, Father.'

Another thud.

'Nothing. I think he's had it.'

25

'OK.'

One of the ambulancemen looked up. 'Sorry, vicar. Good of you to come, but I don't think there's much you can do for him now.'

'I saw him earlier ... if anyone needs me, I'm at the local church.'

'I'll make sure the police know.'

The paramedic had a friendly face, seemingly unaffected by the events which he must witness every day.

Carefully, what remained of Henry Jenkins was placed onto a stretcher and carried up to the waiting ambulance. Just before they carried him away, Marcus approached the stretcher and gently laid a hand on the blanket.

'May you rest in peace, Mr Jenkins.'

There was a momentary pause before the ambulancemen moved on. Marcus followed at a distance.

Behind him, the special squad moved in to clear the rest of the remains. Summoned by the station manager, their job was to move around the tube network, clearing the remains of suicides from the rails. It had to be one of the most unpleasant jobs in the world.

Marcus reached the top of the escalator and just made it out of the door before being sick in the gutter. As he hunched down, recovering, he thought of the man who earlier that day had sat in front of him seeking absolution. He wrenched off his collar and tried to breathe deeply. Behind him, the doors to the station opened and the crowd started to filter in. A disaffected voice rang out.

''Bout bloody time too. Another nutter topped himself. Don't they ever think about the rest of us when they decide to jump?'

Marcus shook his head, trying to shake the images from his mind. The agony, the writhing, the blood pouring from the truncated body. He knew it was useless. He would never be able to wipe them from his consciousness. What he had seen would stay with him for the rest of his life.

I'm going to have to find out what the hell this was all

about, he thought to himself. Mr Jenkins, whoever you were, wherever you are now, I will keep my promise to you.

I'm going to find your demons.

Chapter Four

It was 4.30 pm at 29 Pump Court, and the clerks' room was humming. The two juniors, Sarah and Kevin, were fielding the calls which were coming in at the rate of two a minute. Every call meant work. Work meant fees. And Ron Falconer was on eight per cent of everything which went through Chambers.

He should have been happy, but he had too many problems for that. He lit another cigarette, cradling the phone between his shoulder and his cheek. He knew he shouldn't smoke, his doctor had lectured him often enough: blood pressure way up, he needed to lose weight, cut out the fags. Yes, bloody yes. Of course he should, he wasn't a fool. But how the hell could he with a job like this?

He was dependent on his barristers for everything, and lately he wondered if they had any idea what was wrong. They should bloody well spend a few hours in the clerks' room, listening to what was happening all day.

Cigarette in hand, Ron gripped the phone harder as he listened.

'I've still not had that pleading, Ron. Tell Mr Golightly I'm going elsewhere.'

He'd fobbed the solicitor off for three weeks. Alexander Golightly seemed to be in a trance these days. He was weeks behind with his paperwork. When he was on form, he would churn out written advices and pleadings within the

28

week. Now, though, he was way behind, solicitors screaming for him to get a move on.

'I'll get him to do your papers urgently sir, he has been
in court a lot . . .'

'That's not good enough Ron. I don't want a negligence
action against me for not issuing in time.'

'Leave it with me, I'll get hold of him straightaway.'

'No, too late Ron. Send the papers back. I'll have to
brief someone else as an emergency.'

No way. Not another solicitor going elsewhere. This was
becoming too much to bear. Ron sucked hard on the cigarette, drawing in the nicotine.

'Nick, it will be done. If Golightly can't do it in time,
one of my juniors will. Don't worry.'

There was a pause at the other end of the line.

'OK. But by four on Monday at the latest. If it's not here
by then, I'm going elsewhere.'

'Thanks Nick. It'll be there in good time.' Ron put the
phone down with a sigh. 'Where the fuck is Golightly?'

Sarah had just finished a call. 'No idea. Saw him going
out just before lunch.'

'It's four-bloody-thirty. What's happened to him? He
can't just wander off into the wild blue yonder, not when
the whole world wants him, for God's sake!'

The phone rang again. The question hung in the air as
Sarah answered it.

Ron stared at the wall in front of him and drew deeply on
his cigarette. Behind him, the door opened gently.

'Spare a moment, Ron?'

Even on a day like this, he'd not dream of snapping at
his Head of Chambers. Ron turned, stubbing out the cigarette in a glass ashtray.

'Of course, sir.'

He followed Seb up the stairs to his room on the second
floor. It was one of the smallest in the building. Seb had
been there twenty years and had never sought to progress to
one of the grander rooms on the first floor. He liked it

quiet, he said. And he could just see the river from his window, winding its way past the Embankment. Ron would often find him standing there, just looking out. Never understood it himself. A river's a river, after all. Just a load of water.

'Coffee?'

'Thank you, sir.'

Seb had a percolator running constantly in his room. He seemed to live off the stuff. Quick sandwich at lunch, and supper missed, Ron suspected, as often as eaten. But there always seemed to be a hot cup of coffee available, black as night and laden with sugar.

Seb pushed the scalding cup towards his clerk and sat down. He looked tired, thought Ron. Things not too good at home, probably. Mr Waters had not talked much about it, but the Temple had the most efficient grapevine in the known universe.

Seb looked up at his clerk.

'I need your help, Ron.'

Abby let herself in to her flat and sat at the table by the ancient gas cooker. The kitchen had obviously been installed in the Fifties and must have been state of the art at the time. Now, though, the blue Formica was chipped and lustreless. A long work surface, warped and covered in a crazy turquoise slab design, undulated its way to the yellowing cooker, complete with twenty metal bars above the gas flames, all of which had to be taken out and cleaned with depressing regularity.

Beyond the kitchen was the sleeping area. An ancient, sagging double bed was pushed up to the other side of the kitchen work surface, an even older dismantled put-u-up rolled underneath it. A few old bookshelves, filled with Abby's law purchases, a gas heater and a portable TV completed the furnishings. There was a red carpet, still in quite good condition, with the added advantage that it made the room look warm even when it was freezing. Finally, some rickety French windows led through to the garden, a long, overgrown patch of wilderness which Maggie, her landlady, was constantly threatening to cultivate.

Abby had been there for eighteen months now. She had covered the walls with pictures – bold, bright abstracts popped into plastic frames hung from every available surface. She had Mum's throws – remnants of material she'd picked up on her travels – adding light and vibrancy to the rather bare interior. It was hardly the high life, but the whole thing had a certain charm about it. More importantly, it was the closest thing to a home that she had right now.

Abby shook off her shoes as she sat at the table. She opened one of the cupboards and took out her laptop, bought secondhand from a failed bar student. She started it up and got typing. To her bank manager. Urgently. She connected the PC up to the dot matrix printer and it churned out the letter for her.

Duty done, she changed out of her barrister clothes and into jeans and T-shirt. She hung the black suit carefully in the wardrobe. There was just the one outfit, bought last year at the Liberty sale. Her mother had always said it was worth buying quality rather than quantity. The suit was a size ten, but it had been half price. Abby had lost a stone in order to wear it and had kept the weight off until she'd got the news from Crown Office Row. Then she'd taken to the chocolate biscuits. The waistband was uncomfortably tight now.

She released her hair from the stern plait and let it fall around her shoulders. She had a vague feeling that she should be phoning people, letting them know that she had got another pupillage, telling them about Seb Waters, about the fact that they were trying to expand, about her hopes that she might just find a foothold. But there was nobody to phone.

Mum had died just after Abby had left home for

Cambridge, proud in that special way that only a single parent can be when her child does well. She still missed her like hell. They had been a tiny family, but a happy one. Just the two of them in the council flat all those years.

Harriet Penhaligon had given Abby everything she could. She had been a wanderer at heart, Abby knew. Before she'd become pregnant, she'd travelled all over the world on virtually nothing. Always casual jobs, nothing long term. But Harriet had become pregnant in her late twenties. Estranged from her own parents, she'd found a job in Essex and had settled down in a council flat for the rest of her life. She'd never given any impression that she was unhappy doing so, but Abby knew it must have been quite some sacrifice.

There was no father. Someone had deposited the necessary at some point, of course, but that was as far as it had gone. There had been no need for one, anyhow. They'd managed just fine, the two of them together. Abby had wanted for nothing, at least in terms of emotional sustenance. In fact, if it was possible, she'd done rather too well on that front. With no siblings to cut her down to size and the undivided attention of an adoring mother, Abby knew nothing other than centre stage. Anyone who might try to share it, or even seek to remove her from it, would provoke a reaction that made a hyperactive volcano sound rather tame.

Abby sat back in her chair and thought over the events of the day. If Mum had been alive today, she'd be on the phone right now, asking how it had gone, shrieking with delight that Abby had got the pupillage. She'd have set to, making some suits on her ancient sewing machine and sending her vast quantities of fruit cake in the post. And she'd have listened, just like she always used to. Taking her seriously – her thoughts, her dreams, her hopes and her fears. Abby missed that.

But she was gone, and Abby was quite alone.

Jenny and Florence, Abby's best friends at college, were both abroad working all hours for their commercial law firms. There would be little point in ringing them, even if she could afford the phone bill. And Seamus, dear Seamus, who had pledged his undying devotion throughout their torrid romance at the Inns of Court School of Law, had written after six months of his Birmingham pupillage to tell her that he'd just become engaged to one of his local solicitors.

Still, she reasoned, things have to change. I've moved from student mode to working life and I'll just have to get on with it. At least, she knew, there would be plenty to do. She'd have her own cases at last, and with them would come the chance to put all those years of study into practise.

And there was still the law centre. Whatever happened, she'd keep that going. They'd asked her a few weeks ago if she'd be able to continue once she had sorted out a new pupillage. Abby had promised that she would. It was the only chance she'd had to actually use her legal skills until now. So often she'd been able to give real, practical help to people who needed her – people about to be thrown out of houses or jobs; battered women who didn't know that they could get injunctions; victims of loan sharks who hadn't a clue what to do. She'd helped them all – told them their rights, pointed them in the direction of a sympathetic solicitor if they qualified for legal aid, and sat beside them in court whispering encouragement in bringing their own cases if they didn't. It was the most useful work she'd ever done in her life and there was no way she was going to stop now.

For the moment, though, she had an hour free before she set off for the advice centre in Archway. Abby made herself a cup of coffee and sat at the table, allowing herself to daydream. In a year's time, she knew, she could be an established Temple barrister with a flourishing practice, combining family and criminal work. She would defend the innocent, make sure that errant husbands paid their wives proper maintenance, and encourage judges to change things for the better. All this, and she was going to be paid for it. It could be the best job in the world and was just . . . just within her grasp. She was on the threshold of achieving everything she had ever wanted.

The next six months were going to be the most important of her life.

Chapter Five

The only barrister that Ron actually liked in 29 Pump Court was Mr Waters. As for the rest of them, he had respect, certainly, occasionally admiration, but affection, no.

It was partly circumstance, he knew. They'd joined almost at the same time, Seb as a junior pupil, Ron as a runner – a junior clerk whose job it was to lift, carry and take messages. Twenty years later, they were Head of Chambers and Senior Clerk, respectively. They'd grown up together in a funny sort of way. And if Mr Waters was asking for his help, he'd get it.

'Help with what, sir?'

They were seated at the conference table in Seb's attic room. Mr Waters seemed unusually agitated.

'This Chambers is dying on its feet, isn't it?'

Ron took a deep breath, and nodded.

'We've both spent all our working lives here, Ron. We've got to stop it happening.'

'But how?'

Seb looked at him hard.

'We've got to get back to how we were before Gerry took over as Head. He was too choosy about who he took on in the Eighties. Half his rejects are earning double what I am now. We've lost our critical mass, somehow, got too small. We used to be one of the biggest sets in the Temple, now we're in danger of becoming some tin-pot shambles.

So we're going to start recruiting.'

Ron looked doubtful. 'Could be a risk ... what if new tenants don't get things going? I don't want any more lame ducks – one's quite enough for me.'

Seb smiled momentarily. 'There's no other option, is there? If we carry on like this, we're finished anyhow.'

Ron paused. Then, 'What about Mr Golightly's views? He's very keen on establishing a niche – focusing in on the commercial crime, keeping it select. The money's good, I'll grant him that.'

'And have these Chambers dependent on the whims of some City hustlers? Thank you, but no, Ron. No, we're going to start recruiting. Get around to the pupillage fairs, let it be known that we intend to take on at least one new tenant every year. Then we can try to poach some established people from the Temple. We can do it.'

'And what about the other tenants? They'll take some persuading. Their way of thinking is that any new tenant is a threat to them.'

Seb grinned. 'Leave them to me. I'll just have to get on and rattle their cages.'

'Wouldn't mind being a fly on the wall for that one. Do I take it that Miss Penhaligon has a second six with us now?'

'She has.'

'Without the agreement of the pupillage committee?'

Seb nodded. 'The pupillage committee is run by Alexander Golightly. He'd never have accepted her in a million years and I thank God that he seems to be uncontactable this afternoon.'

'What's her CV like?'

'Brilliant. Starred first. She's been a pupil with Danny Ditchcombe and really impressed him. Her second six fell through so I snapped her up. I took the view that I had to offer her a place pretty damn quick.'

Ron nodded, but paused a moment.

'Not what some people would call top drawer, is she?'

Seb sighed. 'Bloody hell, Ron. This is the new

36

millennium, for God's sake. She was brought up by a single parent on a council housing estate. She went to the local comp, got a scholarship to Cambridge and is here entirely on merit. She's got to have her chance.'

'What about James Dorton? He's the senior pupil. He's expecting a tenancy.'

'He'll just have to live with the competition. Might liven him up a bit. He's been complacent as hell ever since he got here.'

Ron grinned. 'Not forgetting that he's Mr Golightly's godson. No disrespect, sir, but you're going to have to try a bit harder on the diplomatic front.'

'Shit, I had forgotten the godson bit. And you're right, I've never had the time or the inclination to butter up the rest of these Chambers. But, Ron, I need your support on this one. You know as well as I do that you'll need to kick-start things for her. I'm just asking you to give her a fair chance. We need new people.'

Ron paused.

'OK. Fair trial. But you know as well as I do that you can have all the degrees in the world, but still be useless the moment you get on your feet in court. I'll give her a fair start, but that's it. If she can't take it from there, she's out. If the solicitors don't want to use her, there's only so much I can do.'

Seb nodded. 'Yes. I can't ask more than that. Now, what about a pupil master for her?'

Ron sucked in his cheeks. 'Golightly is the only one free. Dengie's got James Dorton. They're the only two approved pupil masters at the moment.'

'Not going to be much fun for her with Golightly, is it?'

The clerk shook his head. 'You said it, sir.'

'Well, it's a second six only. If you get her out into court, she won't see him too much.'

'Who's going to break the news to him?'

Seb grinned. 'Leave it with me.'

Ron went to leave, but hesitated at the door.

'By the way, how are things with your father?'

Seb sighed. 'No change, really. The new nurse seems pretty competent so at least he can stay at home. He'd be lost anywhere else.' He stood and looked out of the window. 'It's hopeless, really, though. He's no idea who I am most of the time. He just drifts along.'

Ron's voice softened. 'Nobody could do anything more, you know . . .'

'Yes, maybe.'

Ron waited but Seb said nothing more. Instead, he looked down at the papers in front of him. Ron took the hint and left, shutting the door quietly behind him.

Seb sighed and sat back in his chair. He looked around his room, so familiar after twenty years. He'd started right here, at this desk, bought from a flea market in Islington when he'd first got his tenancy. The walls were painted a light blue, out of keeping with the rest of the rooms in the building. They were all printed in dark, sepulchral hues – magentas and bottle greens. Oppressive, he found them. Not for him, either, the usual reproduction cartoons of legal characters stuck onto the wall. Everyone had them, yet to him they showed nothing more than a complete lack of imagination. The things weren't even funny.

Instead, his walls were decorated with Hockney prints, his later stuff, particularly, all enormous vistas and long, long lines. Seb would gaze into the pictures often, taking a break from his work. He hated Chambers politics, really loathed it. But he was in charge now, and had to do his best. Something had to happen. Either they recruited, expanded, and took on the other sets, or they would be whittled down to nothing. At the same time, they were going to have to modernise. A decent computer system, rather than the hotch potch that currently existed. Proper e-commerce connections, too. That would cost an awful lot of money and they were going to have to generate some investment capital to see it through properly.

38

Alex Golightly, he knew, would resist. He had his practice, would see no reason why Chambers should be going in a different direction.

Seb sighed. Assigning Golightly a pupil he'd never even met, let alone selected, would not go down well. He'd need to think about the Abby situation carefully.

Slowly, he stood up and looked out of the window. He stretched onto tiptoe and looked over the trees to the river. It was always busy in the summer, tourist boats motoring up and down in a vast, noisy flotilla.

Ron was right. He was going to have to be more diplomatic. There was a lot at stake here and he mustn't blow it all just because he didn't stop and think a little. He'd taken refuge in bluff in the past. Didn't have time to waste on diplomacy. Life would be a whole lot easier if everyone would just say what they wanted and get on with it.

But he had to get this one right, spend a little time thinking it through properly. Alex wouldn't respond to argument, he knew. The only thing Golightly understood was his own self-interest. It had always been that way. So taking on Abby would have to be sold to him in a way that would pander to the man.

She was clearly extremely bright. That could be an advantage for him. He could ask her to research his work, report back to him, and Alex could then take the credit for her labours.

Seb rejected the idea. Abby would be a second six pupil, out doing her own work. Alex would try to dump some of his papers on her, but he'd only get away with that for a bit. Once she had her own practice up and running, she wouldn't have time for his cases, and he'd know that.

What about allure? She was clearly an attractive girl. Even Alex might like the ego trip of having her hang on his every word. But the man he knew thought in terms of money received rather than sexual kudos.

This was going to be difficult. Seb tried another tack. Could Alex suffer through not taking Abby on? Slowly, an idea began to germinate. He reflected, still watching the river from his window.

Yes, it could just work.

Seb grinned and walked back to his desk. He reached for the phone.

'Ron, who is that firm Alex is trying to get work from . . . newish, pretty impressive solicitor called Singerhof . . . yes, Gissinghams, that's it.' He paused a moment. 'What are the chances of persuading Mr Singerhof to send a little case to Miss Penhaligon – nothing grand, perhaps a plea in mitigation?'

He listened to the response.

'Excellent! Well, can you do me a favour? Let Joe Heiney become unable to do it and persuade him to let Abby have a go. It has to be quick though, all in place before I ring Mr Golightly – can you give him a call now? Thanks, Ron. Ring me back when you know for sure.'

Seb put down the phone and grinned. He'd ring Alex at home tonight to break the news.

This was going to be quite enjoyable, really.

Chapter Six

'Medway number one on the port bow, Pascal.'

'*Enfin* . . .'

Pascal de Montchavin breathed a sigh of relief. It was a filthy night, blowing like hell. The moon lit up the white water, scudding across the wave tops. The tide had been against him for the last three hours and the boat had taken an age to get here, thudding her way through the chop. Still, at least it meant that there was nothing else around. The last thing they needed was an audience.

'Thierry, are you ready?'

The diver's face peered up from the gloom below deck. The lights were off to save night vision. Thierry was already in his diving suit, his air canister strapped to his back.

'Leave the stuff below until we're there. It may go through the guard rails if we bring it up too early.'

'Sure.'

'David, as it's quiet, we can stay in the main channel. Just follow the Medway buoys.'

'Yes, skipper.'

The Breton helmsman kept his eyes ahead, steadying the tiller of the yacht. It was a classic cruising design, with good storage and reliable sea-keeping. If anyone thought to ask them, they were just three French friends taking a break, caught out by the weather. On a night like this,

41

though, no one was interested enough to want to know.

'Wind over tide, it's not going to be easy to keep her still, Thierry.' Pascal was on the starboard bow, seemingly impervious to the wind and rain. His long hair, tied in a dark band, streamed behind him. He stood steadily, balancing perfectly as the boat pitched and rolled. Thierry nodded briefly.

'No worries. I'll be as quick as I can.'

There was a rapid, unspoken exchange between them. Thierry raised an eyebrow as the helmsman's face was turned. The weather was ideal for their unfinished business – confused seas, a strong tide. Almost imperceptibly, Pascal nodded. *After the drop.*

Pascal felt the salt spray on his face. It stung for a few seconds and he grimaced. Still, once the drop had been made, they could head off back to Holland without hanging around. He listened as David counted off the buoys. He recognised the number eight, flashing at the edge of the channel, marking the deep water for the river traffic.

'Right, take a north just after the number eight, keep going slowly and we'll have a look at what the tide's doing.'

The Breton had heard this dozens of times. He could navigate his way to the wreck in his sleep now, but Pascal reminded him nevertheless. Nobody was allowed to forget that he was very definitely in charge.

David turned the tiller and they edged their way out of the shipping channel. As they turned to the north, the three men strained to see ahead. Pascal spotted her first.

'*Voila . . . La belle!*'

The three masts were directly ahead, rising out of the water and illuminated in the moonlight.

'Right down, now, there's a yellow buoy.'

David brought the throttle control up almost to vertical, just keeping the engine in gear. Pascal had his compass at the ready, just in case the computerised system failed. Carefully, he called out the bearings to follow, easing the yacht into the place that they always used – just off the bow of the submerged wreck, close to number one hold. Thierry would be finding his way largely by touch. He needed to start from the same place every time they made a drop. It was a dangerous business.

'OK, let's get the stuff up on deck.'

The bags, neatly packed in waterproof plastic, and placed in a large plastic box were brought up from below and positioned carefully on the floor of the cockpit.

'Right, on the count of three . . . un, deux . . .' Pascal watched the computer, waited until the right numbers flashed up.

'. . . trois!'

The diver was gone, executing a neat backward roll, the box tied to his wetsuit belt.

'Just hold her steady.'

Pascal knew it would be difficult. They dare not anchor – there was too much chance of it fouling the wreck. And if the authorities did come along, they'd have no explanation. Instead, the helmsman had to use the engine and the tiller to keep the boat in place, resisting the attempts of current and wind to move it.

Below the yacht, Thierry moved downwards through the murky estuary water. A helmet light provided a weak glow, but he knew his way by now. The first time had been terrible. He'd had to feel his way along the barnacled hull, searching for the holes that he knew were there. He'd had to go into each one, looking for the right place to leave the load, a place that the tides didn't disturb, a little niche where things would lie undiscovered for as long as they needed.

The first time, he'd been frightened. He was next to 3,000 tons of live explosive, stuff which had been lying on the sea floor for over fifty years. It could go up at any time, he knew. Peering through the muddy water, he had seen the boxes of bombs, sorted by size, ammunition made in the USA for the Allies to use in the invasion. But the bombs and bullets had never seen France. Instead, they had sat on the bottom of the Thames Estuary, decade after decade, succumbing to God only knew what chemical reactions.

He'd had to make several visits, each time surveying a different part of the wreck. There was little recorded information he could use – nothing to tell him where he could find a nice, safe little storage facility, away from tides, fishermen and prying eyes. Every time, he'd looked at the boxes, their print still visible, and wondered how long it would be before the whole lot went up. After each visit, he'd sat in the cabin on the trip home, sketching the layout until eventually he had a better idea than the port authority about the state of the wreck.

As a result, he'd been able to decide on the best spot – the number one hold. It was difficult to get to, still loaded with phosphorous smoke bombs and some general purpose bombs. But it had room for more goodies. He'd been able to excavate a hole under one of the bomb boxes. The water in it was still and the stuff was safe there. Even if the authorities sent someone down to take a look at the bombs, they wouldn't find the little niche nestling underneath. As time had gone by, he had made two more holes under other boxes, each a similar size, each perfect for what he had in mind.

Thierry felt his way around the edge of the wreck to the hold and through the large gap on the starboard side. Instantly he felt the effect of the tide weaken. He swam around the side of a stack of boxes and felt his way to the bomb case that he wanted. There it was: heavy, even though it had split open and lost much of its contents. With a struggle, he lifted it and quickly dropped the package into the hole. And there it would stay, with thirty-two others, the two other holes already filled with eighty-three bags each.

Every bag held thousands of high-quality ecstasy tablets, manufactured over the last two years in three Dutch labs, known in the trade for the purity of their products. Ten million pounds worth of illegal drugs sitting undisturbed less than a hundred miles away from one of Europe's premier markets. It was bloody brilliant.

No one went near the place because they were all terrified it was going to go up one day. Pascal took risks, sure, but the chances were that everything was inert by now. It hadn't gone up in over fifty years and he'd gambled on the fact that, unassisted, it wasn't going to go bang now.

Pascal, his oldest friend, wanted to join the big boys. Until now, he'd done well enough, importing his pretty tablets into the UK. But it wasn't enough. He had to have more. And in order to make a serious impact on the London drug scene, he had needed to organise storage; a place where large amounts of drugs could be stored undetected for as long as necessary.

And that had been the rub. Storage anywhere in southeast England carried high risks. First problem was getting it into the country. Customs were too good at searching out the stuff. And anything which got through then had to be safely transported to a quiet location, away from the prying eyes and ears of the British population. And that was pretty near impossible in this crowded region of England. A further problem lay in the sheer number of people needed to pull off such a scheme. The greater the workforce, the higher the chance that one of them had a nice little arrangement with the authorities and they'd arrive at the pick-up to a welcome from fifty members of the Metropolitan police drug squad.

This hiding place, though, was sheer genius. The three of them had spent the last year carefully depositing the tablets in the wreck. Few would venture near it: the odd fisherman maybe, perhaps a diver or two. And those that did would find nothing. Not in the murky, filthy waters of the Thames estuary.

One last check that everything was secure and Thierry was out of the hole. He swam alongside the wreck, picking up his points of reference. Then he swam clear, knowing just where he was going to surface. No point in a lifeline here. It would snag, be too dangerous. In a few moments, hands were helping him back onto the yacht and he was undressing in the warmth of the cabin.

Pascal turned towards David, the helmsman.

'You take some time below. Have a sleep for a few hours.' He took over the helm. The Breton nodded briefly and moved towards the companionway steps.

Pascal turned away from the wind and cranked up the throttle. With the wind behind him now, it was a wild, perfect evening. Business over, he could even hoist the sails and enjoy himself a little. He looked for the buoys marking the shipping lane, and grinned as he felt the boat start to glide along the surface.

A few minutes later, Thierry appeared up the steps, dressed in his warm clothes and oilskins. He handed a steaming cup of coffee to Pascal.

'A good evening's work, *mon ami*.'

'Yes. We're nearly there now.'

'199 bundles, by my calculation.'

Pascal knew instantly. 'Ten million pounds worth at current values.'

He noted the last of the buoys, adjusted the tiller and steered the boat out of the estuary. It was still quiet. Out in the shipping lanes it would be busier, he knew. But there, he would be just a blip on a radar, passing unnoticed by any crew still awake in the navigation room.

'One more drop, and then we deal. Sam's contact will come and see me in Paris.'

'Can you be sure he'll really want so much?'

'Sam seemed sure enough. He wants to make an impact in the market, apparently. And he has the money to do so.'

'Still a risk, non?'

Pascal grinned. 'Maybe. But worth taking. And besides, where would we be if we didn't take a few chances? I'd still be waiting for Papa to die. You'd be washing up on the charter boats or gutting fish at Calais.'

Thierry nodded. 'You may have a point there. But for me, giving all that up was nothing. You – I've never understood. Fourteen generations of Montchavins . . . money . . . a château in the Loire, and you leave it all for this.'

Pascal shrugged. 'I gave up boredom, that's all. Sitting around, endlessly finding pointless amusements for myself. You've no idea . . . it's no existence. And as for the money – I can get that elsewhere, like doing this. And get it sooner. No, Thierry, this is it, life. Pushing on, testing ourselves . . .'

The two men fell silent. The boat was in deeper water now and starting to ride along on its bow wave. The log showed seven knots and Pascal's hair was wet. He didn't care one bit. This was everything he lived for – a successful drop in difficult conditions, a wild ride back to the Dutch coast. Every other pleasure – women, fine wine, exquisite food – they all had their place but were transient details compared with this.

Clouds sped across the face of the moon, mirroring the flume on the waves behind them. Outside, it seemed a world of black and white, in which they and the little boat were entirely alone. Down below there was the orange glow from the cabin light and the warmth from the cooker. In time they would take watches – at least he and Thierry would. For the moment though, he wanted to be up here, listening to the sounds of the wind in the rigging, and the fizz as the white water parted underneath the hull of the yacht.

They were into the channel separation zone now. One side of the imaginary line, the shipping travelled north-east, the other, south-west. This was as deep as it got in the North Sea.

It was time to deal with the remaining business.

Pascal nodded at Thierry. The man reached down for his knife as Pascal attached the tiller to the autohelm. Silently, both men climbed down the companionway steps.

David was sleeping, snoring gently as he rolled from side to side of the settee berth.

47

Thierry took the knife and held it at the Breton's throat.

'Wake up, *mon ami*.'

The snoring stopped and David's eyes opened.

'Just stay very still,' hissed Pascal. He saw the fear in the man's eyes. He struggled, tried to lift his head, then sank back as he felt the steel of the knife right by his jugular.

'What's happening?'

'Just do what we say. Very, very slowly, get up.'

The knife retreated a few centimetres.

'Don't do anything silly, there's nowhere to go.'

The Breton knew this. Had known as soon as he'd woken up to find the knife at his neck. Slowly, he hauled himself out of his sleeping bag. He'd taken off his trousers to get in, and now he stood in the cabin in sweater, pants and socks, Thierry was still holding the knife at his neck.

Pascal lifted the Breton's sweater.

'Take this off. Slowly.'

David obliged, carefully pulling the bulky item of clothing over his shoulders.

'And the T-shirt. Everything.'

'But . . .'

Pascal nodded at Thierry. Quickly, the knife drew lightly across the Breton's neck. Just enough to show they meant business. Not enough to draw blood. Not yet.

The T-shirt came off, followed by the pants and socks. He was naked before them now, shivering. He smelt of fear. Rank, overwhelming fear. He knew what was coming. And he knew there was no way out.

'Please, let me go. Keep the money, keep everything. I'll stay quiet, as God is my witness.'

'Shut it, peasant.'

Pascal first went up the steps and turned at the top to watch David. There was only one way out of this for the Breton.

He took it.

He appeared to stumble and fell forward, up the steps, towards Pascal. In a moment, his fist was clenched and he

48

laid a stinging blow on the skipper's cheek.

The boat lurched into a wave and Pascal lost his footing, stumbling himself to the cockpit sole, and knocking the autohelm. Pascal heard a grinding, whining noise as the machine struggled to reset itself.

The boom. It's going to go.

Instinctively, Pascal turned his head upwards. With the wind behind them, a small course deviation could make the mainsail fill from the other side. It did.

With a crash, the boom came swinging over the cockpit. It caught the side of the Breton's head with a dull thud. He staggered as Pascal looked on. The main sail carried one hell of a lot of power and all of it had been transferred temporarily to the Breton's skull.

Things seemed to happen in slow motion. David's knees bent and his hand moved out, feeling desperately for the grab rail. He missed and lurched forward, catching a foot on the side of the cockpit. It was enough to send him through the guardrails, still clutching for something, anything, to stop his inexorable descent into the water.

Pascal grinned. At least it saved them the trouble of throwing him over. He pulled himself up from the cockpit and looked over the side.

The man hadn't given up yet. After the chaos of the gybe, a rope was trailing overboard and the Breton made for this, grasping it with all his might.

Thierry appeared and touched Pascal's elbow lightly.

'Leave him to me.'

Then he shouted into the dark: 'Farewell, my friend. See you in hell.'

His knife was still out of its sheath. With a last wave at the Breton, he cut the trailing line. There was a scream as the boat moved away from the man overboard.

'Please, for God's sake . . . Let me live . . .'

Pascal and Thierry looked at one another, each scanning the other's face for signs of weakness. There was a twitch of the skipper's lip. Thierry grinned back.

'Silly bastard. Screaming like a woman. Does he really think we're going to go back for him?'

Pascal started to laugh. Low at first, then louder. Soon, Thierry had joined in and the boat sailed on. Behind them, David's screams started to weaken as he gave up.

They were making six knots now, headed for Holland. This far out, David's body would wash up and down with the tides. He'd rot away to oblivion before he got anywhere near land. Even if, by some fluke, his body made it to shore, naked and with no means of identification it would be months before anyone would realise who they were dealing with. They'd planned it that way.

Pascal left the helm to his mate. Thierry could be relied upon. He was loyal. Without Pascal, he knew he'd be nothing. Just another army failure hanging around the Caribbean charter scene, too ugly to score with the women, not bright enough to make any serious money. With Pascal, he had a flat in Paris, a beautiful girlfriend and an account at the Bourse. He could be trusted. Unlike the Breton.

The computer gave out the current position and Pascal noted the fix on the chart. They were perfectly on course. Thierry would take them back safely, around the lethal sandbanks which guarded the Dutch coast. They'd tie up, make a few comments about having to turn back from their cruise because of the weather, and head to France by train.

And then, Paris. At last. A few meals, some women. But most important, The Deal.

The time had come.

Chapter Seven

'Hello Abby, how did it go today?'

Officially, Tom Peters was the caretaker of the community hall. Unofficially, he was its relief cleaner, advertising officer and bouncer. Not bad going for a man in his early seventies.

'Great – I've got the pupillage.'

'Well done! Mind you, they were lucky to get you after that last lot went down the plughole.'

Abby grimaced. 'Maybe . . .'

Tom paused.

'You know, Abby . . . if it does get too much, you will tell me, won't you? I don't want you feeling that you've got to keep doing these sessions come what may.'

Abby touched his elbow lightly.

'Tom, I've been doing this for a year now, there's no way I'm going to stop. The pupillage thing is just something I have to get through to qualify. They might let me loose on a few cases, but it's nothing compared with what we do here. This is what it's really all about.'

He grinned at her. 'In that case, let's get started. There's a bit of a queue.'

Abby followed him through the double doors into the main hall. They had put up some screens at one end to provide limited privacy for those seeking advice. A dozen chairs had been set out a discreet distance from the screen, and all of these were already occupied. Abby sighed. It was clearly going to be a busy evening. There were a couple of regulars who smiled at her. The rest carried on reading the magazines which Tom had brought in.

She marched behind the screen and sat down at a small wooden table. The chair wobbled precariously and she made a mental note to keep her leg rigid to stop it toppling over completely.

When Abby had started the legal advice sessions twelve months previously, she had tried to dress like a lawyer in her one and only Liberty suit and an immaculate shirt. But a few weeks of sitting in the dust of the hall had made her think twice about just how often she could afford to dry clean her clothes. And then there was the journey home to consider. Abby could walk it easily, but a smartly dressed woman in high heels tended to attract the wrong sort of attention after dark in the inner city. So she wore her student clothes – jeans, baggy jumper and old coat – when the weather was cold. She had no more trouble.

Tom's face appeared around the screen.

'Ready?'

'Yes.'

He walked in, a woman following.

'Mrs Nicholls, this is Abby Penhaligon, who will do what she can to help. You just tell her all about it.'

The woman took up position in the seat opposite Abby. Tom retreated to the other side of the screen. Mrs Nicholls looked to be in her mid-forties. Her hair had been bleached a yellowing blonde some time ago, but the roots stood proudly dark. Abby wasn't looking at her hair, though. Most of Mrs Nicholls's face was a dark purple colour. Judging by the way she winced as she sat down, there were similar bruises over the rest of her body, too.

Abby spoke gently. 'Tell me what happened.'

The older woman sighed. 'It's my husband.'

Abby kept quiet. Let the woman tell her own story, in her own time.

'It started a few years ago, when he lost his job. You'd never believe it – he used to be so gentle. But then one night he was in drink and hit me. Said nothing about it in the morning, and there was no more trouble for a bit . . .'

Abby smiled encouragingly.

'. . . but then it got worse. Something will put him in a mood, and when he comes home he belts me. Last night was the worst ever . . .'

Her voice had become so soft that Abby had to lean towards her to hear properly.

'I really thought he was going to kill me.'

Abby spoke carefully. 'How long have you been married?'

'Twenty-five years last May – and we had a big party. Three kids, one still at home.'

'Have you talked to your husband about all this?'

Mrs Nicholls breathed out slowly.

'At first, yes. Like I said, the first time he did it, it was like it never happened by the morning. But the second time . . . I made him talk after. He was crying, you know, begging me to forgive him. He said he'd never do it again, that he was down because he couldn't support us any more . . .'

Abby looked at the woman. 'He's not going to stop, you know.'

A tear started to roll down Mrs Nicholls's face.

'I know.'

'You've got to do something to protect yourself. He can't just use you as a punchbag.'

'What can I do?'

'Get an injunction. There's a law, the Family Law Act, it means that a court can bar him from your house.'

'But where would he go?'

Abby's face was grim. 'That would be his problem.'

Mrs Nicholls persisted, her voice wavering.

'But he's on benefit, he'd never find anywhere to live – I can't have him living on the street.'

53

Abby's response was brisk. 'Look no one's forcing him to hit you like this. If he can't treat you like a human being, he's got to go.'

Mrs Nicholls started to cry. 'But he's all I've got . . . I still love him, you see. I couldn't cope without him. And my boy needs him around the house. I just wanted to know . . . just what my rights were, whether someone could write to him perhaps . . .'

Abby scribbled down a name and address on some paper and passed it over the table. Mrs Nicholls, she knew, would do nothing for the time being. They never did, not in a case like this. All she could hope was that she'd keep the address safe and see the solicitor the next time she was beaten up.

'This is a good family lawyer who works near here. She won't charge you if you're on benefit. She'll talk things through with you – maybe write a letter which might help.'

'OK.' Mrs Nicholls took the piece of paper and stared blankly at the writing.

'Good luck.'

The older woman hurried out of the makeshift room and the next client came in. He was young, off the streets, up on a drugs charge. Abby gave him the name of a solicitor specialising in criminal work. Then she steadily worked her way through two housing cases, one more domestic violence and four petty crimes. Each of these cases she referred to specialists who would do the work on legal aid. Abby would dearly have loved to take up their cases herself, but they had to go to a solicitor rather than a barrister.

At eight-thirty, Tom brought her in a cup of scalding coffee.

'Just one more. Came in about an hour ago. Looks a bit strange, if you ask me. Posh voice, but scruffy-looking.'

Abby nodded. She was developing a headache. Get through this last one and home to bed, she thought. She put her head in her hands and started to massage her temples.

Then she looked up and met Marcus Kirkwall for the first time.

54

He stood hesitantly at the edge of the screen, as if waiting for permission to come in. Abby looked at him carefully, taking in the worn jeans and scruffy leather jacket. His dark hair looked a little unkempt, but otherwise he seemed just fine to her. Tall, slim body, tanned-looking skin. No tie, a black shirt without a collar.

'Hello, I'm Marcus Kirkwall.'

He looked at her, and instantly she noticed his eyes. They were the most piercing blue she'd ever seen.

'Hi, Abby Penhaligon. Come in, take a pew.'

He grinned slightly.

'So you know what I do?'

Abby looked at him questioningly.

'No, why should I?'

'The pew reference.'

'What?' She was lost now.

'I'm a vicar.'

'Oh!' Abby was flummoxed. She'd had little to do with vicars since she was at primary school.

'I'm sorry . . . I didn't mean to offend . . .'

'None taken.'

'And I had no idea you were a vicar. Shouldn't you wear, um . . .'

'A dog collar? I took it off earlier. You'll have to take me on trust, I'm afraid.'

'I see.' Abby was regaining her composure fast. She didn't want to look idiotic in front of this man one bit.

'So how can I help?'

Marcus coughed slightly to clear his throat. His right hand reached up to a lock of hair at his temple, and he pushed it back intently. His hands, she noticed, were large and powerful, his nails clean and carefully kept. Quickly, she looked back at his face. He was struggling to keep control.

'Forgive me if I'm not completely coherent at the moment.'

She looked to his right hand again, now placed on the

table. It had started to tremble, making the table rock quickly to and fro. Marcus was looking at the wall behind her, his face set in grim lines. Whatever was troubling him was pretty bad. He was clearly a man of considerable self-control, but even he was on the verge of losing it.

'Tell me, please, Marcus.' She spoke softly, placing her hands in front of his on the table. Gently, she moved them towards him, until her fingertips touched his. At her touch, he started slightly and seemed to come back into her world.

'I've just taken a confession.'

Damn, she thought. He must be Catholic. But surely they were priests, not vicars?

'He came to see me this afternoon. Wanted a Catholic priest, but stumbled into my whist afternoon in the church hall.'

'Who?'

'I'd never met him before. Henry Jenkins, he said he was called.'

'So what happened? I mean, why . . .'

'He told me he'd murdered a man, someone called Jacobs. Then he'd framed someone else, an Abraham James.'

Abby started to take notes.

'He came to see me to ask me to make sure that the conviction is overturned and that justice is done.'

Abby was nodding as she wrote.

'Well, if he's prepared to say so in court, you can go with him to a solicitor and start the appeal process straight away.'

'He's dead.'

'What?'

'He went from seeing me and jumped under a tube train. I saw him after . . . It was bad.'

'Oh my God.'

Abby gently put her hands on top of his, feeling the trembling worsen. She shook her head.

'Come with me.'

He looked at her blankly.

'I'm taking you for a drink. Now.'

Mutely, he followed as Abby traversed the hall, saying a quick goodnight to an astonished Tom. There was a pub just along the street, a typical London place – flock wallpaper, a circular bar, the air thick with smoke. She sat him down in a quiet corner and bought two brandies.

Abby wanted to steer clear of the day's events for the moment, let him calm down a bit.

'Tell me about yourself. Where are you from?'

He smiled lightly. 'Cornwall. And you?'

'Basildon. You may have heard of it.'

'Certainly have. Is the law centre your job?'

Abby shook her head. 'No. I'm in the last stages of qualifying as a barrister. I just do the centre for the hell of it, really.' She grimaced. Technically, she'd just blasphemed. Funny how easy it was to do. She usually didn't notice. She took a sip of her brandy. He took the cue and raised his own glass to his lips. 'You don't look much like a vicar.'

He gulped back some of his drink and put his glass down on the table.

'What do you mean by that?'

'Well, I'm no expert, but most I've seen dress a little more . . . well, more old fashioned, I suppose.'

'You mean middle England, middle class, sherry before lunch and don't frighten the dogs darling?'

Abby laughed. 'Yes. But you must be from that class.'

Marcus smiled. If she knew, she'd be horrified. Better keep quiet. He nodded: 'Yes, I was, but that doesn't mean that I stayed that way.'

'Come on. You're English. Your class defines you for life.'

'Rubbish!'

'Which school did you go to?'

'Winchester. But if I ever have children, they'll go to the local state.'

'Oh yes? The number of people at university like you

57

was amazing. I'd put money on all of them changing their minds before they're twenty-five.'

'I'm thirty-six and haven't changed yet. And which university did you go to?'

'Cambridge.'

'Which makes you middle class, too. Barrister from ancient university.'

Ouch, that hurt.

'Course not. I just went there because I was bright, not because I went to public school.'

'And what are you going to do when you get established. Commercial work?'

'Bugger that. Real law is what I'm going to do. Real law with people in it – crime and family.' Abby took another sip. She was rather enjoying this. 'I don't believe in God, by the way.'

He looked at her, scanning her face carefully.

'Why did you say it just like that?'

'How do you mean?'

'Were you just trying to shock me?'

Abby blushed. 'No. Of course not.'

Marcus looked into his drink. 'I didn't believe in God until I was twenty-eight.'

'Well, I never will. I don't know how you can cling to a belief. Look around you – see how people live. How can you think that some kind deity is in charge of it all?'

Marcus smiled. 'How very rational you are, Miss Penhaligon.'

Abby's eyes glinted. 'Don't patronise me.'

'I wouldn't dream of it. But don't you wonder what the point of it all is?'

'The point is biological. We're a life form. We're born, we have children, we die. We have to die to allow the species to evolve. That's the point. Talk of nice floaty places afterwards is just to placate the masses.'

'But you don't *know*, not for sure, do you?'

Abby grinned. 'Maybe. But neither do you.'

58

'Touché. Abby, can we stop arguing for a moment? Not that I don't enjoy it, but I was trying to get your advice rather than convert you.'

'OK. So you want to overturn the murder conviction. When was it?'

Marcus frowned. 'I don't know, exactly. It must have been around 1945 or '46, I'd have thought. The murder itself was on VE night . . .'

'*1945!*'

'Yes.'

Abby sighed. 'Marcus, that's virtually impossible. All the trial records will have gone. And the man who was imprisoned is probably dead by now, anyhow. Even if he is alive, it's so long ago, he'll have got on with his own life, probably wouldn't want people turning up trying to re-open the past.'

There was a long silence. Marcus shook his head gently.

'But I've got to try . . . Abby, I promised this man that I would do my best. If there is the slightest chance of putting this right, I've got to go for it. Where should I start?'

Abby sat back in her chair and thought carefully.

'Well, I suppose the first thing would be to find the prisoner. What was the name again?'

'Abraham James.'

'Any idea where he was sent?'

'No.'

'Try press records. Get up to the newspaper reference library at Colindale and read the old reports. They might say where he went.'

Marcus was nodding. 'Good idea. And there may be some church connections that will tell me what happened to him after his release.'

'Yes. Then, if you can find him, you'll have to ask if he wants an appeal to be brought. After all this time, he may just want to leave it in the past.'

'And if he does want to bring an appeal? Do you do that sort of work?'

Abby smiled. 'Not directly. You'd have to go to a solicitor to start with. It's then up to both yourself and the solicitor which barrister you want. But that's a long way ahead. You've got to find your man first.'

'There are diocesan solicitors, Dinkwaters, I'll go to them. But I'll ask them to brief you, if you'd like, Abby.'

'Well, I'm hardly going to say no to a case like this!'

He took another sip of the brandy.

'Can I have your phone number? Work, if you prefer . . .'

Abby scribbled down the address and phone number of 29 Pump Court. Then she added her home address and phone number. She was hardly likely to get stalked by a vicar, after all. He nodded.

'Thanks for bringing me here. I'm glad I came to see you.'

'Did you know about the advice evening?'

'No. I was just walking past and saw the sign. I'd say it was divine intervention, but you'd tell me not to be so daft.'

He was grinning as he said it. Then, rather awkwardly, he spoke again.

'I've been given a couple of tickets for a concert at Wembley the night after tomorrow. Would you like to come?'

Abby looked up at him. She hadn't been asked on a date for ages. But she hardly knew the guy. For all she knew, he could be bogus – a nutter who picked up girls by pretending to be a vicar.

Get a grip, she thought to herself. This man's as genuine as rain in Manchester. And besides, he's bloody good looking.

'I'd love to.'

'Really?'

'Really.'

'Great!'

A thought suddenly struck Abby.

'It's not gospel music, is it? Or Cliff? I'm not into that sort of thing . . .'

Marcus laughed. 'No, just some straightforward rockers. Page and Plant, used to be in Led Zeppelin. Is that OK? If you don't fancy it, we can always go somewhere else.'

'No, that's brilliant. I'd love to go, Marcus.'

They made the arrangements and went their separate ways outside the pub. Abby refused his offer to walk her home, but instantly regretted it as she set off alone along the dark streets.

Still, things were looking up. A new pupillage and a date, both on the same day. It had to be a good sign, it really did.

Chapter Eight

'Darling, would you pour me a sherry?'

'Of course, darling. Be there in a mo.'

Alexander Golightly was on his best behaviour. There was nothing like an afternoon in a mistress's bed to improve uxorial conduct, he was discovering.

He poured a large schooner and took it through to the sitting room. The Hon. Lucinda was sitting on one of the chintz sofas, chosen by her from Harrods earlier in the year. Lucinda was in a good mood, having spent most of the day at her health club. Tennis to start with, a gossipy lunch and then a spell in the sauna and jacuzzi, apparently. Whilst he'd been in bed with Rita. Alex still trembled at the thought.

'Are you well, darling? You look a little pale.'

'No, not at all. Just a busy day.'

'Of course. Well, let's have supper in a moment, and perhaps I can rejuvenate you later ...' She smiled that awful smile, the one which displayed her long teeth in all their equine charm.

'Oh dear, I'm so sorry. I've got to work tonight, darling. Going to be a late night, I'm afraid.'

'Oh.'

Lucinda tended not to complain when he had to work into the night. It was part of the lot of the barrister, she knew. They were only certain which case they were doing the night before it was on. So the preparation – reading the statements, teasing out the inconsistencies, devising the cross-examination – all of this had to be done late into the night. And she couldn't moan too much – it paid for the house and the health club, after all. In time, if he got to the High Court Bench, it might even make a Lady of her.

Just then, the phone rang.

'I'll get it.'

Alexander raced to the phone before the answering machine cut in. He wouldn't put it past Rita to leave some incriminating message.

'Alex, it's Seb.'

'Hello.'

Alex's tone was cautious. He'd never liked Seb, particularly since the man had got silk before him. He'd been applying to become a QC for years, and been politely rejected each time with the usual thin envelope from the Lord Chancellor's Department. Seb had got it on his first application – the longed-for 'thickie' envelope. Stuffed with details of the silk ceremony, you'd know before you'd opened it that you'd made it. And because he was the only silk, Seb had been the automatic choice to take over Chambers when their previous Head had got his High Court appointment.

'Alex, I thought I'd ring you at home. I've taken on a new pupil – she was looking for somewhere urgently after that Crown Office Row débâcle. I was against her in a murder this week and she was superb. I didn't want to pass up the opportunity.'

Alex spluttered, 'But what about the pupillage committee? These things have to go through us.'

'Too urgent, I'm afraid. This was a special case.'

'What about Dorton?'

'Don't worry. There's enough work for two pupils at the moment. In fact, Ron was quite clear that we need extra bodies.'

'So she's a second six?'

'Yes . . . And Alex, Ron and I felt that you would be the appropriate pupil master.'

Seb paused. He could only imagine the colour that Alex's face was becoming.

'But that's outrageous! You can't simply foist some rookie on me! I haven't got time, you know the demands of my practice . . .'

'I'm sorry, Alex, but she will be out of the way doing her own work. I hadn't realised you'd object so strongly.'

'Well I do. You should have checked. I simply cannot take on a pupil. I *will* not.'

Seb smiled. Alex was going into pompous mode. Time to put the plan into action.

'Then don't worry, I'll cancel her. Such a pity, though – she's already got a brief from Mark Singerhof at Gissinghams.'

There was a pause at the other end.

'Mark Singerhof?'

'Yes. Apparently, he'd heard of her through some paper she'd written at Cambridge. When Ron mentioned she was joining us, he immediately asked to instruct her. I don't know what he'll think if I have to tell him that she's gone elsewhere . . .'

Five seconds went by. Seb counted them as he waited.

'Bloody hell, Seb. He's just sent me a new fraud . . . We'll look like a bunch of incompetents to him . . . You really have put me in an impossible situation.'

Seb kept quiet. There was a sigh down the phone line. Seb's smile broadened into a grin.

'All right. She can by my pupil, rather than have our Chambers look foolish. But Seb, don't do this again. The committee is there for a reason, you know.'

'Of course, Alex. So sorry.'

Alex gripped the receiver hard. The bastard was smiling. He could hear it in his voice.

Seb put down the phone with a grin. Mission accomplished.

64

The next Chambers meeting was going to be a memorable one. Time for a drink before bed. He padded barefoot into the sitting room and picked up the whisky bottle.

Just then, there was a loud crash. He jumped, dropping the bottle, which smashed around his feet. He winced as a shaft of pain lanced through him.

Shit. Blood everywhere. Seb hobbled to the kitchen, looking for the first aid box. There was a hell of a draught. He turned around to find the back door open, swinging in the wind. There was another crash as it rebounded off the wall. Seb walked towards it, trying not to cry out each time his injured foot touched the floor.

It was a windy night. He must have failed to shut the door properly. He pulled it to and locked it.

Back in the kitchen, Seb found the first aid box. Damn, there was still glass in the cut. Best thing would have been to get Dad's nurse to sort it out, but it was her night off. He'd have to do it himself. And he hated blood. Dad had always thought it the funniest thing ever. A six-foot man who fainted at the sight of blood. Ridiculous.

He got the tweezers and looked again at the glass. On a count of three. Come on, man, grow up. One, two . . . three. Quickly in, tweezers clamped around it and pull like hell. Yes, got the bloody thing, here it is. Oh shit, everything's going a bit wobbly at the edges, I know what's coming . . .

He was out for about twenty minutes. He came to on the kitchen floor, freezing cold and with a splitting headache. Damn. He sat for a while, looking away from his foot, waiting until he felt vaguely human again.

As he sat, the old thoughts came back again. He hated being on his own. It had struck him lately just what a sad specimen he was. No one to argue with, maybe, but no one to care either. He could have lain there all night and nobody would have known. Dad might have found him in the morning if he'd gone for one of his wanders. But that was it.

65

Even life with Clarrie had to be better than this. It was probably his fault anyhow, that things had gone the way they had, now he thought about it properly. She'd wanted children so much. And when she'd finally found out it could never be, he hadn't been there for her. He'd been up in his study, night after night, building his career. It had worked well, to a degree. He had raced up the ladder, getting work that half the Temple coveted. But it had ruined his marriage. Clarrie had turned to others for company, had hardened, become cynical.

It was his fault. Things could have been so different if he'd had more sense, seen it from her point of view. All he had now was a healthy bank balance, a decent house in pretty countryside, and a father with Alzheimer's. Sum total: bugger all. At least in what mattered.

The bleeding had stopped, finally. A quick rinse in the shower and he could get away without having to dress the wound. Gingerly, Seb made for the stairs.

He'd just check Dad's flat on the way. He always did it. Sometimes, Dad was awake. Occasionally, he'd even know who he was and be able to have the semblance of a conversation. More often, though, he'd either be asleep or staring blankly at the wall opposite, rambling incoherently.

Still, at least there was room for him to live in the house. The flat had been intended for use by a nanny, a big plus for Clarrie when they'd bought the place way back. They'd gone out on a limb for this house, borrowed what had seemed at the time to be a vast amount to get it. It was beautiful, granted – a beamed farmhouse just into Suffolk, but handy for the fast trains into London.

Now it was largely empty, the nursery used not by four young children as planned, but by a retired bank manager in his late seventies who didn't know what day of the week it was.

Quietly, Seb opened the door. Dad wasn't in the sitting room. Probably gone to bed. He tiptoed through to the bedroom.

He wasn't there. The bed was still made up.

Seb's heart started to beat faster. He hurried back to the sitting room and out onto the landing. Toilet? Bathroom? Both empty.

'Dad?'

Silence.

'Dad!'

Shit. Why did the nurse have to be off tonight?

He thought back. He'd passed out for a while. He'd had a cut on his foot. He'd dropped the bottle.

The door. The door had been open.

Dad must have gone out.

He had a dreadful feeling in his stomach, like the night he'd come home to find the letter from Clarrie. He hobbled down the stairs, and pushed his feet into some outdoor shoes. Bloody hell, that hurt. He grabbed some trousers from the tumble dryer, a jumper from the radiator. Quickly, he threw them on, over his pyjamas.

The wind gusted around him as he stood outside the door.

'Dad! Are you out there?'

No answer.

Seb set out across the garden. It was pitch black now and he couldn't see a thing.

Where the hell would the old man have gone?

He stopped and tried to look around him. There was an acre and a half of garden around the house. In front, a lane leading down to the village and the pub.

Seb set off for the village, calling down the lane for his father. The village was two miles away. After half an hour, he knew it was a mistake. His foot was agony, the cut rubbing on the upper of the shoe. He could feel liquid. It must be bleeding again. He was walking at a snail's pace. It was bloody hopeless.

'Dad! For God's sake, Dad . . . are you there?'

No good. He started to walk back to the house. It would have to be the police now.

67

The young officer turned up an hour later. Seb had given the details and found a torch with which to start looking. Radio messages were sent, and cars told to patrol the lanes, looking out for an elderly and confused man.

'You wait here, sir. That foot looks pretty nasty.'

But he couldn't just sit there. The only member of his family, alone out there somewhere, and he'd just let him go.

Seb had put his slippers on. They were the most comfortable things he could find, but he couldn't go far in them. Still, he could help. Do his bit.

The officer had made straight for the front garden. There was a pond there and Seb knew what the man was thinking. He couldn't bear to be out there, not if they found a body. Please God, please. He's all I have. Without him, I really am on my own.

He opened the back door and paused. Dad would have gone left or right here. Left to the front garden, the pond and the road. Right to the back garden. No immediate hazards there, so the police were concentrating on the front. He padded off down the lawn at the back. There was a bite to the wind – lazy wind, he'd heard one of the locals call it – and it went through you rather than bothering to go round. He shivered.

What did Dad usually do when he came out here? At first, he'd like to wander round the garden, pulling up weeds as he went. Funny, he'd been able to do that long after the Alzheimer's had set in. Somehow he'd remember which plants were weeds, even though he thought the Prime Minister was Mr Baldwin. But lately, with increasing frailty, Dad had tended to concentrate on the rose bower.

It had been put in by Clarrie years ago – an old wooden seat, roses growing around it, tubs, a trellis, beautifully fragrant on still summer evenings.

It was a long way in the dark, right down to the bottom of the lawn. Seb stumbled and fell. Quickly, he pulled himself back up again. He wished he'd not lent his torch to

68

the police officer. It was so black, he could almost feel the darkness, soft, velvety, entombing him.

Funny, he'd never realised how noisy the garden was at night. The larger shrubs were bending away from the gusts of wind, the stems groaning as they leaned. A thousand leaves rustled in unison and the branches of the enormous ash tree creaked under the strain.

Ouch! Something caught his left arm. Seb pulled it back and felt the thorn trace its way through his skin. He'd reached the rose bower.

He stopped for a moment, trying to make out shapes in the darkness. If he moved a few steps, slightly to the right, he should just clip the seat . . . yes, there it was.

Seb moved towards it gingerly, his right hand out, feeling for the back of the seat. He had his bearings now. Yes, there was the top of the wood, rough, gnarled. He ran his palm along the top.

He stopped. There was an obstruction. Slumped on the seat. A soft pyjama jacket and under it, a shoulder. Very, very cold.

Dad.

Seb hobbled to the edge of the bower and hollered so loud his throat hurt.

'Come quickly! Bottom of the garden. Now! Please . . .'

Chapter Nine

Abby woke at five-thirty. There was a strange feeling in the pit of her stomach and it took her a while to work out why. Of course! The first day of her new pupillage.

She knew that she wouldn't get back to sleep, so she got out of bed and changed into her running clothes. She hadn't run for a few days and could do with a decent workout. Shed some of the pounds those biscuits had put on.

Once dressed, Abby made her way up the basement steps and onto the busy street. She broke into a steady trot and made her way up the hill to the Angel. There were a few street people about, most still asleep in doorways. Some yelled out to her as she passed and she did her best to ignore them. On she went, past the traffic lights and up to Camden Passage. She was starting to tire a little now, but forced herself to go farther, pounding her way back towards the tube station.

Downhill all the way now, she thought to herself. Back over the road and a sprint to the flat. She arrived at her door, her lungs feeling as though they were going to burst. It was the best way to start the day.

Marcus, too, was awake early. He had a mums' and toddlers' service at two, so he would have to get up to Colindale shortly. The Rectory was a gloomy Victorian building, next door to the church. He'd had a quiet night for once, apart from the dreams which came every time he nodded off. The same thing each time – trains, blood, death, damnation. But he'd spent years being tortured by bad dreams. And at least he'd not had to get up and tend to an unexpected visitor. Often, the homeless or unhappy would knock at his door, deep into the night. It was always opened to them, and often Marcus would wake in the morning to find his downstairs rooms turned into an unofficial hostel. Today, though, it was empty.

It was, however, very untidy indeed. Marcus looked at the state of the place in the early morning light. It was almost enough to send him back to bed. He'd certainly slipped since his navy days, he knew. Then, he had lived an exemplary service life – his boots polished and stacked in just the right place every night, his bed made as soon as he climbed out of it, even his toothbrush cleaned after use and placed back on the right side of a gleaming glass.

This is just not good enough, he thought to himself. He started with the living room, putting the books back on the shelves and polishing the tables. The house seemed to accumulate dust like nobody's business. Then the same for the dining room – easier now, because he so rarely used it; and finally the kitchen, which was a complete tip.

Afterwards, he sat back as he ate his breakfast. It certainly seemed much cheerier now. Perhaps he ought to buy a few things for it – some pictures, maybe, or even some furniture. Anything to give the place a bit of life.

Maybe he would buy something today, if he had time. There was a place up the road that might have a few pictures. But for now, to business. It would be good to have a blast on the old bike.

He was going in the opposite direction to the traffic flow and made good speed. By ten o'clock, Marcus was waiting outside the newspaper library at Colindale, right on the northern outskirts of London.

Abby, by now showered, breakfasted and dressed in her

71

black suit, walked to Chambers. It was a glorious morning, although the air had a bite to it. The shops in Chancery Lane were still shut as she walked past. She stopped briefly to look at the robes in the window of Ede and Ravenscroft. This shop supplied many of the barristers' and judges' white wigs, although she'd had to buy her own secondhand. Further down, on the corner of Fleet Street, she looked in the window of Hammicks, the legal bookshop.

The traffic on Fleet Street was already heavy, taxis and buses ploughing their way up to the Royal Courts of Justice on the Strand. The road ran from the City, with its towers and commerce, through the legal arena of the Temple and the courts, and on into the heart of the West End, with its theatres and palaces.

She crossed the road and dived through the old gate into the Temple. The paperman, as always, stood on the corner, daily papers and magazines at the ready. Once past the hustle of Fleet Street, Abby slowed her pace, enjoying the peace of the Temple. The church, one of the most ancient in London, was on her left. She thought of Marcus and wondered whether he was up yet.

Abby paused briefly outside the entrance to 29 Pump Court. She might stay here six months. Or if things went right, it could be forty years or more. The outcome would depend on her.

'Miss Penhaligon! Good to see you nice and early. Shall I take you to your room? Mr Golightly has agreed to be your pupil master and he'll be in later.'

Ron smiled his greeting. Excellent start, he thought to himself. Mr Waters himself used to get in at eight when he was a pupil. James Dorton wouldn't materialise for another two hours yet.

He led Abby up to the first floor and opened the door off the left side of the staircase.

'Here we are, ma'am – if you take that empty desk in the corner. I've got a little matter of a mitigation in Chippington

72

for you tomorrow – the papers should be with us soon. In the meantime, make yourself at home. Coffee room's downstairs.'

Abby paused, frowning.

'Not ma'am, please . . . why not Abby?'

Ron shook his head. 'Goodness gracious . . . you're a barrister, the choice is sir or ma'am.'

'But I don't want to be ma'am. I'm not the Queen, you know.'

'Miss Dengie is ma'am.'

This was getting surreal, thought Abby.

'Abby.' She tried to make her voice sound firm and unyielding.

'All right, ma'am.'

Obviously not unyielding enough. I'll have to work on that one, she thought to herself.

Ron, smiling gently, shut the door as he left. Abby sat down tentatively at the desk. It was old, leather bound. There were some bare shelves beside it, set into an alcove. Abby imagined them groaning with work.

Her pupil master's desk was on the other side of the room, its back to the large Georgian window. She'd never heard of Mr Golightly and wondered what he would be like.

Since it was her second six months of pupillage, she would spend little time with him, she knew. But this Mr Golightly would have a lot to live up to, after Daniel. Still, judging from the papers on his shelves, he was pretty busy. Abby stood up and cautiously moved over to his desk. There was a set open, the red tape carelessly thrown over an ashtray. Abby looked at the uppermost page. Looked like crime, she noted with relief. Commercial fraud, judging by the number of bank statements in the exhibits.

As she read on, the door opened loudly. Startled, Abby looked up.

'Hi Miss Penhaligon – just come to say hello!'

It was a friendly face, surrounded by rather angelic, blond, wavy hair.

'I'm Joe Heiney, junior tenant. Ron told me you were starting today.'

Abby moved towards him and smiled.

'Yes – do call me Abby.'

'Abby it is, then. Must say, good to see you so bright and early. Alex – your pupil master – doesn't usually roll in until two minutes before ten.'

She smiled. 'I thought it would be good to settle in. What sort of work do you do?'

Joe sat on Abby's desk. She took the cue and perched on Golightly's.

'General crime – crown court work all over the place, really. I was Seb's last pupil before he took silk, and just carried on doing a lower level version of his practice, really.'

'Is there plenty of work around?'

He nodded quickly. 'Lots – particularly at the lower end. And the criminal stuff pays quicker too, which is always a help when you're starting out.'

'Who are the other tenants?'

'There are a few based at various other points in the country – they rarely come in, other than for the AGM. The ones you'll see most here are Rita, Alex and Seb, of course.'

He paused and looked at her carefully. 'Rita you'll have to watch.' He had lowered his voice conspiratorially.

'Why?'

'She's got a bit of a reputation as a drawbridge merchant.'

'A what?'

'Women in Chambers. I've got in, got a good practice, so I'll pull up the drawbridge to stop anyone else coming in. That sort of mentality.'

'Oh.'

'Don't worry, though. We all expect it of her so it doesn't really make much difference.'

'What sort of work does she do?'

74

'She's always done a lot of family cases. She doesn't really like them, though. Thinks she's not earning enough. In the last few years she's been spreading her wings a little, trying other areas of work.'

'And what about Alexander Golightly?'

Joe paused.

'Well, he's quite a traditional sort of chap. Went to Eton, then Oxford. Lives in Surrey with an Honourable wife. OK though. He does a lot of commercial crime – quite good stuff. Rita's got her eye on the same sort of thing.'

Joe looked at his watch.

'Anyhow, I'll catch you later. I've got a conference at ten, so I'd better get ready. When you get your papers for tomorrow, bring them in to me if you want so I can give you a few ideas – first time on your feet is always pretty awful.'

'Thanks. I did a tiny bit at the end of my first six, though.' Abby smiled as he left the room.

Just before ten, the door crashed open and a furious-looking man came in. He walked straight past her desk and plumped himself into his chair, slinging his papers down. He was large, with balding grey hair Brylcreamed into place, a stubby nose and flaccid jowls. He'd obviously cut himself shaving, and there was a tiny patch of tissue on one cheek.

Only after he'd sat down did he acknowledge Abby's presence.

'I'm Golightly. You must be Penhaligon.'

Abby tried to smile. 'Yes, Abby.'

'Hrrmph. Have they got you any work yet?'

'No, I'm waiting for the DX. I've got a case in Chippington tomorrow.'

'Yes, I know. Well, make yourself useful in the meantime. Cup of coffee, white, two sugars.'

Abby tried to be gracious, although this was rather different to life with Daniel. Still, it was the first day. She left the room and found her way to the coffee room. There,

75

she poured a cup from the filter machine and unearthed the milk and sugar.

'There you go.' Abby placed the cup carefully in front of Alex. She had no idea what to call him. She couldn't use his first name without a cue from him. But there was no way she was going to refer to him as Golightly. She knew other members of the Bar used surnames only, but she was buggered if she was going to carry on as though she was at some third rate public school.

As she stood uselessly in front of the desk, he grunted at her.

'Stay there a moment.'

He extended an arm towards his shelving and took a large set of papers from the top.

'Here you are. Read through this – it's a commercial fraud. Insider trading at the stock market. I'd like you to go through the bank statements and prepare a schedule of entries and withdrawals of the sums in the charges.'

'OK.'

'And let me give you a tip. If you want to get on at the Bar, you may want to dress a bit better.'

Abby was stung. 'Sorry?'

'Good. So just pop down to a decent ladies' outfitters and get a couple of new suits.'

She reddened. Bloody cheek. She stood up straight and looked him in the eye.

'No, I wasn't apologising. I wanted you to explain what you meant just now.'

There was an oppressive silence as Alex glared at her.

'Well, just trying to point out the obvious. Do you have a problem with me trying to guide you in the right direction?'

Abby was furious. Who was this pompous fool to start lecturing her on what she wore? Her eyes flashed.

'Is there something wrong with this suit?'

'Well, put it this way. No judge is going to take you seriously if you turn up in last year's cast-offs. Particularly when it doesn't even fit you properly . . . can I suggest the next size up?'

Abby was fuming. 'And with what do you suggest I buy these magnificent outfits?' Her voice hung in the air.

He was momentarily silenced.

'Surely your parents can help out.'

'I only had one. She's dead.'

Even Alex went a bit pink at that. Serve him bloody well right, she thought to herself. he dropped his eyes and looked at something on his desk.

'Well, just trying some friendly advice. Now, I'd like those schedules by nine tomorrow, if you don't mind.'

'But I'm in court tomorrow.'

'Then pop them in before you leave.'

His tone had lifted at the end of his last remark. He was clearly starting to lose whatever patience he'd started out with. Abby sniffed and took the papers back to her desk. She sat for an hour, trying to make sense of the dodgy transactions. She'd never undertaken work like this before, but there was no way she was going to ask for assistance. Not from him.

At eleven, the door opened and a young man walked over to Alex's desk. Her pupil master looked up and smiled.

'James, dear boy. How are you this morning? Do thank your mother for that lovely meal at the weekend. The crème brulée was a triumph, an absolute marvel.'

James grinned. 'Nothing's too much for the old god-father.'

'James, do meet Miss Penhaligon, who's with us for the next six months.'

James turned to face Abby. He was a tall, gangling young man, still with a trace of acne around the chin.

'Pleased to meet you.'

He seemed pleasant enough. Abby had met many like him at university. Educated to perfection but still not particularly bright.

'Hello.'

'James is here on a second six with a view. That means that as soon as he's finished his pupillage, he'll be joining us permanently.'

Alex was rubbing her nose in it now. She was here for six months only, he had said; James would be asked to stay. Seb hadn't mentioned anything like that. Her face started to redden. Slowly, she stood up.

'Going somewhere?'

She turned towards Alex. 'Am I expected to ask your permission before I leave the room?'

He smiled sardonically. 'Just a polite enquiry.'

'I'm in court tomorrow. My papers are ready.'

'Make sure you finish my work before you deal with anything else . . . it's a big case.'

Abby's eyes flashed. Her patience finally deserted her.

'Let's get this clear, Mr Golightly. I'm going to represent my own clients to the best of my ability. I'm not going to skip preparing their cases just to save you some work.'

Alex looked horrified. Good, serve him right. With that, she turned on her heel and clumped down the stairs.

'Here you are, ma'am.'

'It's Abby, Ron . . .'

'Yes, ma'am.'

With a grin, he handed Abby her first brief.

'I hope it's the first of many.'

'Thanks, Ron.'

Abby looked at the neat bundle of papers. In the Crown Court at Chippington, it said. R v Winter. Brief to counsel for the Defendant. And there was her name – Miss Abby Penhaligon, 29 Pump Court, Temple, London. Then the solicitors, Gissinghams, in Chippington.

She held the brief close to her chest as she raced back up the stairs. She felt like an Oscar winner. Thank you Mr Winter, for offending and needing her services. Thank you Gissinghams, for briefing a pupil barrister they'd never heard of. And thank you even to the Queen for graciously deciding, through the magnificent Crown Prosecution Service, to bring Mr Winter to Court.

She went into Alex's room and sat down at her desk. James had left, but her pupil master was still there, pointedly ignoring her. Well, sod him, she thought. She was back on familiar territory. Out on a limb, on her own. Better not weaken, Abby, or he'll walk all over you.

Her tutor at Cambridge had once gently suggested that she should be prepared to consider the wider picture, make a few concessions, jolly things along a bit. There were times, he said, when people might get the wrong impression about her, imagine that she had a bit of a chip on her shoulder when of course that was far from the truth . . . She'd not had the faintest idea what he was talking about.

Carefully, Abby untied the red tape and opened out her first brief. Dean Winter was up before the judge for the twenty-second time in his fifteen-year career as a professional burglar. Abby looked through his list of previous convictions. He had started out at fourteen with a clutch of taking without consents. At eighteen he had graduated to using credit cards – the problem being that he didn't actually own the ones he so frequently used. The usual attempts had been made to point out the error of his ways to Dean – probation, suspended sentences, community service orders. Clearly, none had had the slightest effect. From the age of twenty-two, he had been dealt with solely through prison sentences. There was no logical reason why he should incur anything less now.

Dean – Abby felt she knew him well enough for first names having read through his history – had been caught on video camera stealing from an unattended till in a clothes shop. An opportunistic crime, committed when he'd seen the keys left in the till lock. A report had been prepared on him. It made for pretty uninspiring reading. Couldn't suggest any non-custodial sentence . . . This was code for 'he's got to go inside for a bit'.

Abby took a pen and started to note down relevant

79

points. He was pleading guilty, so he would get a discount for not wasting anyone's time. It was an opportunistic crime. He'd been out of trouble – well, at least undetected – for almost a year. Presumably somewhere in the brief would be reference to a newly pregnant girlfriend whom he planned to marry in the near future.

Alex stood up.

'Just off for lunch with James. Don't forget the schedules, will you? If you can find the time from your flourishing practice, that is . . .'

'No,' muttered Abby. No chance of lunch from him then. Daniel Ditchcombe had always said it was tradition that the pupil master buy lunch for two each day, even if it was just a snack. Abby was already starting to regret her earlier outburst. She needed him on her side, after all. It hand't been a very good start. Damn. Not for the first time, she cursed her lack of tact.

Just then, her telephone extension rang.

'Abby, Joe here. Fancy a sandwich?'

He appeared in her room a few minutes later.

'How's the first day going?' He saw the brief spread out in front of her. 'Mind if I take a look?'

'No – I'd be interested to hear what you think.'

He read intently, his face not moving. He started with the statement, then looked through the previous convictions. The report came last.

'Well, it's got to be imprisonment, I'd say.'

'What about community service? It was a spur of the moment offence.'

'Maybe, but you won't persuade many judges to go for a CSO with that type of offending history. I'd say that it's a case of getting the shortest possible prison sentence.'

Abby pressed a little. 'I planned to talk about the nature of the offence, then move through his previous convictions.'

Joe nodded carefully. 'Keep it short, though. It's a busy court and the judge will have a lot of sentencing work. The

80

other thing which leaps out from the precons – previous convictions – is the fact that none of the offences involved violence. That's quite unusual in a record that long.'

'Yes.'

Abby kicked herself. She'd been studying the papers for an hour and hadn't noticed that fact.

Joe looked at the other papers strewn around her desk.

'So, Alex has got you working already, has he?'

'Yes.'

'And is he being totally charming and helpful?'

Abby muttered in answer. 'Not entirely. But I think I may have overreacted, too.'

'Ah. Look, there's a certain amount of politics going on with him at the moment – he's got some strange ideas about where Chambers is going. He'll move on to a new fad before long. Just hang on in there, he's quite harmless really. And do some of his work, but don't go mad. You'll have to concentrate on building up your own practice.'

Abby nodded.

'Lunch?'

Chapter Ten

It had been far too long a night. Seb had spent it on an orange plastic chair in the waiting area of the hospital. He'd dozed for a while, but most of the time he'd sat, still and aching. Every time the swing door opened in front of him, he'd braced himself, waiting for bad news. Each time, though, it was a false alarm.

The ambulance had taken a while to find the house. It was set back a long way from the road, the sign too small. He'd thought about replacing it for years but had never got round to it somehow. When they'd finally got there, they'd found a pulse, but it had been terribly weak. They'd wrapped Dad in some foil material and rushed him to the hospital. Seb had followed in his car, taking a last look at his father as he was bundled into the ambulance, his eyes grey and cold.

But the hospital staff seemed to have some hope left. Dad had gone into Accident and Emergency. Core temperature very low, they said, but stable. He was still alive. All they could do now was wait.

Seb tried to shift his position on the plastic chair. His foot was still hurting like hell. Maybe someone here would bandage it up. Everyone at the hospital had seemed so busy through the night, it had seemed too trivial to mention. He looked at his watch. Five o'clock. Four hours since Dad had arrived. Surely they must know what his chances were by now? A nurse came through the doors and Seb looked at her, trying to meet her eyes. She smiled blankly at him. Just like all the others. Must be their way of dealing with things. Every morning, they must see the relatives lined up outside the department. Some struck lucky and would get a second chance; others would be about to join the ranks of the recently bereaved. Christ, it was grim.

He'd ring Ron in a moment. He was due in court, but he couldn't leave his father. His junior would just have to do his best. If they changed the running order, they could deal with his witnesses first. It would be a bit of a muddle, but there was no way he could leave.

'Mr Waters?'

A young girl in a white coat stood at the entrance to the waiting area. She couldn't be qualified, surely?

Seb nodded.

'Would you like to come with me?'

He scoured her face. Happy? Sad? Nothing. Just exhaustion. She walked briskly, not looking behind to check that he was following. She led him into an empty cubicle.

At that point, he knew.

'I'm sorry . . . we seemed to be winning for a while, but twenty minutes ago, your father had a heart attack. There was nothing we could do . . .'

She mouthed the platitudes. Seb watched her face move, heard the words, but took nothing in.

'Are you OK? I can prescribe you something. It's all been a bit of a shock, I know.'

'No. No thank you.'

There was an awkward silence, broken only by an insistent beeping noise from the doctor's pager.

She rolled her eyes and grimaced. He nodded at her.

'Please don't worry, I'll be fine.'

She hurried out of the cubicle.

Seb leaned against the empty bed. Idly, he wondered if it had happened in here; if this little white world had been the last thing his father had seen. He prayed not. It was so

83

small, so sterile, just a place for those passing through.

On the other side of the curtain, Seb could hear the sounds of the hospital: pagers beeping unpredictably; a shouted greeting to a ward cleaner; a yelp of pain followed by soft words from a nurse. Life was continuing; it had to. Of course it did. But for him, somehow, it had stopped for a few moments.

Seb felt the tears pricking the back of his eyelids. He had never felt so alone in his life. Slowly, he opened the curtain and shuffled out. No one noticed as he left.

Home, home.

Automatically, he pointed his car in the right direction and drove. The lanes were quiet, the air clear. It was going to be a beautiful day.

He'd ring Ron from home. He'd understand. He was due in court, but it was no good. His junior would cope. He just didn't care all of a sudden.

He drove up the driveway, past the gates it had taken the ambulance so long to find. The door opened easily and he walked through to the kitchen. His blood was still on the floor from last night.

He looked at the red stain and felt himself start to shake. Then he wept, desperate, uncontrollable tears, which fell from his face to the floor below. There was nobody to hear, nobody to comfort.

Dad's room. He had to go there now. He'd never do it otherwise.

Silently, he climbed the stairs. The door was open, just as he'd left it last night. He crossed the threshold.

The room still felt as though it was Dad's. It smelt of him. His clothes were hanging in the wardrobe. His favourite chair was by the door, the one he'd brought with him from his own house after Mother had died. There were some pictures on the wall, prints from the classics.

He sat in the chair and looked around the room. Not a lot to show for a life: some savings, a few pictures and some furniture. And one child who'd failed miserably at marriage

84

and had no children. God, the old man must have been disappointed at how it had turned out.

He left the room and went towards the bathroom. The house was eerily silent. The nurse would turn up soon and he'd have to tell her. But at least there would be someone else around.

He ran the shower cold and hard and climbed in, oblivious to the shock. Quickly, he cleansed himself, scrubbing until he was immaculate. Still the house was quiet. Too quiet. A silence which became overwhelming. The house was way out of the village, standing alone. He'd thought once that it would be a good thing, that he would find peace here. But peace didn't come from outside. In fact, silence just made it worse. He needed life around him, noises, shouting, cars. Anything to get away from what was going on in his mind.

He sat down and put his head in his hands. He couldn't stand it any longer. He'd go to work. It would save explanations, problems. He'd leave a note for the nurse, let her know what had happened. And at least he'd be out of this place for a few hours. And then there was the Chambers meeting to chair. He'd not get home until about eight tonight.

The thought was comforting.

Chapter Eleven

Marcus Kirkwall was having a most productive morning at the Colindale newspaper library. He had found himself a good spot, close to the librarian. Dressed for once in a suit and dog collar, he had no difficulty in obtaining her help in tracking down the newspapers from the 1940s.

He'd ploughed through all the locals for the months following VE day. It had been an education in itself. The real war was in the papers, he'd decided. It was not in the talk of treaties, super-power negotiations or where the King was spending his summer. No, here was the real story of a country at the end of a long, hard war: families coping without their men; women making meals from virtually nothing at all; the relentless cheeriness – chin up at all costs, even if you had lost everything. They'd won the war in Europe, although the Japs were still fighting. Soon, it would all be over if everyone could just hang on and do their best.

The VE celebrations were splashed all over the front pages of the local papers as well as the nationals. Pictures of street parties, smiling children, worn out women. It wasn't until five pages later that he found what he was looking for. A couple of columns, headed with a photo.

'*Senior reporter found dead.*'

Magnus scanned the report quickly. Denny Jacobs had been found dead in the newspaper offices. Police suspected foul play, it said, without giving any details. Probably didn't want to give too much away. He'd left a wife, Isobel, who was expecting their first child.

Marcus shook his head to clear it. There had been a murder on VE night at the newspaper offices. Henry had been telling the truth.

It had really happened.

He had to find the report of the trial. It must have happened a few months later. Quickly, Marcus returned to the desk, ready for the next batch.

This was where it started to get difficult. He could only guess when the trial would have happened. He decided to begin in December 1945, and read through the weekly editions, forcing himself to scan every item in the news pages to make sure that he didn't miss it.

March 1946. Page two: there it was! Marcus read it right through, as quickly as he could.

'Manslaughter of Denny Jacobs: reporter convicted.'

It was all there, in the rather dry tone of the papers in those days. Abraham James, a junior reporter, had pleaded guilty to the manslaughter of Denny Jacobs on VE night. He had admitted drinking to excess and becoming involved in an argument with his boss. He had lost control of himself and had struck him with a knife, killing him.

He had no previous convictions, and the prosecution accepted that he had lost control, which was why they were prepared to accept a plea of guilty to manslaughter. He was sentenced to twenty years' imprisonment. Before he left the court for Dartmoor, he was asked if he had anything to say, but apparently stayed silent.

Marcus put down the paper and stared hard at the desk in front of him. Henry had not been making up some drunken tale. There really had been a murder and a trial all that time ago. Well, if he was right on that, the chances were he was right on what had really happened.

Marcus stretched back in his chair and closed his eyes. It was a mistake. The scene at the tube station was there in an instant. He started to shake.

Don't worry, Henry. I'm getting there.

Marcus raced through the mothers' and toddlers' service later that day, ending with the fastest version of *Jesus Wants Me For A Sunbeam* that anyone could ever recall. Afterwards, he ran back to the Vicarage and started to investigate in earnest.

The chaplain at Dartmoor was very helpful. He'd check the records, he said. If he found an address, he'd contact the man direct and find out if he would agree to Marcus contacting him. Marcus thanked him and hung up. At least he'd have something to report to Abby the following evening.

He sat back in his chair. He had to know more. Someone who knew about the extra cargo and would be ready to talk. They'd have to give the court some explanation, surely? Some reason why Henry had acted as he did? He had Henry's words, of course, but he couldn't tell everything, not without breaking his promise to the man.

The classifieds in the local papers would have to be the first step. There might be people around who could help him. He'd have a go, at least.

He set to composing a message. Information sought, it said, on events surrounding the sinking of the *Richard Montgomery* off Sheerness in 1944. He kept it vague. He'd need as much as possible. If there was anyone – anyone who knew about the extra cargo – it would be a godsend. Then he rang Directory Enquiries for the Southend local papers.

The advert needed to go in quickly. They'd have to give it prominence, though. Cost was no object – it would be the first time he'd dipped into Henry's money, sitting safely in the bank.

He was finally getting the show on the road.

Rest in peace, Henry.

Trestle tables were laid out along the side of Inner Temple Hall, loaded with a cold buffet. Abby and Joe moved along, selecting from the display.

They found seats near the entrance.

'Have you heard about Seb?' asked Joe.

'No – what is it?'

'His father died last night . . . he'd been suffering from Alzheimer's and was living with Seb. He'd gone out into the garden at night, apparently, got exposure.'

Abby shook her head. 'That's awful . . . poor Seb.'

'Ron said he was pretty upset about the whole thing.'

Abby paused.

'It's awful losing a parent. I once read somewhere that you can only understand what it is to be alone when your last surviving parent has died.'

Joe thought for a moment, then looked carefully at Abby.

'I can understand that.'

Tactfully, he changed the subject.

'Any more work in the pipeline?'

Abby nodded. 'If I ever surface from Alex's paperwork.' Joe frowned. 'Don't let him offload too much. By all means do the odd set, but if he starts expecting you to run that side of his practice, tell him where to get off.'

'But I'd quite like a tenancy at the end of this, Joe. The last thing I need is a duff report from my pupil master. I went a bit far this morning, telling him I wouldn't do his work.'

'But you've got to stick up for yourself. People will respect you for that.'

He paused.

'What's this other work, anyhow?'

Abby frowned. 'Well, it may never happen . . . I do some work at a legal advice centre in Archway and we had a vicar in who'd taken a confession. This man admitted to a murder, and to framing somebody for it. He wanted things to be set right. It was pretty awful – killed himself, right after he'd spoken to the vicar.'

'Goodness . . .'

'But the murder took place in 1945 – that's the first problem.'

Joe smiled. 'Bit out of time for getting leave to appeal
. . . but in an exceptional case, you'd still get it.'

'Maybe. The second problem is going to be finding the
man who took the rap. He could be dead for all I know.'

Joe did the calculation.

'Fifty-five years. He may well be, but it's worth trying
to find him. A private detective might be able to help.'

'If we don't find him ourselves, that could be the next
option. This vicar is going to try and find out which prison
he went to, and see if the chaplain there can help.'

'Good idea. He sounds pretty resourceful, this vicar.'

Abby nodded. 'Yes, extremely. His name's Marcus
Kirkwall.'

Joe paused.

'A case like this would be a pretty good start for a pupil
. . . even Alex would find it difficult to object to your being
taken on permanently if you dragged something like that
into Chambers and made a success of it.'

Abby smiled. 'Just goes to show that we should all do a
stint at the law centre now and then.'

Joe put up his hands. 'Don't get at me . . . I've been
doing pro-bono work ever since I was a student. Now, Alex
. . . I'd like to see him having a go. Can you imagine it,
him in a church hall of a Thursday evening?'

They laughed together.

Chapter Twelve

Pascal de Montchavin was glad to be back in Paris. His home city, civilised, cultured, with real women, not English frumps or American neurotics. He stood a while on the Pont Neuf, watching the Seine with its armada of tourist craft floating by. *Dieu*, it was great to be back.

It was eleven in the morning. Almost time for his appointment. He walked towards the Pompidou Centre on the other side of the river. He'd chosen the venue for the meeting, but he needed to check it out, just to be sure. George might be planning on bringing a few accomplices. If he did, the deal was off. They had to be alone.

Pascal strode over the bridge. He was wearing one of his Armani suits. A shame to buy Italian, but they looked good on him, he knew. It was a dark grey colour, cut to perfection. He was wearing a Dior shirt, in a light blue, with the top button casually undone and no tie. His long dark hair was loose around his shoulders, framing his face and giving it a certain ambiguity. He was handsome, beautiful – a look made of fine lines and high cheekbones, which was just plain good looking, whatever the current vogue.

Some American tourists watched as he crossed the bridge.

'Must be famous,' he heard one of them say. He flashed a grin at the girl who had spoken who looked as though she was going to faint on the spot. God, they were so obvious.

He reached the edge of the square ten minutes later. The Pompidou was busy and crowds were milling around outside. The café was not busy yet – just a few elderly men and the *patron*. Pascal walked to the bar casually. He raised an eyebrow at the *patron*, who shook his head almost imperceptibly. Pascal nodded and passed a five hundred franc note over the counter before taking his usual corner table.

George arrived at 11.30 precisely. Pascal watched him negotiate his way through the tables to the bar. He was a big man, well over six feet tall, and broad with it. He was dressed in chinos and a polo shirt – unremarkable clothes, as ever. Good. Just a tourist doing the sights, common enough in Paris in the late spring.

Pascal had dealt with George many times before. They'd met first in the Grenadines, on the boats. George had been working for a rival charter firm, and they'd got to know each other over a few beers one quiet evening. They came from remarkably similar backgrounds. Both had titled fathers, with estates in the country. Both had gone to top boarding schools, and had left at the earliest possible opportunity. They knew each other inside out from the first time they met.

George had been operating a particularly profitable side-line, supplying cocaine to his customers. They expected it. The idle rich, too stupid even to sail the boats they had hired, needed something to pass the time. Something to persuade them that they were all witty, attractive and devastatingly clever. George had met that need well enough, but as word of his procurement abilities spread, he had needed more supply lines.

Pascal had come in at that stage, using his connections back in France. They'd operated together for a year or so, splitting the profits. George, though, wanted to get back to England. He'd grown sick of the sun, the beaches, the exquisite yet neurotic women. And so he'd carried on his

92

little sideline in England. Pascal knew it was even more profitable there. London was a major player in the European drug scene and George had made the most of it. He'd struck gold with ecstasy, getting into it just as the new club scene took off. Although he prided himself on being able to supply anything – coke, heroin, acid – the real business for him was in Es.

Pascal had returned to France three years later. George had made contact pretty quickly, and had rapidly become his best customer. Pascal could trust him. He'd drive a hard bargain, but he'd see it through. No funny business, either.

The *patron* nodded at George and motioned towards Pascal with his head. George walked into the gloom and took a chair at the table.

'Pascal, a pleasure, as always.'

'It's all mine, George.'

They spoke in English. George, as a patrician Englishman, spoke execrable French.

'Good. How much have you got for me?'

No mucking around either. Always straight to the point.

'One million tablets.'

George breathed out slowly. He knew better than to ask how they could produce such a vast quantity without using an articulated lorry. Customs had got much better at catching them and they had long abandoned that route.

'Quality?'

'A-1. It's all from Hans's lab. Top grade.'

'And how much are you asking?'

'Fifteen million. Sterling. Half by the end of next week. The rest two weeks later.'

George didn't need a calculator.

'That's way over the market value!'

'Then I'll take it elsewhere.'

'What are the delivery arrangements?'

Pascal looked hard at George. 'They are stored in a safe location within one hundred miles of London. Collection

93

from that point will be your responsibility. We will stop using the location and you will be free to continue as long as you need it.'

'How accessible is the storage place?'

'All I'm going to tell you is that you'll need a diver and marine transport.'

George nodded. 'That's going to add to my expenses.'

'Maybe. But the risk is lower than land-based storage.'

The Englishman paused a moment.

'I've got to have the storage. There's no point in having that much material unless the storage is perfect.'

Pascal held his gaze. 'It is. My word on that. And once I have the money, you'll have the free run of it. You can keep the stuff there as long as you want to.'

George nodded slowly. 'Five million.'

Pascal stood up. George sighed.

'OK. Eight.'

Pascal shook his head and started to move away.

'Come back.'

Pascal took his seat again. 'This had better be your best offer, George. I don't have time to fuck around.'

'Twelve, but that's it. Twelve million pounds.'

The Frenchman smiled to himself. The rumours were right. George was low on stock. Others were starting to dominate the market. The ecstasy trade in London was flourishing and dealers were only interested in quantity at the moment. They were cutting George out. That's why he was prepared to pay so much. He nodded slowly.

'Done. Payment of six to the usual account by the end of next week or it's off.'

'And when will you give me the location?'

'When I've made the last drop. It'll be within the month. Then it's all yours.'

The Englishman sighed. 'OK. Better come up with the goods, though. I'm relying on you.'

Pascal nodded. 'And now, what shall we do, mon ami?'

It was always this way. Pascal knew that George had a

particular need; a high class brothel with the roughest women he'd ever met. It kept him coming back to Paris. All in all, it was to be encouraged.

'I have the number right here, George.'

'We're meant to start now. I'm in a hurry.'

It was six pm. Alex didn't want to wait for Seb any longer. If the man was going to be late for the Chambers meeting, then he was certainly not going to hang on.

'Alex, for God's sake. His father died this morning.'

Alex would hear none of it. His face was red, his neck sweaty.

'Well, nobody's forcing him to chair the meeting. How long is he going to be, for heaven's sake?

Rita strode in. She was wearing a black suit, with a scarlet Hermès scarf slung casually across the shoulders. As ever, she was made up to within an inch of her life. A puce gash ran across her lips, and her face was powdered a strange white colour. At five foot nothing, her heels must have been six inches at least, tapering down to the tiniest point. She attracted and repulsed Alex in equal measure.

As a teenager, Alex went on a school trip to Paris. There, like many of his classmates, he had his first sexual experience with a prostitute picked up in the Pigalle. He had had fantasies of taking the woman to heights she had never reached before; of being thanked; of being lauded as the new Casanova. In fact, he had lasted no more than ten seconds up against a wall with her.

The memory, though, had stayed with him, and was just as potent decades later. More so, in fact. Twenty years of middle-class sex with the Hon. Lucinda had made him yearn for the passion of those ten seconds in Paris like never before.

That afternoon with Rita had rekindled those feelings like never before. He hated himself for it. The woman was a complete tart, he knew. She was past it, mutton dressed as

95

lamb. And her reputation reached far beyond the Temple. But what she had made him feel that afternoon was just incomparable. He prayed by the hour for another experience like it.

'Ah, everyone's here. Excellent.'

Seb breezed into the room without so much as a word of apology. Alex seethed quietly. He had never forgiven the man for getting silk before him and he had a nasty feeling that politics had had something to do with it. He had stood (as a Tory, naturally) for Parliament ten years ago. It had been his first try and they had put him in some hopeless Welsh constituency where he had polled precisely 2,384 votes – behind even the Monster Raving Looney Party. He'd applied to other local branches since, but had never had another go. He knew, though, that he was marked as a Conservative supporter. And while that may have been acceptable during the eighteen years of Conservative rule, with the new regime, he doubted it really helped. He had considered a Damascan conversion to New Labour, but knew that Lucinda wouldn't let him.

Seb cleared his throat and looked down the long library table. They always had Chambers meetings in this room, as it was the largest in the building. Meetings were always badly attended, though. Very few of the tenants had any real interest in making group decisions. They had their practices up and running, and once they had their brief for the next day, they were on the first train home. Tonight, he saw, there was Rita, Alex, looking distinctly sulky, Joe and Nigel Monroving, their oldest tenant, with a family practice which had been failing for twenty years. Nigel sat in his usual place at the end of the table. None of them mentioned Seb's father. He was relieved. Thank heavens for English reserve.

'Right. Recruitment first. In an urgent move I've taken on a pupil called Abby Penhaligon. She needed a decision immediately and came with excellent references. Starred first at Cambridge, second in her year at Bar School —'

96

Nigel's querulous voice cut in. 'Another woman? We've already got Miss Dengie.'

'No reason not to have another one, Nigel. We have to select on merit.'

'How very politically correct, Seb.' Alex smirked and lit a cigarette. Seb, a lifelong non-smoker, tried to ignore him.

Joe threw in some support.

'Well I met her today and she seems excellent to me. Intelligent, personable, obviously going to do well.'

Alex leant back in his chair.

'Are we talking about the same person? I met her today – no formal introduction, I should mention, even though I'm apparently her pupil master – and she sat and sulked for two hours. And so badly dressed – couldn't even find a suit to fit her.'

Seb took up the flow again, ignoring Alex.

'As I said, I took the decision on merit. And also because we are going to have to recruit aggressively. We've lost three key practitioners and if we are going to continue to attract work, we must fill those spaces.'

Rita spoke for the first time. 'This may well be a good time to think about whether we just want to carry on as before, you know.'

'What do you mean?'

Rita took her time. 'Alex and I . . . .' she smiled slowly at him, '. . . are actually developing a niche in commercial crime. And I have to say that it's rather a goldmine.'

Alex nodded quickly. 'Absolutely. It's heavy duty work, with good clients who are often paying privately. There's a lot of it around for the right people.'

Nigel sat up. 'Should I be moving into it?'

Christ, there are limits, thought Alex.

'Well, what I was about to say,' said Rita quickly, 'was that maybe we should aim not to recruit, but to stay small and move into the commercial crime niche. Existing tenants can run their practices as they please, but we direct our group efforts into developing that area.'

97

Seb shook his head. 'This has always been a generalist set, Rita. There are real dangers in putting all our eggs into one basket – what if we don't attract enough work or the Serious Fraud Office is disbanded? It's too risky.'

'I can't agree with recruitment just for the sake of it,' said Alex.

'But a small set can't be generalist. We won't be able to offer an across the board service.' Joe looked intently at Alex as he spoke.

'Are you saying that we've offered this girl some sort of tenancy?' asked Alex.

Seb was quick into the breach.

'Of course not. We've got to see what she's like on her feet. But I don't mind anyone knowing that my plan is for pupils who do well to be taken on. It's the best way to expand.'

'But what about James? He's been offered his pupillage with a view.'

Alex was being quite insistent. Joe rolled his eyes.

'Not by us, he hasn't. You may have told him something, but as far as I'm concerned, he was given a second six full stop. And I was against him yesterday on an injunction. He was all over the place – asked for a power of arrest when my client gave an undertaking.'

'That's a mistake we've all made,' said Nigel. Rita tried to hide a smile.

'Well anyway, we need to give both of them a chance to show what they can do' said Seb, fairly. 'But in the meantime, I'm going to put out feelers for some established practitioners. Sorry, Rita, if you want to develop a niche with Alex . . .' he waited and watched with pleasure as Alex blushed, '. . . the rest of Chambers won't be joining you. Now, I think that's a reasonable place to leave things, don't you?'

The meeting ended and Seb went back to his room to prepare his trial for the next day.

Rita walked quietly up to Alex's chair.

'Never mind, we'll just keep on pressing . . . talking of which, have you got time to pop round before you go home?'

Her voice was husky and full of potential. Alex's heart lifted. He stood up and followed her out of the room.

Chapter Thirteen

Pascal was asleep when the shit started to hit the fan. It was seven in the morning. He'd sorted George out, dropping him outside the building and leaving him to it. Then he'd gone to celebrate and had met a Dior model, out without her chaperone for the night. She was all of seventeen, and beautiful with it. Now she was next to him, sleeping off the night's activity. She barely moved when the phone next to Pascal rang.

It was Sam, the English contact.

'I'm sending you a fax. Now.'

The line clicked. Pascal sprung out of bed and walked into the study, throwing on a robe. The fax was already churning out its material. He read it quickly.

The blood seemed to drain from his face.

Not now. Please God. Not at this moment.

He put the sheet of paper under a book and moved back to the bedroom. Patrice was just waking.

'*Cheri* . . .' She reached her arms out to him.

'No, you have to go.'

'What?'

'Just go. Now.'

'But why . . . do you not love me now it's morning?'

He looked at her coldly. Why did they always think he loved them?

'I don't love you. I want you to go now.'

100

She moved suddenly, as though she'd been hit. Quickly, she climbed out of bed and put her clothes back on. Crumpled and dirty, they clung to her anorexic body. With as much dignity as she could muster, she left the flat without a word.

He had to speak to Thierry and Sam, sort out what they were going to do. It could be nothing, but if it meant the wreck was going to attract attention . . . *Merde*! and so close to the deal. One more drop . . . the final shipment was almost ready, for God's sake.

Pascal reached for the phone and punched in Sam's number. He tried to keep his voice casual, just in case anyone might be listening. They'd planned for a hitch, so he knew what to say.

'Sam, I'd forgotten it was your birthday – why don't you come over on Eurostar for the day? See you – around lunchtime?'

Sam got the message instantly and said he was on his way.

Then Pascal was on the line to Thierry. He'd be there at noon.

He went back to the fax and studied it once more. Some local newspaper, by the look of it. An advert in the personal columns: Information wanted on the *Richard Montgomery*.

Nothing more. Could be anything. Might even be code for something completely different. People communicated in strange ways, he knew. But it was worrying.

He stood up and moved over to the window. Paris was starting to get moving and he watched the workers walking on the pavement below. He thought. Hard.

This could be a real problem. Thank goodness Sam was doing his job properly. If he hadn't had someone based in England, this threat would have gone unnoticed. The last thing he needed was interest in the wreck. God only knew what it could lead to.

Quickly, he climbed into some old jeans, carefully hung

101

up in his wardrobe by the cleaner. They were tight on him, and he knew he looked good. His chest, muscled and hairless, was soon covered by a spotless T-shirt. His hair hung around his shoulders, framing his dark features. He wouldn't bother tying it back this morning.

There was no food in the flat. He didn't cook. There was a state of the art kitchen but he'd never even turned the cooker on. Never intended to, either. No need to in Paris.

Quickly, he left for the *boulangerie* on the corner.

Sam put down the phone and thought hard, too. The original cutting was by the fax machine. He'd seen it only thirty minutes before. Fifty-six bloody years that wreck had sat there, and nobody had expressed any interest in the thing for at least the last twenty. Yet now, at the very point when twelve million quids' worth of ecstasy was sitting in the wreck, some joker wanted information about it.

It had to be the police. Someone must have seen them, kept a log of their visits. But that would have been impossible. Pascal had used different boats, chartering them under made-up names so that he couldn't be traced. No one had ever been near the wreck when they'd been making drops.

David, the Breton? Pascal hadn't trusted him, that was for sure. Maybe he'd said something before his little swim and the authorities were on to them. But why this way? It made no sense.

Sam didn't like it. Not one bit. He had a nasty feeling that everything was about to go very wrong indeed.

His passport was in his jacket pocket already. Sam took his credit card and set off for the station. There, he mingled with the commuters and found a seat by a window.

Thank goodness he'd seen the advert. Someone had paid well for it. It was large, in bold type, grabbed the attention. Whoever had done it wanted information all right.

Sam badly needed the deal to go through. He had to have some money, and soon. He ran a small fishing boat, but had been hit hard by the new quotas. An ex-wife, three children and a child support agency assessment had made it impossible for him to meet the marine mortgage instalments a while back. He'd been stupid, hiding the letters from the finance company in a drawer, knowing it was just a matter of time before they re-possessed the boat.

Thierry had popped up just at the right moment. He'd known him for years, seen him around the fish markets before the Frenchman had left for the Caribbean. They'd done a little business then. Fags and spirits from France, stuffed into the bilges. It had brought in some welcome extra cash. He'd missed it when his mate had been away.

Then Thierry had returned. He'd got in touch and suggested a new line. Drugs. More of a risk, sure, but then the rewards were greater. Running a fishing boat out of a quiet English port was an ideal cover and they'd done a bit of trade. He'd motor over, bilges full of the stuff, and leave the boat wherever he was told for a few hours. He'd return to clean bilges and a good injection into an offshore bank account.

It had helped for a bit, that money. But he needed more and was starting to worry about the risks. Sooner or later, he knew, there would be a tip off and he'd return to the boat to find it full of customs officials. He wanted to get out before that happened. But get out rich. Very rich indeed. Rich enough never to have to put to sea again.

He'd met Pascal a year ago. There had been no need to before, with Thierry acting as middle-man, but this time a face-to-face meeting was necessary. The stakes were too high. A long project with a hell of a reward at the end of it: you didn't play in that league without wanting to check out your partners.

Each of them had liked what the other had to say. A big, safe deal and get out of the business for the time being.

And they were so close now. Two weeks and the money would be there. Three million pounds for him, then out. All he had to do was lie low in England and monitor things. He motored past the wreck several times a week and kept an eye on it. Any potential problems were noted and sent on to Pascal.

Well, this one had potential all right.

And if the worst came to the worst, he was on hand. With a large boat close to the drugs, they needed him as a fallback. If the heat got too much, with Thierry ready to dive he could get to the wreck and offload the stuff in a few nights. He'd sounded confident when asked about this by Pascal. And so he ought to be. It was a form of fishing, after all.

What he never admitted was that the wreck frightened him. All those years, sitting there with its lethal load of explosives just waiting to go up. No one could agree how bad it would be, but 3,000 tons would make one hell of a bang.

What terrified him most, though, was the appearance of the wreck. The masts still rose above the water, and there was seaweed hanging from them. It looked like some ghostly sailing ship, particularly when the moon was up. Fanciful nonsense, he knew, but it didn't stop him shuddering every time he saw it.

The Southend train ground into Liverpool Street, shrieking to a stop. Sam was off quickly, mingling with the commuters. He had dressed casually but smartly, hoping that he would not stand out too much on Eurostar. Soon, his short, burly frame was making its way across the main concourse.

As he did so, he passed Abby. Neither of them knew each other, of course, and they'd only ever meet once. She was up early to catch the Chippington train, her wig and gown in her bag, along with some sentencing reports and an Archbold, the bible of the criminal lawyer.

Flying solo at last! It had been nerve-wracking enough doing that cross-examination with Daniel. But there, at least, he was around to pick up the pieces if it all went wrong. This was a different proposition altogether. She'd

104

rehearsed her plea in mitigation most of the night. She knew it off by heart. She'd rung National Train Enquiries and was on far too early a train, but you never knew when there might be problems.

Abby sat in the deserted carriage as it snaked its way out through the East End. She tried to look out of the window, but couldn't stop going over her speech. Round and round her head it went. Then she started to get that awful gnawing feeling in the pit of her stomach. She'd gulped down breakfast much too quickly. Now she was feeling sick.

She forced herself to look out of the window. But it was no good. She dashed into the train toilet and threw up into a smelly metal sink.

After what seemed like a hundred years, the train drew into Chippington. Abby walked from the station, found her way to the court and entered through the smoked glass doors. The usher recorded her name – counsel for Mr Winter – and directed her to the robing room.

She sat in the corner of a vast modern room, strewn with haphazardly placed tables, wig tins and coats. Carefully, she put on her collarette – a white linen arrangement designed as a feminine alternative to the wing collar. Then her black gown, almost unused, and one very new-looking wig. There were twenty or so other barristers milling around the robing room by the time she was ready. They chatted, smoked and relaxed. Abby was the only one obviously preparing for her hearing as she ran a final check through her authorities.

She left the robing room and entered the waiting area, a large, square space in the centre of the court building. She checked the name of her solicitor and approached a few likely candidates.

'Mr Singerhof? Mr Winter?'

She was about to give up for the time being when she felt a tap on her shoulder.

'You must be Abby Penhaligon.'

She turned around to find a tall, slightly stooping man at her shoulder. He smiled a greeting.

'Mark Singerhof. Pleasure to meet you.'

'Hello – is our client here yet?'

'No, he won't put in an appearance until the last minute. He'll be relishing his last few moments of freedom, I expect. Can I get you a coffee?'

She followed him upstairs to the coffee bar. Already, it was packed with solicitors and barristers sharing the latest gossip. They found a seat at one end.

'Is this your first case?'

Abby thought about pretending, but realised it was pointless.

'Afraid so. Thank you for briefing me.'

'Not at all – it's a pretty academic exercise with Mr Winter, anyhow. But it's nice to give a career a start, particularly with the sort of build-up your clerk was giving you.'

'Really?'

'Yes – first class brain, allied with common sense – very rare in a barrister, I'd have to say!'

Abby laughed. 'Which judge have we got?'

'Mr Assistant Recorder Steinberg-Massey, it says. Never come across him myself, but he's unlikely to do anything remarkable as an AR.'

Abby shook her head. Assistant recorders were part-time judges – usually barristers. They were looking to make their way up the ladder to a full-time appointment and needed to show they were a safe pair of hands.

'Is there a Miss Penhaligon?'

Abby looked up. A barrister was calling her name. He was short, squat with a pugnacious face.

'Here.'

'Oh Jesus, it's Simon Manacute,' muttered Mark.

The other barrister stopped by the table.

'I'm prosecuting you in Winter. Guilty plea, you've had the precons I take it?'

Abby nodded, trying to look at home with the slang. Daniel had told her on her first day that the previous convictions were one of the most important documents in any plea of mitigation.

'Not seen you before – you done much court work?'

Abby went puce. 'Enough,' she muttered.

'Good. See you in court, as they say.'

'He's a shit,' Mark told her. 'Arrogant, pompous. None of the local firms use him. He'll try and bully you.'

'Even on a plea?'

'Yes, just for the hell of it. Listen to how he opens the case and stand up if he gets it wrong.'

'Thanks.'

'Hi, Mark.'

A twenty-something man in jeans and a bomber jacket appeared at the table.

'Dean – thought it was about time you showed up. This is Miss Penhaligon, she's representing you today.'

'Wotcha.'

Dean took the seat next to Abby.

'Don't worry, love. I know I'm going down. Just been seeing off the missus properly, if you know what I mean.'

'Spare us, Dean.' Mark grimaced.

Abby spoke. 'One of the things I noticed was that you've never had a precon for violence – is that right?'

'Yes. I just nick things. Don't want to start beating people up.'

They walked down to the entrance and milled around for a while. There seemed to be an awful lot of cases, all up for sentence only. The poor assistant recorder was probably bored to tears. Thank goodness her speech was short. She tried to make polite conversation with her solicitor and client, but the minutes dragged by interminably.

And then, finally, they were in. Dean was put into the dock. The judge entered and Simon Manacute started to speak.

'Guilty plea, Your Honour. The defendant reached over

to take money from an unattended till in a clothing shop last October eighteenth. In doing so, he pushed some elderly ladies out of the way.'

Abby's blood went cold. No he bloody well didn't.

Don't let him get away with it.

She stood up. 'May it please Your Honour . . .'

All eyes turned to her as Manacute went silent. But I can't just let this go by, she thought to herself.

'That's not right!'

Oh goodness, I don't sound like a lawyer, she thought. Why didn't I prepare for this? She felt her face redden. Then all the words vanished from her head. She froze. And the more she thought about it, the more difficult it became to say anything. Anything coherent, at least.

The judge raised an eyebrow. A press reporter coughed. Pull yourself together, silly woman, she told herself. He's only a judge. An assistant recorder who no doubt thinks dreadful thoughts, uses the toilet and sings in the bath, just like the rest of us. Get a grip . . .

Abby coughed lightly to clear her throat. Then the dam seemed to break and the phrases – the ones she had subconsciously digested during her first six months' pupillage – churned their way out.

'I hesitate to interrupt my learned friend . . .' with a gracious smile thrown in for good measure, '. . . but I have to indicate, Your Honour, that he has made an unfortunate mistake in opening the case this morning. My client did not push anyone out of the way – this was not an offence of violence, in any sense.'

Then she sat down. Manacute was back up on his feet.

'I'm so sorry, your Honour . . .'

The prosecutor's face had reddened. It was his turn to look foolish. Abby listened carefully as he continued. This time, he kept to the straight and narrow.

'Yes, Miss Penhaligon.'

The judge was looking at her impassively. Abby stood up again and took a deep breath. Keep your voice loud. Don't fiddle with your hands. Try to keep your tone deep. Do not, under any circumstances, squeak. Exude confidence. For God's sake, act like you're a professional.

All the mantras came back to Abby as she started her speech. She was half expecting someone to butt in and correct her, as they had in her training sessions at Bar School, but nothing happened, and she continued. On to the section about no precons for violence. Past that to the renewed family responsibilities and the understanding that his conduct must improve. Through it all, Abby looked towards the front of the court. Dean was behind her, in the dock. She couldn't see him and hoped like hell he was looking chastened and willing to change his ways.

She was on her feet for fifteen minutes, but it felt like an hour. By the end, Abby was conscious of sweat running down her body.

'Unless I can help Your Honour any further . . .' she finished impeccably. Code for 'that's my lot, Judge'. Her notes were still open in front of her. She hadn't looked down at them once.

The assistant recorder nodded briefly and prepared to pass sentence.

'Before I'd heard from your barrister today, prison seemed to be the only option. But having heard Miss Penhaligon's mitigation, I am going to sentence you to two hundred hours' community service. You are a lucky man to have such an astute counsel.'

He glared at Simon Manacute.

'And I'm extremely grateful to Miss Penhaligon for taking the trouble to correct prosecution counsel when he opened this case.'

Abby had gone bright red.

'Well done,' hissed her solicitor.

Dean gave her a thumbs up from the dock.

Abby could have floated all the way back to London. Instead, she left on the train, the congratulations still ringing in her ears. Thank God, she thought to herself.

109

Thank God I stopped that prosecutor.

She grinned across the empty carriage. 'I can do it,' she thought to herself. 'I really can do it!'

The only time she'd spoken in court before, she'd had a stroke of luck with her local knowledge. And she'd had Daniel right there, ready to help if she froze. This time, it had been the real thing. With a real client and a proper judge thinking about a real period of imprisonment.

And when it had come to it, she'd been OK. Better than that. Something had happened once she had got into her stride. She'd forgotten who she was, where she came from, the overdraft, everything. It was as though the world had shrunk to a point where all that existed was her and the task she had to do. Just her, a judge and an argument to run.

Abby grinned once more. 'I can do this job.'

Sam reached Paris just after lunch and made his way directly from the Gare du Nord to the café. Pascal had told him the name and given him directions many months ago. They'd never met there before. It was for emergencies only.

Pascal was there already, sitting at the back, a small glass of pastis in front of him. Thierry was with him, his face unshaven.

Sam took the third chair and Pascal started the meeting.

'Thierry, how long would it take you to get everything off the wreck?'

The other Frenchman thought for a few moments.

'It would be one hell of a job, now. One hundred and ninety-nine and I'm the only diver . . . I'd need to make one hundred journeys out of the hull if I carried two bags each time. I'd need several nights. Each round trip, boat to wreck and back again is at least twenty minutes.'

Pascal shook his head. 'It would be too much of a risk going back there, night after night. The port authorities will pick us up.'

Sam looked up from the table. 'Hell of a risk just leaving

them there though, if people are getting interested in the boat. I think the police have got on to it somehow.'

Thierry grinned. 'Maybe you're just panicking, Sam. For all we know, it's just some local historian who wants to know more about what happened to the boat. Why the hell would the police start putting adverts in the local paper?'

Pascal drummed his fingers on the table.

'We don't know what's going on. It could be the police, it could be something completely harmless. All we know is that somebody is interested in the wreck. And that's bad news for us.' He looked at the other two men. 'Leaving the drugs where they are may well be risky. Taking them off is dangerous, too. We could end up alerting the authorities to a problem they didn't even know existed.'

He paused.

'And then there's the problem of storage if we get them all off the boat. That's going to be impossible at short notice. And George will want a safe place for the drugs – that was part of the deal. I wouldn't put it past him to try and re-negotiate once he discovers what's happened.'

He took a sip from his drink and put it down again on the table, smoothing out a crease in the cloth with his index finger.

'We don't know enough yet to make a decision. There's twelve million pounds of trade there – I'm not going to decide anything until I have the best possible information.'

Sam spoke. 'But how can we find out more?'

Pascal looked up. 'We respond to the advert. I'll call the number, make up some story. Perhaps I've got some elderly relative who remembers the wreck. I need to know more about what they want so that I can speak to her about it all, find out if she can help them. Yes, that's how I'll play it.'

The other two were nodding.

'And then?' asked Thierry.

Pascal shrugged. 'And then, we'll have three options. If they're harmless, we ignore them. If it's the police, or customs, we'll just have to lift the drugs off and take a chance.'

'And the third?' Sam looked bemused.

'If it's not the police, but whoever it is does pose a risk, we eliminate them. Quickly.'

Thierry grinned. 'That sounds good to me.'

Pascal sat back in his chair. 'I'm going to go to the London flat tomorrow, as soon as I've got in touch with whoever placed this advert. I'll stay in London until the decision is made. You two get back to England tonight. Separate trains. Join me at the flat tomorrow evening and be ready to stay for at least two nights. Once I can get a response from whoever put this advert in, we'll be ready to do whatever's necessary. We need to sort this out quickly, before it becomes a problem.'

With that, Pascal pushed back his chair and left the café. His comrades drank up slowly and left at a discreet distance. Sam made straight for the Gare du Nord, looking over his shoulder as he went.

Chapter Fourteen

Abby was still on a high as she walked back to Chambers from the tube. Everything seemed perfect. The sun was high in the sky, birds were singing and she was going to make it as a barrister.

She popped her head round the door to the clerks' room to tell them she was back. Ron stood up.

'Miss Penhaligon – community service, I hear! Your solicitor has been on the phone already, he was so pleased. He's got a trial coming up soon in the Magistrates Court and wants you to do that. Well done!'

Abby smiled. 'Thanks – anything in for tomorrow?'

'We'll let you know. Mr Golightly is in Birmingham today, but I think Mr Waters might want a word.'

Abby looked surprised. 'He's back, is he? I heard about . . . well, about his father.'

Ron dropped his voice. 'Yes, he was in court yesterday and came in late to chair a meeting. He says he wants to carry on as usual.'

Abby climbed the stairs to Seb's room. She knocked before she entered – bad form, she knew, but it didn't feel right to go barging in. She'd been told in her first pupillage that barristers had to look on their Chambers as their home. As you didn't knock on doors at home, you shouldn't in Chambers, either. It seemed rather to miss the point though, however nice the thought, that a set of Chambers was not a home, and she'd heard no end of tales of embarrassing scenes resulting from the simple precaution of failing to knock first.

Seb looked up from the papers on his desk and smiled at her. He was very tired, it was obvious. He had huge bags under rather red eyes. Tie slightly off centre, and there was a sagging between the shoulders which even his immaculately cut suit couldn't disguise.

'Abby . . . grab yourself a chair. Sorry I didn't see you yesterday, but I hear you made a good start in Chippington today.'

Abby paused for a moment, unsure what to say.

'I'm sorry about your father.'

He nodded slowly, and their eyes met. God, he just looked so sad.

'Thank you. He was living with me . . .'

The QC's voice faltered a little. She watched him carefully.

'Seb, I know about it, My mother died when I was eighteen. She was all I had.'

Seb was looking over her head. His voice, when he spoke, was distant.

'He just wandered off into the garden at night. I should have stopped him. I could have, I just could have . . .'

Abby touched his hand lightly. 'Sometimes things just happen, you know. You shouldn't blame yourself.'

He forced himself out of his reverie.

'Sorry, Abby. Perhaps you're right. Anyhow, tell me about the case – did you enjoy it?'

'Seb, it was great . . . I knew I could do it, but somehow there was this thought that maybe I wouldn't be able to . . .'

He smiled, but not with his eyes, she saw.

'I know, don't worry. Until it's for real, you're never quite sure. And there are a few who get this far before they find out they can't go through with it.'

Abby grinned. 'What are you doing?'

'I'm starting an appeal tomorrow – a murder conviction

114

from Manchester. I'm just checking to see if there's been any new cases on translation evidence. My heart's not in it, though, I've got to say.'

Abby paused.

'Can I ask you something – about a case?'

Seb put down his pen. 'Please do. Anything for a break.'

'I was doing a session at the law centre the other night – it's usually small-time domestic and criminal stuff, but this time a vicar came in. He'd taken a confession from a man who said that, in the forties, he'd killed someone and framed someone else. Anyhow, he made his confession, asked the vicar to bring the appeal ... and then killed himself – right after.'

Seb breathed out slowly. 'Sounds pretty heavy duty. What did you tell the vicar to do?'

'I suggested he check the story, find out if there was a murder conviction. If there was, he'll need to find the client, although chances are he's dead by now.'

Seb nodded. 'Sounds impeccable advice to me.'

Abby paused.

'If there's something in it – and if the man who was convicted wants to bring an appeal – and if they want me in on it – would you be interested in coming in as the silk?'

Seb grinned. 'That's three "ifs" – but if they all come off, I'd be delighted. Let me know what happens on it, Abby, it sounds a fantastic case. It'll give me some ammunition for dealing with certain other tenants here, too.'

The phone went. Seb picked it up.

'It's Ron, for you, Abby.'

'Miss Penhaligon, I've got some papers for an injunction tomorrow. The solicitors are happy for you to take it on, so they're ready when you want them.'

'Great. I'll come right down.'

Seb looked up. 'Another solicitor crying out for your services? Well done.'

'Just an injunction. Mind you, it'll keep the bank manager happy.'

115

Abby raced down to the clerks' room and picked up the papers. They didn't look too bad – around fifty pages, neatly tied up in the usual red tape. More work. But another case meant another cheque – in the fullness of time, mind you. Some cases took years to pay.

Abby took the papers up to her room. She was desperate to open the tape and start preparing. But first, she knew, she had to get Alex's work out of the way. Damn. Mentally, she gave herself until four.

She opened the lever arch file and started noting down more transactions, working through her lunch hour and ignoring the clatterings on the staircase outside. She was trying to match up withdrawals from one account with payments in to another. Most tallied, but every now and then a withdrawal seemed to go astray. Carefully, she noted each one, writing down the account page reference in her blue notebook. By three o'clock, she had found fifteen discrepancies, adding up to nearly a million pounds. She'd left her laptop in the room overnight, and neatly typed up a schedule, setting out the entries and withdrawals. By four, it was finished. She also had a splitting headache.

She was just thinking about making herself a cup of tea when the door crashed open and Alex came in. He nodded at her briefly before settling himself down in his large oak chair.

Abby took the schedule over to him. She tried a tentative smile.

'All done. There's about a million gone astray.'

Golightly ran his eye down the schedule. Then, looking directly at her, he tossed it onto the floor.

'Hmm. Well, I won't be using that in front of the jury then.' He turned to Abby. 'Could you make me a cup of tea? White, two sugars, you know the score.'

Abby turned on her heel and left, her face red with fury. This was fucking Dickensian, she thought to herself. I'm doing his bloody work for him, no attempt to thank me, just go away and make the sodding tea like a good girl. She

116

made two cups and stalked back to the room, deliberately slopping as much of his into the saucer as she could.

'Just down there. And I've got some more papers here, Abby. It's a personal injury claim – God knows why they sent it to me, I don't do that sort of work any more. Anyhow, could you just draft an Advice and settle the pleadings? The limitation date runs out next week, so it'd better be ready by tomorrow.'

He was punching numbers into the phone before she could answer. 'Darling? Only me. Look, I'm going to have to stay late tonight. Be back as soon as I can, though.' He hung up and was out of the door within seconds.

Abby ignored the personal injury papers and opened her second brief. She was acting, it said, for a Miss Karen Morely, who was living with her partner of six months in her council flat in Islington. Only, he'd started beating her up. He wouldn't leave the flat, and she needed to get an injunction to force him out. Abby read through the statement carefully, noting the important points. There was nothing from the boyfriend yet.

She started to prepare her opening speech. As the applicant's barrister, she had the right to tell the judge all about the case, so it was important that she had all the facts at her fingertips. Carefully, she noted the dates, checked the tenancy document, and scanned the medical report.

Alex's personal injury papers sat on her desk, daring her to ignore them. Limitation date, he had said. That meant that the plaintiff could lose the right to bring the claim unless the proceedings were started quickly. Christ, she thought. What if Alex relies upon me to do it, and forgets all about them? They might sue me. Hardly the best way to start a career. With a sigh, she wrapped up her own papers and started to go through Alex's.

God, it just took so long. The accident seemed to involve every vehicle in London, and she had to tally them all with the right registration numbers and the police plan. Then she had to set out the claim in reasonably plain language – list

117

her allegations of negligence, the injuries and out-of-pocket expenses. Abby worked on as darkness fell outside.

There was a knock at her door.

'Just off now, Miss Penhaligon. Here's a key.'

Abby started and looked up.

'Oh . . . thanks, Ron.'

'Everything all right, miss?'

'Yes, fine. I'll just finish this for Mr Golightly and then I'll be off. I'm ready for the injunction.'

'Good, that's the spirit . . .' he paused at the door.

Abby looked at her watch. Seven-thirty already.

Shit.

Her date with Marcus. He was picking her up now. Or rather, he wasn't.

She flew out of the room, and almost fell down the stairs past a startled Ron. She raced out of the Temple and into Fleet Street. No time for a bus. She had a twenty pound note in her pocket. It would have to be a taxi.

The black cab clattered its way north to the flat. Marcus was there, sitting on the wall, kicking his heels nonchalantly against the brickwork. He was in jeans and a leather jacket, she noticed.

She paid off the driver and climbed out of the cab.

'Marcus, I'm really sorry . . .'

He grinned at her. 'What happened?'

'I just got dumped with some extra work . . . I had to stay and do it.'

She decided not to tell him she'd forgotten as well.

'Never mind. Are you ready?'

'Yes.'

'Here's your helmet.'

'My what?'

He held up a blue and white full-face motorbike helmet.

'Ever been on a bike?'

Abby could feel the blood draining from her face.

'No.'

'Scared?'

118

She looked at him direct. 'Course not.' Then she focused on the gleaming machine beside him. It looked as though it had come straight from a race track. 'What sort of bike is it?'

'It's a Fireblade. Top speed one-sixty. But I promise not to frighten you. We'd better leg it, though, if we're going to get there in time. Are you going to change?'

Abby looked down at her black suit. It wouldn't look too dignified on a motorbike.

'Sure.'

She was back ten minutes later in some old jeans and a denim jacket. Marcus grinned at her again, this time from the seat of the bike. The pillion space looked about the size of a postage stamp.

Carefully, she put her foot on a protruberance from the machine. The next question was how to get on without falling straight off. Gently, she grabbed his shoulder and swung her leg over the seat.

'What do I hold on to?' she hissed.

'Me.'

No way, she thought to herself. There is no way I'm going to be the passive girl clinging on to the bloke in front. I would rather fall off the back than have that happen.

He opened the throttle and the bike seemed to take off. There was no way it could still be in contact with the street, she thought. Her body seemed to be pushed backwards by the speed, and she felt her jeans start to slip along the seat away from him. Instinctively, she reached out, grabbing Marcus round his stomach and pulling herself back on to the seat.

He stopped at the end of the road and she realised that her eyes were tight shut. She was suddenly aware that she was gripping him like he was going out of fashion. She moved her body up towards him, relaxing her hands slightly. Her legs were touching his, she knew, but all social conventions seemed irrelevant for the moment.

119

Then he was away again, this time shooting up the High Street. He overtook several cars and forced his way to the front of the traffic. Again, they got away without trouble, haring down the hill away from the lights. Abby tried to peek over his shoulder at the speed gauge. It was wildly out, she knew. It said he was doing 30, but he had to be doing 110, at least. What the hell would Chambers say if she was prosecuted for aiding and abetting? Would it be better to just jump off and seek a sympathy vote for the broken limbs?

They were on to the North Circular now, winding their way round to Wembley. Abby had to admit, it was a whole lot quicker than taking the bus. And, gradually, it was starting to become fun. When he wasn't accelerating hard, she could feel the warmth of the early summer air as they moved along. And, now she'd had time to think about it, perhaps he wasn't going quite as fast as she'd thought.

The concert had just started when they got there. As they went in, they bypassed the burger stalls and found their entrance gate. Abby gasped at the vastness of the place. She'd never been in a room this big. There had to be thousands just standing in front of the stage. And at the sides, all the seats were filled.

It was dark in the auditorium, but as they found their seats, the stage erupted into pure white light. Then it went dark again, before pink and purple strobes started to flash. Suddenly, a guitar chord rang out, echoing around the auditorium. Then a scream as it picked up and proceeded into a new register. The bass cut in – hard, throbbing, loud enough to shake her chair. And then they were on, the band racing their way through music she'd not heard for years.

Abby looked around her. It was a largely male audience, most of them in their thirties by the look of them. Quite a few, she realised, looked worryingly nerdy, with a tendency to play air guitar and mouth the words.

She glanced at Marcus. At least he wasn't joining in. Instead, he watched the stage intently.

120

She had to admit to herself, he was the best looking man she could see there. Tall and solid, without being fat. His hair was dark and flopped down rather sweetly over one side of his face. In another life, she thought, if I was into God and prayers and vicarage tea parties, I could rather fancy you, Marcus Kirkwall.

He moved to look at her and quickly she turned her head away.

By eleven, it was over. The band had given at least six encores and everyone had started to file out of the building.

'What did you think of it?'

She grinned. 'Brilliant – thank you for taking me!'

They started to walk down the steps from their seats.

'I'm starving. Fancy some food?'

Abby realised that she'd only had a sandwich all day.

'Mmm, yes.'

'I've got something cooking at home – that all right?'

'Brilliant.'

The bike was waiting for them, and this time Abby managed to mount it a little more elegantly. Marcus started the engine and they roared off back towards Archway. The night was still warm, the lights of the traffic merging to create a panorama of colour against the dark violet sky. Marcus rode quickly, but she was no longer frightened as he weaved past the slower cars.

They drew up outside a Victorian villa in a tree-lined street. This must be the Vicarage, she thought to herself, as he drove through the open gate and came to a halt.

She hopped off the bike. As he locked the bike up, Abby took off her helmet and shook her hair free.

'That was fantastic, Marcus.'

He grinned. 'I hope you like casserole.'

She followed him into a cavernous hall, covered in an ancient red carpet. Stacked along one side were books by the dozen and Abby quickly scanned the titles as she passed. They seemed to be in no particular order, Harold Robbins propped up against Stephen Hawking. At the end was a stack of magazines, mostly bike related by the look of it.

The kitchen was at the back of the house, enormous and warm. There was a huge Aga and Marcus went straight to it, oven cloth in hand. Carefully, he lifted out a heavy-looking casserole, and took the lid off.

'That smells good.'

'Chicken with a few herbs. This is the first vicarage I've lived in with an Aga – my mother used to have one so she wrote down all her old recipes for me. Now, there's some baked potatoes and salad, if you'd like.'

Abby sat at the scrubbed pine table and looked around her. Again, there were books piled everywhere, and a collection of framed posters on the wall: old railway adverts, the east coast resorts in their heyday – sun and sand, stripy bathing costumes, and plump holidaymakers. They looked very new, somehow.

Abby tasted the casserole. 'This is good, Marcus.'

He smiled at her. 'Excellent. Well, as I said, my mother has to take responsibility. I've only started to learn to cook since I left the navy. Everything was done for us there and I was shamefully ignorant.'

'You've obviously learned fast.'

'Do you cook much?'

Abby paused, remembering Sunday lunches at home. Just her and Mum, but they always had a roast. Perfectly done – Yorkshire puddings risen, meat just right. Then Mum had become ill and they'd stopped. She'd had a go herself once, flustering her way around the tiny kitchen. But it had been awful – the meat overcooked, the greens soggy. Mum had chewed her way through it, doing the best she could. Abby hadn't tried again.

'Not really.'

Absurdly, she felt hot tears pricking at her eyelids. Change the subject, Abby, quick, before you embarrass yourself.

'So Marcus, about that murder appeal . . . I spoke to my

122

head of Chambers, Seb Waters. He's a silk, a QC that is, only does crime, and I asked him what he thought. He seemed very interested – if we can take it further, he'd be ideal to take the case on.'

'With you or instead of you?'

'With me. Silks usually have a junior barrister, but the choice is really up to whichever solicitors you use. I can't tout for business.'

Marcus grinned. 'No need to. But I've been making progress. I went up to the newspaper reference library. There was a trial just when he said there was, and a conviction, just as he said. Abraham James.'

He paused, and looked directly at her. Those eyes, she thought. It was extraordinary. She'd never seen a colour like it before. Then he spoke, his voice quiet.

'It was for real, Abby.' He looked down. 'The awful thing is, I'd wondered at first if he was telling the truth. He seemed ... unstable, ill. I came close to just ignoring it, not following it up. It was after ... after the tube that I started to believe him ...'

Abby swallowed hard. 'So, we've got to find Abraham James.'

Marcus nodded. 'He went to Dartmoor on a life sentence. I've contacted the chaplain there, who's going to check through their records. And I've put an ad in the local paper in Southend to see if anyone remembers anything about the case. It'll have appeared this morning.'

Abby spoke softly. 'He may have died, you know.'

'Yes, maybe. But we've got to try.'

She nodded. 'Yes, I know.'

He looked away for a moment. When he spoke again, his tone was brighter, perhaps a little forced.

'Anyhow, how did your first proper case go?'

Abby grinned. 'It was just brilliant, Marcus. Really. I was sick on the train, I was so worried, but once I got there, it was OK. I stood up, and there was a bit of a moment, but then ... I just can't describe it, it was fantastic. And the judge gave him community service, rather than banging him up . . .'

'So have you got any more cases in the pipeline?'

'Yes, I've got an injunction tomorrow, so there'll be some money to put towards the overdraft.' She looked at her watch. 'Talking of which, I need to get away, really, if I'm in court tomorrow.'

He nodded. 'Thanks for coming with me.'

She looked across the table. 'It was great, a wonderful evening, Marcus.'

Inwardly she wondered what she'd do if he made a pass. There was no one around, and it would be so easy to sneak upstairs. She felt herself go red and hoped he hadn't noticed.

He followed her along the tiled hall, and leaned across her briefly to open the door. Both of them jumped back from the contact, each looking away from the other.

'Well, see you soon . . .'

Abby smiled. 'Yes, thanks again, Marcus.'

'My pleasure.'

They waited on the doorstep, each unwilling to end the evening. Finally, with an embarrassed, stilted wave, Abby turned and set off down the street.

Chapter Fifteen

Marcus looked out of his window for what must have been the twentieth time that morning. Sermonising had never been his forte, and he made himself sit down and write his piece for fifteen minutes a day. Then, conscience clear, he could move on to more important things.

But today, his heart was not in the meaning of the Damascan conversion. It focused rather more easily on the thought of a young blonde barrister. The vision of Abby shaking free her hair the evening before would stay with him for ever. It seemed to him like gold suddenly turned into moving waves, impelling him to touch it, run his fingers through it. God, if she'd known what he'd been thinking at the end of the evening, she'd never visit again.

He'd never felt this vulnerable before. Not since just after Jennifer. There had been girlfriends, certainly. Any number of them. Usually with names like Annabel, Clarissa or Sophie, a bridge-playing mother and a Jacobean place in Gloucestershire. To which he'd be invited for chilly weekends spent making small talk over miniscule cups of tea. He'd never been able to work out if the traditional night-time bedhopping was performed in search of sex or was more a case of desperately needing some bodily warmth.

He'd taken some girls home to Cornwall, too. They'd

been welcomed at the old manor house, had made polite if confused noises at the sight of his father's paintings and endured tours of the garden with his mother.

But he wasn't really part of their set, he knew. And they'd all come to realise it in the end. He may have been the oldest son of an Earl with a family seat in Cornwall and some of SW1's most expensive freeholds, but somehow he could never perform whatever role it was they expected of him. There was just something about him that made it impossible for him to slot into the world around him. Nature or nurture, he'd never known which. Quite possibly a bit of both, given his eccentric parents. But he was loved by them and that counted for a lot.

He'd always been serious. That was no problem at home. Father was either away or painting; Mother spent her days gardening, constantly fighting a losing battle in the ten acres to which the public came on bank holidays. He'd grown up, contented, secure, free, but essentially serious. That was seen as a problem by some, although he'd never understood why.

Marcus was passionate, though. Intensely, outrageously so. His father had recognised the trait as coming from himself. In him, it had been transformed into blotches of colour which miraculously took on the form of light and texture. He was wise, though, and knew that his son would reject that outlet. A boy like Marcus would need to plough his own furrow in life.

So, at the age of eight, he'd bought Marcus his first violin. Just a three-quarter size, the tone dubious. But Marcus had taken the offering, practising hour after hour, racing through the work set by his teacher. By the age of twelve, he was leading his county orchestra whenever he could make it back from Winchester. By fifteen, he was giving concerts, and the subsequent scholarship to the Royal College of Music was merely a formality.

London, though, had been a shock. His parents had taken him there only twice during his childhood. When the time came for him to move to the capital, he hated the noise, the grime, the constant activity of the city. But it was the poverty that really affected him. Coming out of Paddington Station at the beginning of his first term, he'd seen the beggars, filthy, stinking, their bottles beside them. He'd stride past, violin in one hand and suitcase in the other, feeling guilty as hell.

Like so many students, he'd taken to busking to raise some drinking money. They'd play in the underground stations, rotating around the regular pitches, one eye open for the transport police. It was more organised than he'd thought – pitches would be booked in advance in tiny scribbled script on advertising hoardings. The most lucrative were on the tourist trail – South Kensington, of course, on the way to the museums, Oxford Circus, Piccadilly. He'd set up for an hour at each pitch, his violin case open for the money, a flask of hot coffee beside him to warm him up in the cold weather.

It was amusing to watch as people passed. Most would ignore him, of course, pretending in their very British way that he was not there, and that the beautiful sound all around them was a figment of somebody else's imagination. Others would smile to themselves, and in some embarrassment, place 20p in his violin case. The children were the best. They would stand in front of him, some trying to make him laugh, others just listening, entranced. For them, he would play his best, pushing his bow hard into the strings, working, coaxing the sound out of the instrument, pausing on the cadenzas as the echo reverberated off the hard walls.

It was while he was playing that he got to know Jennifer. He'd first seen her at Piccadilly, when she'd walked past him, clearly listening and casting surreptitious glances back as she walked along the passageway. He'd gone back the next day to play at the same spot, working his way through the Brahms concerto in D, his favourite piece. She'd come past him again, but this time she'd stopped.

127

He had been into the third movement, the Allegro Giocoso, and had been concentrating so hard that he hadn't noticed her until he finished. Then, sweat pouring down his body, he had been surprised to hear a solitary handclap.

She was there in front of him, wearing the same clothes she'd had on the previous day – a black micro mini, fishnet tights and a boob tube. Her hair was wild, flung behind her, and her makeup heavy-looking even in the dim light of the passage.

'Thank you,' murmured Marcus.

'No, it's me who is thanking *you*. I've never heard Brahms played like that – you have a wonderful talent.'

Marcus had been momentarily startled, and she had laughed gently at him.

'Don't you expect a tart to know about Brahms?'

'Look, I don't expect anyone to know too much about him, tart or whatever.'

She coughed slightly and he looked at her once more. Beneath the makeup, he could see she was no older than him. He gesticulated towards his flask.

'Fancy a coffee?'

They sat down companionably, backs to the wall as commuters surged past.

'I used to play at home,' she explained.

'Where's that?'

'It was near Birmingham. Not any more, though.'

Her voice was southern counties, almost prep school in tone.

'Why did you leave?'

She took a sip of the coffee before answering.

'Usual reasons. My mother re-married, he's a bastard. So I left.'

Marcus paused.

'Ran away?'

'I suppose so.'

'Does your mother know where you are?'

128

It was as though he'd hit her. She stood up in an instant, her coffee spilling onto the concrete.

'Just fuck off, nosy. It's none of your business any fucking how.'

'I'm sorry . . . look . . .'

But she had already stalked off up the passageway and he was too late.

He hadn't seen her then for months. Finally, though, one day in the summer he finished the sonata in G at Piccadilly tube station to find her grinning in front of him.

'Brahms again . . . really, you must widen your repertoire.'

She was changed. Thinner, paler. Clothes a little dowdier.

'Good to see you again. Can I interest you in some more coffee if I promise not to be so fucking nosy?'

She smiled at him again, but her eyes were dull.

'You may, but you can be as nosy as you like.'

'Are you all right?'

'Nothing a few grammes won't put right. Have you got a tenner?'

Oh, shit.

'Please.'

There was about twenty pounds in the case – she could see it – so there was no point in saying he didn't have enough. But giving her money to shoot up . . . yet he'd sound like a pompous prat if he said no, he knew it.

'I'm not asking you to give it. I'll earn it off you.'

He looked at her questioningly.

'Hand relief, that's a tenner. Here, now, nobody'll see.'

Her hand was already reaching toward him. Worse, he could feel himself responding. Instinctively, he moved away.

'All right, full intercourse but you'll have to go through my pimp, Tony. That's twenty quid. Or oral, that's fifteen. Extra services on demand . . .'

She was reeling off a list. Marcus felt sick.

'Just have the tenner, but tell me about yourself.'

'Like what?'

'Like how old you are.'

'I'm nineteen.'

'Your name?'

'Jennifer Stubbs.'

'And how you've ended up here.'

'Like I said, my step-father's a bastard.'

'So . . .'

'So I arrived at Euston Station ten months ago. Someone offered me a light, said there was a party going on at King's Cross. I went, met a few people, got a bit high and stayed the night.'

Marcus waited. He wanted to hear, knew she would tell him, but only in her own time. If he pressed too hard, she'd be gone in an instant, just like last time,

'And the next day, I got high again. I'd only done dope and speed before, but they'd got some heroin so I gave it a go. It was brilliant, I could do anything.'

She looked away from him.

'Like I say, that was ten months ago. I stayed for a while, then Tony – it was his flat – said that I owed him some rent and my share of the heroin. It came to five hundred pounds.'

Marcus breathed out slowly. 'So what did you do?'

'Nothing I could bloody well do, was there? He said I'd have to earn it, that he could fix me up with a few men and I'd get the money back in no time at all, then I could be off and get on with my life.' She took a sip of the coffee. 'It was all so bloody easy. He just told me to go upstairs and there was some bloke already there . . .'

Jennifer looked away. When she spoke again her voice was trembling.

'I just shut my eyes and lay there. I didn't have to do a thing. It took about two minutes and he'd done. Just put his trousers back on and went downstairs. He must have paid Tony, because the next thing I knew, I only owed four

130

hundred and eighty and Tony was saying there were three more.'

Marcus shuddered.

'And I just carried on. After a bit, I didn't really notice, and it was easy. By the end of the day, I'd earned a hundred quid.'

Marcus's voice was quiet. 'But you're still with Tony.'

'Yes.' She stared at him blankly. 'Trouble is, I get to the end of the day and I need more drugs. And they cost money. Tony can get them for me, really cheap. And the business is there, so it's easier than doing anything else – finding somewhere to live, all that crap.'

She looked past him and her voice softened.

'It's not me really. I pretend I'm someone else – that's what the punters want anyhow. All women do it, not just tarts. It's easy when I do that.'

'So why do you need the tenner today?'

She looked at him. 'He'll only give me heroin once a day. It's not enough, Not now.'

Marcus reached towards his violin case and found ten pounds in change. He handed it to her.

'You can get off it, you know.'

'Yes, some day.'

Then she was off, scurrying along the passageway to her next fix. And he'd done nothing. Not that time, or those that followed. Just let her walk away. Time after time he'd re-lived it.

I should have done something. Anything. How can I call myself a human being when I let her walk away to her death? I despise myself. I am worthless. There is no point in my existence.

Marcus heard the phone ringing, dragging him back into the present. He stood up and hurried to the hall. 'Hello, the Vicarage.'

'I saw your advert . . . about the *Richard Montgomery*.'

Instantly Marcus was on the alert. The voice sounded young, French, male.

131

'Yes, thank you for calling, I'm trying to find out some information about the ship.'

There was a pause at the end of the line before the Frenchman replied.

'Tell me what you need to know. My mother is in Paris, very old now. But she told me about the ship. She's English, lived in Southend during the war and remembers it sinking. But you have to tell me what you need to know so I can ask. She's ill now, can't travel, but I can go to her . . . she hates the phone, but I visit all the time and could ask her whatever you need to know . . .'

Quickly, Marcus thought it through. Surely there was no harm in the truth?'

'I'm trying to help a man. He was convicted of murder in the 1940s, and it was all to do with the ship. I need to find people who can tell me what was on it when it went down, and whether anything was removed.'

There was a pause at the other end of the line.

'It sounds a little, how you say, vague.'

Marcus could hear the beginnings of contempt. He replied, his voice firm and efficient-sounding.

'It has to be at the moment. I'm working on instructions from our legal team. We have a barrister, Abby Penhaligon, and a leading QC, Mr Seb Waters.'

The voice sounded a little more impressed. 'Perhaps they could tell me what I need to ask my mother?'

'Yes, maybe. They're in Chambers at 29 Pump Court in London. I'm sure they'll be grateful for any information you can give them. Perhaps you'd like Miss Penhaligon to speak to you direct? If you'd like to give me your phone number, I'll ask her to ring you straightaway.'

The voice sounded much warmer now. 'I'm just about to leave on business for a few days – I think it's better if I get in touch with these people myself.'

'Maybe. Well, thank you.'

Abby's injunction was scheduled third. So she had a bit of a wait, not made any easier by the nagging feeling that her client was becoming increasingly worried. The court was old, grimy, devoid of interview rooms. All Karen Morely could do was sit in the waiting room, shaking every time the door opened.

Suddenly, a tall, thickset man entered.

'That's him.'

'Mr Singleton?' asked Abby, turning to face him.

'Who's asking?'

'I'm representing Miss Morely . . . I was just wondering if you had a lawyer.'

The man towered over her.

'No I fucking don't. Load of tossers, you lot. No, I'll defend myself, plead not guilty.' He looked across at Karen Morely. 'She's a lying cow anyhow.'

Karen started to sob quietly. Oh for an interview room, thought Abby. Why the hell did her client have to endure this? It was her bloody flat, after all.

'Mr Singleton, it's only fair that you understand what we're asking for. Miss Morely needs the flat back . . . do you agree that the tenancy is in her name?'

'Just save it for the court, darling, all right?'

Abby felt herself redden. 'Come on,' she muttered to Karen. 'Let's not wait here.'

They trooped out and lurked beside the courtroom door. At last, the case was called.

'May it please Your Honour, I represent Miss Morely in this application for an injunction. There is a sworn statement . . .'

The judge stopped her.

'Is it defended?'

Singleton spoke from his seat. 'You bet it is.'

The judge sighed and smiled weakly at Abby over his glasses.

'Then you'd better call your client.'

Karen was ushered into the witness box where she swore to tell the truth.

133

'Are the contents of your statement correct?'

'Yes.'

'And you are currently living in a refuge?'

'Yes. I haven't returned to the flat since he hit me. That was last Wednesday.'

The judge looked at the respondent. 'Any cross-examination, Mr Singleton?'

'Yes there is. You've been shagging someone else, you silly bitch.'

'No, I haven't.'

'What's this then?'

He waved around a letter. Karen started to look rather sheepish.

'Let me read from it. "Dearest Kevin, I can't wait until you're back home and we can get together again. We had a great time when you came round here – Darren's away in two weeks, so can you call?"'

Abby stood up. 'Your Honour, that's hardly a matter of relevance. Nothing gives someone the right to strike another—'

'Let him finish, Miss Penhaligon.'

Darren Singleton continued. 'So you *have* been screwing around.'

'Only the once. And that didn't give you the right to hit me, you bastard.'

'And how did I get this?'

Singleton rolled up his sleeve to show a long, curving scar. Karen recoiled visibly.

'Not from me.'

The judge intervened.

'What are you saying happened, Mr Singleton?'

'What I'm saying is that I got home to find her in a strop, telling me I had to go. I was packing a bag, then I found that letter in a drawer. I showed it to her, then she starts threatening me with a bloody knife.'

'Perhaps you'd like to go into the witness box, Mr Singleton. Any questions, Miss Penhaligon?'

134

Abby took a moment to collect her thoughts. Normally, she would have prepared a cross-examination. The opposition would have served a statement, giving her time to look for inconsistencies, shreds of evidence which could be developed and woven into her own case. Here, he'd just come up with this. What was it she'd been told? Let your mind go blank for a moment, then think like hell.

'Why did she go after you with the knife?'

'Stands to reason – I found the letter.'

Abby pushed harder. 'But you were going anyhow. She wanted you to go, on your evidence. Why should she be so upset that you'd found out she was seeing someone else?'

He looked slightly taken aback for a moment. A direct hit by the look of it. Abby decided to press her advantage.

'Show us the arm again.'

He obliged, and Abby saw the stitch marks down the side of the ugly scar.

'It's been stitched. Where?'

'St Thomas's hospital.'

'When?'

'Right after the attack. Last week, Wednesday.'

'So they'll provide a medical report, will they?'

She was way into the danger zone. If everything tallied – if he could get a medical report confirming the date – she was in real trouble. But there was something about him that encouraged her to pursue the point.

'Well?'

'They may not remember . . .'

'They'll have records . . . Mr Singleton, you are on oath, and what you say can be checked. When did you have your arm stitched up? Perhaps we could approach the hospital . . .'

He muttered his answer. 'Last Saturday.'

'Speak up.'

'Last Saturday.'

'So you've just told a pack of lies. The applicant wasn't anywhere near you on Saturday.'

His face was pink with fury now.

135

'She's just a slag.'

The insult always made Abby furious. It was the standard term of abuse – a slag, someone who slept around. The male equivalent, of course, was a stud, a superhero.

The judge intervened again.

'Miss Penhaligon, I think I've formed a view.'

She took the hint and sat down.

'Injunction granted, the respondent to vacate by noon tomorrow.'

'Then fuck you, Judge.'

Abby grinned at the judge as Singleton stalked out of the court.

Alexander Golightly, sitting in Chambers that Thursday lunchtime, was feeling distinctly uncomfortable. He just couldn't bear the thought of another weekend in Surrey with the Hon. Lucinda. There was only so long a chap could hide behind his copy of *The Times*. Eventually, she'd expect to talk, go out, play bridge. He'd have to admire her hair, zip her into some appalling dress which had cost a bloody fortune. It would be just like every other weekend. Dull dull dull. He could have screamed.

He stared at the papers in front of him. The case was hopeless. Any doubts he'd had had been obliterated by the work of that pupil. The SFO barrister would be carrying out the same exercise, marrying up the account movements. It all came to the same thing: an overwhelming case. And all of it against his client.

That said, there was still hope. There had to be or Mr Ronnie Keyton would not be paying him £250 an hour. That hope lay in the fact that the case would be heard by a jury; a combination of individuals drawn from South London, who, with a bit of luck, would either have no financial nous at all, or who would see Ronnie as one of their own, undeserving of a conviction. He'd heard the tales, half believing them – the CPS dropping cases of handling stolen goods in certain areas of the capital, fearing that any jury from the area would fail to see that the accused had done anything wrong. Burglary was a crime, sure; handling, though – well, that was just doing your best to make ends meet. Stands to reason.

He could always plead pressure of work to Lucinda and lock himself in the study. But spending the weekend engrossed in Mr Keyton's financial affairs was almost as bad as spending it in his wife's company.

He knew what he really wanted, above all else: a long weekend in Rita's bed. He'd been due to spend tonight in town anyhow, but he was dreading going home tomorrow. Not when he could be with Rita.

Once the idea had struck, there was no getting away from it. Every time he turned a page, he thought of her on those crumpled sheets. He would shut his eyes and she'd be there, makeup smudged, her skin blotchy, looking like a harridan but totally, absolutely insatiable. Wanting more and more of him, refusing to let him stop.

Women just didn't act like that. Not the women he'd known, anyhow. Although come to think of it, he'd not known many. But he could imagine that his life with Lucinda was no different to the lives led by all the men in his street. It was there in everything they did – the sherries, the fawn cardigans, the golf on Sunday mornings, and the relief that it was Monday morning once more. They were like neutered tom cats, plodding around inoffensively, taking the line of least resistance. When did it happen, he wondered? When did this transformation from rampant beast to tamed old boy occur? Thirty? Forty? Fifty?

None of them had Rita, though. None of them would be living as he did, aware that at any time she could appear, seeking him out, whisking him off to a hotel for an afternoon – when he would go to heaven for a few hours.

It was no good. He wanted more. Lucinda could stuff her stupid sherries for a weekend. He pressed the numbers into the phone. Good, she was out. He could leave a message on the answerphone.

137

He wondered if she'd ever had an affair. She had plenty of opportunity, now he thought of it. No job, no children, all the time in the world. And she'd kept herself in trim, always put on makeup, and had her hair done every week. Well, good luck to her, he thought. Mentally, he prepared the message.

'Darling, I'm terribly sorry, but the clerks have arranged a conference through Saturday and Sunday to get ready for the Keyton case. I am absolutely furious, but I think I'll have to stay up in town for the weekend as well as tonight, and have a real old session getting through everything. Sorry to be such a bore, but I'll make it up to you.'

Yes, that should do it. Good. And now, lunch. Maybe he could see what Rita was doing tonight. Pick up a bottle of Krug and a few flowers in Fleet Street. Yes. Things were looking much better, now he'd made his mind up. Humming to himself, he hurried down the stairs.

Abby, returning from her injunction hearing, watched Alexander Golightly make his way across the Temple car park. Good, she thought, he's not noticed me. He'll only make me do some more unpaid work.

She reached Chambers and popped her head around the clerks' room door.

'Victory?' asked Ron.

'Yes.' Abby grinned at him.

'Well, well, no stopping the girl! If you'd like to go up to your room, I think there are some more pleadings for you from Mr Golightly.'

Her smile disappeared. Still, she had the afternoon to work on them. She trudged up the stairs. Her desk was groaning under the weight of Alexander's papers, neatly bundled and tied up with the ever present red ribbon. He'd left a note: '*Please draft the specials on this.*'

Wonderful. She knew what he was doing. He didn't like this work. He wanted to develop his crime niche, but didn't dare abandon the personal injury work. It was his safety net. So he needed to find a mug who would keep his practice going. What a bastard.

Abby started leafing through the papers, trying to find the documents which she needed to work out the client's loss of earnings. She'd never meet this mythical person, and certainly never see any money for sorting out his claim.

God, it was so frustrating. She wanted to be out there, doing battle. Yet she was dependent upon others. Ron, of course, although she couldn't complain there. But she needed Alex's support. When it came to the crunch, the rest of Chambers would want to know what he thought of her. He was exactly the sort of man she loathed – lazy, rude, handed a living on a plate whilst she had to struggle – yet she had to get him on her side. God, the system stank at times. Stick to her ideals and remain an outsider for ever, or take the broader view. Somehow, she just couldn't bring herself to do the latter. And living on the outside had one striking advantage: she was the only person there.

Abby stood up and walked over to open the window behind Alexander's desk. It was old, and the sash needed replacing. She pushed hard and jolted the window up. As she looked out, she saw a black Saab convertible purr into the car park and nudge its way into a space. One day, she thought. One day I'll have one of those.

The figure getting out of the car looked familiar. He was also clearly lost, looking at the lists of names on the Chambers' doors around him. Then he turned and she saw his face.

Marcus! God, she'd no idea someone in a dog collar could look so good. She watched him as he walked up the steps to 29 Pump Court. Quickly, she raced through to the loo and did the best she could to tidy herself up before heading for the stairs.

Ron was just starting to walk up.

'Ah, Miss, just coming to look for you – you weren't at your phone. Some vicar in the waiting room, there is.'

139

Abby ran down the stairs and pushed open the door.

'Marcus . . . what is it?'

He was standing by the window, dwarfing the room. As Abby entered, he grinned.

'I had to come straight away ... I had a phone call from Dartmoor. They've got an address for Abraham James, it's a few years old but the chances are he's still there. He was released on licence so he has to tell them if he moves.'

'Where is he?'

'Colchester, Essex. Not far from your patch. Shall we go?'

'When?'

'Now . . . come on, let's do it.'

'But I can't see a client direct . . .'

'He's not a client at the moment . . . and he may not even be there. And I'll buy you a meal at a pub on the way if you say yes.'

He was like a seven-year-old with his infectious enthusiasm. Before she knew it, Abby was in the front seat of the Saab, watching Marcus weave his way expertly through the East End traffic. He seemed to know his way around the back streets, racing around one-way systems, keeping the car moving smoothly, overtaking in the blink of an eye.

'How do you know your way around here?' asked Abby, as he raced up past Leyton tube station.

He grinned. 'Well, it's a while since I was here, but I spent a couple of years as a despatch rider before I went into the navy. You get to know all the rat runs.'

That explains the bike, she thought. No wonder he got to Wembley so quickly the other night. But a car like this cost a bomb. Surely vicars didn't get paid that much? Rewards in heaven rather than on earth, she'd always assumed. Perhaps there was a little more to him than met the eye . . .

'I didn't even know you had a car.'

'Hidden in the garage. Not a lot of point in using it for the daily stuff, but I need something reasonable to get down

140

to Cornwall now and then. What would you like on the CD?'

'What have you got?'

He motioned towards the glove compartment and Abby rifled through the CDs slung inside it. Mozart, Beethoven . . . all classical, mainly string quartets. She took one at random and slotted it into the player.

A gentle beginning, pastoral, then dramatic long chords from the whole orchestra, building up dramatically, then some woodwind, gently changing the pace, sweetly filling the car. Marcus was silent, a muscle moving in his cheek. Abby sat back in the seat and closed her eyes, letting the music waft over her.

Some timpani, gentle minor chords, slight crescendo. Strings moving quickly, threateningly, building up. Then, gloriously, a solo violin, soaring up through the registers, reaching higher and higher. Abby thought of a skylark over a summer cornfield.

'It's beautiful.'

'Do you know it?' asked Marcus.

'No,' she admitted.

'It's Brahms's violin concerto. It's the only violin concerto he ever wrote. Much of the stuff he did was for piano – that was his instrument. But he wrote this, and three sonatas for the violin. Fiendishly difficult, all of them, but glorious.'

He moved the car through the gears and onto a faster road, accelerating away from a roundabout.

'Tell me more,' asked Abby.

'About Brahms? Born in 1833, from a poor family – you'd approve of him, Abby. He fell in love with Schumann's wife, held a torch for her for the rest of his life. She was meant to have loved him too, but they never got together. Listen to that note – it's practically impossible to get . . .'

'Do you play?'

He kept his eyes on the road.

141

'I did. Not now.'

Abby opened her mouth to ask why, but something in his tone discouraged her. Instead, she closed her eyes again and listened as the violin worked its way through some smooth, sweet-sounding melodies. She felt herself relaxing, imagined herself back in that cornfield with the skylark overhead . . .

'We're here. Abby, wake up . . .'

The car was still, the engine off. Abby opened her eyes, her brain befuddled as she caught her bearings.

'You've been asleep for the last hour . . .'

She lifted her head and brushed back her hair which had fallen forward over her face. She hoped she hadn't snored or dribbled. She sat up straight. They were parked outside a row of houses on what looked to be a council estate.

'Are you sure this is his place?'

'It's the address the chaplain gave me. He shouldn't have told me really . . .'

They got out of the car and Abby followed Marcus to the door. It was the middle house of a row of five, all identical, in dark red brick with metal windows. From inside, they could hear the sound of a Hoover whining.

'Somebody in, at least,' muttered Marcus.

He rang the doorbell, holding the buzzer down so that it could be heard over the noise. Abby peered through the opaque glass as best she could. At last, a muzzy shape appeared on the other side and the door opened hesitantly, still on the security chain.

'Mr James?'

He peered suspiciously out through pebble-thick glasses. Then he seemed to catch sight of Marcus's dog collar. Thank goodness, thought Abby. That thing seems to act as a passport; doors opened, expressions changed, language moderated.

'Mr James?' repeated Marcus. 'Can we come in? We've some important news for you.'

142

Chapter Sixteen

The three of them sat perched on the living room furniture, coffee cups balanced on their knees. Abby had kept quiet, letting Marcus do the talking. Her eyes had wandered around what she could see of the house. It was depressingly familiar. A small living room, dominated by a large rug. A tile hearth, enveloping an ancient Parkray which had to be filled with coal twice a day to heat the water. Beige walls, some pictures hanging from a rail, unlined garish curtains. The architecture was almost identical to Abby's old home, but the inside was totally different. Mum's place, for all their lack of money, had been tidy, bright and clean. She'd made curtains which hung properly outside bleached nets; for pictures, she'd bought frames for some of Abby's better offerings. She had always been making something for the house – a new bedspread, some lace to cover a small table, some frills to hang from a curtain pole. She'd kept her bits and pieces from her travels, and every bare surface had a photograph – usually of Abby, or of the two of them.

Abraham James, though, had no such photos. Probably had no family; or if he had, they'd long ago disowned him. The walls were in need of some paint and the carpet had a large stain in the middle. It was dusty and smelt of smoke. He'd lit up shortly after Marcus had started to speak and his hand shook slightly as he listened.

'It was such a long time ago . . .'

Abraham James paused.

'I've never really talked about this ... no one would have been interested. Ex-cons going on about how they never did it ...'

'Tell us what happened.'

The old man took a long drag on his cigarette and waited for the nicotine hit. He breathed out slowly. His voice was low and quiet, a little weak.

'I was working on the newspaper. I'd grown up in Grays, gone to the grammar school there, got a job on the paper at Southend. I'd been there about six years, must have been about twenty-four. I'd been a conscientious objector and had been allowed not to fight.

'I got arrested after VE night. There'd been an office party, a hell of a do. We'd spent the war doling out so much bad news, it just seemed a chance to let it all go again. Anyhow, my boss was Denny, Denny Jacobs. He'd taken me on. He was good, had really helped me get started in the job, given me some good work. Well, we were both at the party, and in the morning I woke up in his office. He was there, next to me, dead.'

Marcus kept silent as the old man looked into the distance.

'I had a hell of a hangover. I must have been so drunk that I'd passed out. I'd spent the night on the floor and the first thing I smelt when I woke was blood. I'll never forget it.'

'How had he died?'

'A knife. There was one right bloody well beside me.'

Marcus took a deep breath.

'Did you kill him?'

Another drag on the cigarette.

'I'll never know for sure. That's what I've wanted to know for the last fifty-odd years. I can't believe that I'd do something like that. I was a real idealist, those days.'

He looked up. 'I'd always been a pacifist. I wouldn't fight – I just felt it was wrong. I know it was dreadful for

144

those that went, but those of us who objected – "conshies",
they called us – we had to put up with quite a bit at home.
You know, poison pen letters, abuse on the streets. They
interviewed us all to make sure we had thought through the
pacifism thing, not just putting it on for an easy time. I
passed the interview, put up with all the comments . . . I
just believed so deeply that it was wrong to kill, I was
prepared to put up with anything to avoid it. So I just can't
believe that I would have been capable of murdering a man
. . . however much I hated him.'

Marcus look at him closely as he continued.

'But, the only thing was, I did have the motive.'

'What do you mean?'

Abraham James looked at Marcus carefully, his eyes
meeting the vicar's. He took his time, and spoke slowly.

'I was in love with his wife.'

There was silence for a few moments.

'Really in love. Like she was the love of my life. Isobel,
her name was. She was younger than him, just the most
beautiful woman I'd ever met. I can remember her so
clearly.'

He took a sip of his coffee before continuing.

'I can still remember the first time we met. I'd come into
Denny's office and they were talking together. I must have
looked a right Charlie – I couldn't speak, couldn't stop
myself staring at her.'

Abby spoke gently. 'Did she love you too?'

Abraham turned towards her and smiled.

'Yes, she did. Denny used to invite me round for supper
on Fridays. I'd always help Isobel with the washing up and
we just got talking. It started to get personal, and I began to
realise that she felt something for me, too. We would meet
for walks some weekends. One day, she told me that she
loved me and wanted to be with me.'

The cigarette was finished and Abraham stubbed out the
remains.

'I really loved her, you know. Funny thing was, we

145

never did anything, though – I mean, go to bed together. Stupid really. It was the war, that sort of thing was going on all over the place. All this stuff about the liberated society is rubbish – in the war, you wouldn't believe what went on. But we didn't. I wanted to wait until we were together properly. But we never had our chance.'

'What happened?'

'A few nights before the party, she told me she was pregnant. They'd given up hoping, her and Denny, but there it was. And there was no way she was going to deny that child its father.'

His voice was trembling. 'So, I do sometimes wonder if it was me that killed him after all. I . . . I'd never felt so angry before. Maybe I did it. That's what I find so difficult.'

Marcus reached over and put his hand on Abraham's.

'It wasn't you. The man who did it has told me.'

Abraham James shut his eyes for a few moments. When they opened, a solitary tear escaped.

'My God!'

There was silence. Abby and Marcus were quiet. Abraham looked down at the carpet for a few moments. Finally, he spoke, his voice low but controlled.

'All these years, I have lived with that question. Now I finally know the answer.'

Marcus kept his hand on Abraham's.

'I can tell you some of what happened. It was Henry Jenkins who killed him.'

'Henry Jenkins?' Abraham James's head came up sharply.

'Yes. He was the policeman investigating the murder, I think.'

'Yes,' said the older man. He sat back in his chair. 'The bastard,' he said softly. 'What a complete bastard.'

He looked at Marcus. 'Why did he do it?'

Marcus spoke carefully. 'Denny was about to bring you in on a story he was running. A story about the *Richard Montgomery*.'

'The wreck off Southend?'

'Yes. Did he speak to you about it?'

'Not as far as I remember. There were stories about it, of course – people looting the ship. And there was a rumour that it had some secret cargo ... I always wondered if perhaps it was some nuclear material, kept hush hush. But to answer your question, no, Denny hadn't talked about a big story on it.'

Marcus continued. 'Well, you were about to be given some information by your boss, which Henry didn't want you to know. So he stabbed Denny and framed you.'

'And the bastard told me that unless I pleaded guilty, chances were I'd hang ... my God. And to think, I was so grateful when he agreed that all the stuff about Isobel and me wouldn't come out. I'd been petrified it would ruin her, to have all that over the papers.'

He looked across at Abby, his eyes overflowing with sadness.

'But the worst thing was, I thought perhaps I had done it after all, finding out about Isobel, losing her.'

'What happened to her?' asked Abby.

'She never spoke to me again. Said I'd murdered her child's father. She went back to her parents, had the baby. Probably married again.'

Marcus leaned forward. 'I spoke to Henry a few days ago. He wants you to bring an appeal. He's admitted the murder to me and has asked me to make it public.'

'But will he say so in court?'

'Not any more. Shortly after he confessed to me, he killed himself.'

There was a low rasping noise as Abraham breathed out.

'So he had his demons, too, then.'

Marcus nodded slowly.

'If you want to bring the appeal, Abraham, Abby and I will help you. Or you can go off and see your own lawyer. But what's important is that I will certainly say in court what Henry told me. I know that he was telling the truth.'

147

'I've no money,' said Abraham. Bitterness had crept into his voice. 'Nothing to show for my life.'

Abby was about to tell him about legal aid but Marcus got in first.

'I'm going to pay.'

'What?'

'Henry gave me the money to pay for your appeal. It's enough to cover the costs.'

Abby looked up, startled.

'But where did he get it from?'

Marcus paused.

'That, I'm afraid, I can't say. But I think you ought to appeal, Abraham. You'll clear your name. There will still be people around who will want to know what really happened that night.'

'Isobel.'

Abraham's eyes started to fill with tears.

'Maybe.'

He grasped Marcus's hand.

'Yes. Thank God. I will appeal.'

Seb Waters sat on his father's bed. He'd thought it would be easy to come back into the flat now. He'd done so on the day of his death, thought that would be it. But it was still painful. Deeply so.

It had to be done, though. The clothes could be bagged up and sent to the charity shop in the village, Most of his father's belongings would have to go, and soon. If he didn't throw them out now, he knew he never would.

It took him until midday to sort out the clothes. Photos could be kept, put in a drawer for posterity. After Seb died, he knew, they'd mean nothing to anyone. Until then, he'd keep them.

Now for the desk. Dad was like him, a terrible hoarder. Receipts, guarantees ten years out of date. Bank statements, pages of the things. All straight into the bin.

The desk itself was a beautiful Georgian antique, inherited

from his father's own mother. It would be Seb's now. The locks were still working, every key still in place. He'd seen a similar one on TV a few weeks ago valued at over £30,000. According to the programme, it would have a hidden drawer, just . . . delicately, he pushed his hand to the back of the main drawer . . . here.

Gently, he pulled the drawer front open. His arm was fully extended and he had to feel his way.

There was something in it. Particularly long forgotten junk, knowing his father. Seb's fingers clasped around some papers, and gently pulled them out. As they came out the front of the desk, a small black and white photograph fell to the floor.

It was four o'clock by the time they had finished. Marcus started up the engine and the car moved silently off towards the dual carriageway.

'Shall we stop on the way back for something to eat?' asked Marcus.

'Yes, good idea. I'm starving.'

From under her fringe, Abby watched him as he drove. He was concentrating hard for the car was moving at speed. She looked around the interior. It was messy, papers strewn around the back, some discarded Galaxy wrappers and an old copy of the Observer supplement.

Abby looked back at him and their eyes met momentarily.

'So, where does our man go from here?' he asked, breaking the silence.

'He goes to a firm of solicitors, preferably with you. Do you know anyone?'

'There are the diocesan solicitors, Dinkwaters – they're a firm that does the legal work for the church. They're quite big – I'm sure they'll have a criminal department. I'll give them a ring tomorrow.'

'Good. But it won't be cheap, Marcus. Wouldn't it be better if he puts in an application for legal aid? With a

149

manslaughter conviction and such strong evidence, he'll get it . . . '

Marcus shook his head. 'No. Like I said, the money's not a problem.'

Abby paused.

'Where *did* Henry get the money from?'

'I'm not saying.'

'But you can tell me. I've got a duty of confidentiality, too, you know.'

'Not like me. And I'm not telling.'

His jaw was clenched and his words terse. Abby bridled.

'Surely we can't operate on the same case with secrets between us?'

'Abby, I have to. I can't tell you. And that's it, so stop hassling me.'

'Well in that case, I don't feel like eating. Just drop me back at Chambers. I've got work to do.'

'Yes, your ladyship.'

They drove back in silence. Abby was fuming. Bloody cheek, she thought to herself. Turns up and assumes I'll be only too delighted to traipse off to the back end of beyond at the drop of a hat, sit through a meeting with a potential client and all the bloody way back again, and then he starts withholding information.

The journey back seemed endless. At every traffic light, they both looked ahead, avoiding each other's eyes. As time went on, Abby started to see the funny side, but she wasn't going to crumble first. He had to know that she could out-sulk him, and know it fast.

'I'll get out here.'

They were in Fleet Street and she was opening the door almost before he had stopped.

'Bye then.'

What a bastard, she thought. He doesn't seem at all bothered. Probably hasn't even noticed. She slammed the door without looking back and stalked off. It was six o'clock.

'Enjoy your away day, did you ma'am?' enquired Ron.

Kevin, the junior clerk, was looking at a fee note as though it contained a message from Mars. Suddenly, Abby realised what they were all thinking.

'It wasn't what it looked like . . . It's diocesan work . . .' she stumbled, praying that a brief would come in, if only to save her reputation.

'Must say, takes all sorts. Never seen a vicar in a Saab convertible myself. Still, funny what people like to dress up as, and it's not for us to judge, ma'am. Meet him on the internet did you?'

Abby felt herself go bright red. 'Any work for me tomorrow?'

Ron gestured towards her pigeon hole. 'Yes. A return of Miss Dengie's. A nice little ancillary relief for you.'

'Thank you.'

She took the brief from its resting place. She'd never done an ancillary relief before – looked like it was going to be a long night boning up on the law. Dividing up family assets after the collapse of a marriage was notoriously difficult – an area littered with legal and emotional minefields.

She skimmed over the title: Davies v Davies. Northby County Court. Northby?

'Has this been transferred to London?'

'No ma'am, early train for you. All part of the job, you know. Could be worse, it's only about two hours from Liverpool Street.'

Abby sighed inwardly. She could do with a quiet Friday after her first few days. Still, one day she'd get paid for it all.

She trudged upstairs, brief in hand. At her desk, Alexander's papers remained, just as she'd left them. They'd have to wait for a bit. Maybe she could take them home over the weekend.

She opened the brief and started to read. She was for Mr Davies. Or, more to the point, Rita Dengie had been, but was apparently unavailable to cover the case at the last minute. Brilliant. The client would feel he was getting a second-best barrister.

Abby read through the statements. It looked as though there was a house worth about £50,000 after a marriage of thirty years, while Mr Davies had a business and a pension worth £80,000. The wife wanted the house. Sounded reasonable enough to her.

She turned to Rita's Advice, prepared months ago, and read it through with a growing sense of incredulity. The pension was not a liquid asset, it said confidently, and could not be looked at in the same way as the house. In fact, it ought not to form part of the calculations. Mr Davies should offer a sale of the house and £30,000, enough to re-house the wife in a small flat. She'd have to get a job and raise a mortgage, of course. There were suspicions, in any event, that she had a new relationship.

Abby read the Advice through several times. Sure, she'd not done an ancillary relief before. But she knew perfectly well that after a long marriage, the court would want to ensure that the wife had a decent slice of what was available. And the pension was going to loom large in a judge's mind, surely?

She went through the statements again, taking notes this time. Then she started to trawl through the exhibits. There were pages and pages of bank statements, and she had to check each entry, looking for something out of the ordinary: cheques coming in from an unknown source might be from a rich lover; large amounts going out each month might be heading for a secret savings account. By ten o'clock, she had found nothing. She was also famished. Sod it, she'd have to eat before she could do anything more. She'd grab a kebab on the way home.

Seb Waters stared at the photograph: a chubby, pretty baby in her mother's arms.

Only the mother was Ellie.

Ellie.

It had been the summer of '77. He'd been eighteen, home from school and at a loose end before going up to

152

Cambridge. Ellie had floated through his life for a glorious, heady eight weeks.

She'd been ten years older than him, spending the summer working at the local pub. Then she was off, she told him, probably to Goa. She seemed so free to him, a boy whose life had been planned since before conception. And so powerful, too. He was entranced, in love for what he knew now was the only time in his life.

He'd tentatively asked her for a date, and she'd accepted. He was in unknown territory from there on. But she'd returned his love, with nothing asked or expected.

They'd gone to bed very soon. She was child of the sixties, love was not there to be withheld; it was free, unconditional, but never for keeps. Except in his memory. He'd often wondered what had happened to her, whether she'd made it to Goa.

And here she was with a baby. Accompanying the photograph was a yellowing letter, addressed to his parents. He read it quickly.

My God. He put a hand on the bed to steady himself whilst he read it through again.

Ellie had had his child.

Chapter Seventeen

Papers were strewn all over the table of the train as Abby continued to prepare. She'd fallen asleep over the bloody things last night and woken up cold and stiff at three in the morning. She'd had to get up at six to catch the train, so she was not at her best.

Still, the two hours' work on the journey had helped a little. Abby knew she had a case, but she had her doubts about Rita's approach. If it was me, she thought, I'd let the wife take the house and call it quits. Still, Rita's the tenant and I'm just the pupil.

The train pulled into Northby at 9.20. Abby, yet to see any money for all the work she'd done that week, decided to walk to the court. She asked for directions at the station and walked in the sunshine through the Cathedral Close and on to the modern court complex. Then she made her way through the security screen and up the stairs to the family courts.

Abby checked in with the usher. As she turned away, an elderly-looking man approached.

'Miss Penhaligon? I'm clerking for your solicitors. Mr Davies is in an interview room. Let me show you through.'

She followed him into a cell-like room, bare except for a plastic desk and some chairs. And her client. He was accompanied by a large blonde lady who appeared to be hanging on to his every word.

'Mr Davies, this is Miss Penhaligon.'

The client gave her a look as though she'd just risen from a pile of ordure.

'I'm not happy about this.'

'What seems to be the problem?' asked Abby, trying not to sound too much like a doctor.

'I have been represented by Miss Dengie. I was expecting her this morning. Then I'm told ten minutes ago that she's sent you in her place.'

'It's not quite like that, Mr Davies.' She tried to keep her voice reasonable. 'Often, barristers do find that the courts list two cases in which they're involved at the same time. When that happens, someone else does have to step in. Let me assure you, I've read through the papers most carefully.'

'And you agree with Miss Dengie, do you?'

Oh Christ.

'Miss Dengie took the view that your case should be argued in a particular way and I will present it accordingly.'

Pompous enough for you? she thought.

Mr Davies looked momentarily shocked, but recovered himself quickly.

'Well, I'm not happy. If you don't get what Miss Dengie says you should, I'll take this further.'

'And may I ask who this lady is?' countered Abby sweetly.

'I'm Mr Davies' personal assistant,' grinned the blonde toothily. And I'm a flying sausage, thought Abby.

There was a knock at the door and a besuited male gesticulated for Abby to come outside. She excused herself.

'Not met you before. I think I'm against you in Davies. Dovely-Walters is the name.'

'Oh, pleased to meet you. I'm Abby Penhaligon.'

He moved away from the door to the interview room and looked Abby straight in the face. If anyone else tells me they were expecting Rita Dengie I shall hit them, she thought.

'Just to let you know, there's no change in our position.

155

The pension outweighs the house by several thousand. Your client's at a cost risk, you know.'

Of course she bloody well knew. Make the wrong offer in an ancillary relief these days and you were very likely to find yourself paying not only for your own lawyers, but for the other side's. But she could hardly tell Mr Davies that Rita had got it very wrong indeed.

'The pension doesn't kick in for several years yet.'

'So what? It's got a CETV of eighty-thousand pounds. We've got Deputy District Judge Pilcher today. He's very sensible, will have no problem in giving us what we seek. It's the obvious solution, and all your client has done is rack up costs unnecessarily. It's quite outrageous. I've had to come out from London to argue a case that should have been settled a full year ago.'

Abby longed for the peace of the criminal courts. Give her a nice non-violent thief any day rather than this living hell, where it was difficult to tell who was the most obnoxious, her client or her opponent.

'I'll take instructions,' she muttered, diving back into the room where she addressed her client once again. 'They've offered for Mrs Davies to keep the house, and you the pension.'

'I know that. Are you backtracking, saying I ought to take it?'

Abby took a deep breath. 'Well, if the court agrees with her, you could find that you'll be ordered to pay her costs.'

Mr Davies was starting to go very red indeed.

'No one told me that before. How much are we talking about?'

Abby raised her palms upwards. 'That depends. Several thousand.'

'And how high is the risk of that happening?'

'I have to say, Mr Davies, different judges take different views. Some could well agree with you; others might go for your wife's approach. But you do have to be aware of the risk of costs.'

Mr Davies stood up. 'I'm being mucked around here. I'm not daft. I've got one lawyer saying one thing, another saying something totally bloody different.' He looked at her suspiciously. 'How long have you been doing this job then?'

Oh shit. Still, since he was obviously going to complain about her, she'd better not lie about it.

'Four days.'

It didn't register for a moment. When it did, he had to sit down.

'Say that again.'

'Four days.'

No point in softening the blow, telling him how good the training was, how she'd trailed one of the top barristers in the country for six months. No point at all. And besides, he was so revolting that she got a sadistic pleasure from his realisation that he was about to be represented by an idiot with only four days experience in the job.

'And Miss Dengie?'

'About twenty years.'

'Then it's bloody obvious, isn't it? But you'd better bloody well put it over properly. If I lose this, I'm going to hold you personally responsible.'

Whilst Abby sweated profusely in Northby, Marcus was sitting in the Georgian splendour of Dinkwater and Co., solicitors to several of the London and home counties diocese. They could help, it transpired. Certainly, they'd given up legal aid crime many years ago, but as it was a private situation . . .

They gratefully accepted a cheque for the money in the special account – Henry's money. For now, it would repose peacefully in the firm's client account. And if there was a barrister and a silk that the Reverend Kirkwall felt should act, of course, they would issue immediate instructions. Now, what was the address again?

*

157

Seb looked into the mirror in his father's room. All these bloody years and nobody had said a thing. Ellie had written, told them what had happened, how happy she was, how she sought nothing, just wanted them to be aware that their son was a father and perhaps he ought to know. She was sorry to write to them, meant no offence, but she didn't know where to contact him, it said.

He'd been blissfully unaware, trawling through his law books at university when his child had been born, when that letter had been written.

They'd not told him. They'd never bloody well told him.

Calm down, calm down. There had to be a reason. He forced himself to think rationally. They hadn't known Ellie. They'd known she was a barmaid, that was all. Never spoken to her, never had the chance to get to know her.

They'd have thought she wanted marriage, money. That she wanted to interfere with their plans for him. Class – it had to come down to class. She'd be a drudge, old before her time, dragging their boy down.

If only. If only they'd known her.

Ellie wouldn't have expected anything from him. She was strong enough to cope. She'd meant what she'd said in her letter, but they'd not believed her.

Who was this child? Mentally, he added up the years: twenty-three. He turned the photograph over. There was Ellie's writing again, faded to a light blue over the years, but he could just make it out if he held it up to the light.

Born 18th May, 1977.
Abigail Elizabeth Penhaligon.

The usher came to release Abby from the conference room at eleven o'clock, and led her into a large, modern room. The judge sat facing them, wearing a dark grey suit. He frowned over the top of his glasses. Abby tried to smile. He frowned even more. Somehow, she knew, this was not going to go well.

The application was being made by Mrs Davies, so her

158

barrister opened the case. He'd prepared a list of assets, which made it patently clear that the obvious solution was for her to have the house. At the end of the opening, the judge looked quizzically at Abby.

'And what do you say, Miss, er, Penhaligon?'

Abby tried to sound confident.

'We say that the pension can't be looked at in the same way as the house, sir. It's not a realisable asset.'

'Are you querying the value?'

'No.' Of course not, I'd be bloody mad to.

'Then how are you saying I should look at it?'

'As an asset with a value, but with the proviso that it can't yet be realised. I'll be inviting you not to attach too much weight to it.'

The judge looked distinctly unimpressed.

'Very well then. We'd better get on.'

Mrs Davies gave her evidence. About the thirty years of marriage. About her husband's three affairs. About him leaving her for his secretary last year. About his refusing to pay the mortgage on the house until the court ordered him to. About the fact that she'd been relying upon their grown-up children to bail her out every month. It was all there: every nail in the coffin of Abby's case. Finally, her barrister had finished his questions. 'If you'll just stay there, Mrs Davies, you may be asked some more questions.'

The deserted wife sat calmly awaiting Abby's cross-examination. The trouble was, there was very little to ask. The bank accounts all added up perfectly. There were no offshore trusts, no purchases of jewellery, no holidays in the Maldives. All Abby had were her instructions.

'You've got a new partner, haven't you, Mrs Davies?'

A placid stare back. 'No, I haven't.'

Ah. Better try again.

'A younger man called Sam.'

Mrs Davies started to laugh.

Oh God, being laughed at in cross-examination. This was becoming humiliating.

159

'Sam is one of my son's friends. He's gay. Good-looking, mind you.'

Even the deputy district judge smiled at that.

'Isn't it right that he's moved in with you?'

'Well, he had the spare room for a month when his house got re-possessed after he lost his job. He couldn't pay any rent as he was on benefits. He got a new job six months ago, and now he's renting a place near Swaffham.'

Bang goes the rich toyboy theory. It had always seemed unlikely. Better try another tack. Her opponent grinned at her irritatingly across the table. Abby took a deep breath and carried on.

'Now, about the pension . . .'

Chapter Eighteen

Seb studied his face in the mirror. He looked a sight, he knew; bags around his eyes, sallow skin. But his life had just been transformed, changed utterly in the course of ten minutes.

He was no longer alone. She had to be his daughter. It was so obvious, now he thought of it. Looking at her was like looking at her mother twenty-three years ago: bright, beautiful. The way she held her head, took her time when she needed it. That inner confidence, the knowledge that she was anybody's equal.

He'd tell her. Ring her up. He reached for the phone, his hand trembling.

'Ron, it's me, is Miss Penhaligon there?'

'No sir, she's at Northby County Court at the moment. Shall I ask her to call you when she gets back?'

Damn. Still, it would be better to do this to her face rather than over the phone.

'No, don't worry. I'll come in later to pick up my papers, so I'll catch her then.'

She could move in with him. He could sort out her money problems with one cheque. They'd be in Chambers together . . . he could lead her in some cases. Goodness, they could catch up on lost time.

He had a family at last.

*

Marcus had raced up the A12 to Colchester once again. Abraham was at home – Marcus got the impression he rarely left the place. Marcus ran through the chat he'd had with the solicitors and gave Abraham some forms to sign to get the ball rolling.

After a quick cup of tea, he drove towards the town centre and made for the library. A large, modern building in the middle of a Seventies' shopping precinct, he knew that it had a famed collection of local history books. He trawled through the shelves, leafing through anything which might deal with the wreck.

'Can I help you?'

It was one of the librarians.

'I'm just trying to find out about a shipwreck off Southend . . . it was called the *Richard Montgomery*.'

'The liberty ship which went down in the war?'

'Yes – you obviously know about it?'

'A little. It's an odd story, really, sitting there in the middle of the Estuary like a time tomb.'

Marcus looked up at the man, astonished.

'How do you mean?'

'Don't you know? It ran aground in the war loaded with thousands of tons of explosive. They couldn't save the ship, which broke its back. They just had to leave the explosives aboard.'

'I knew it had carried explosives, but I'd no idea they were still on board today. Why didn't they move them?'

'Firstly, it was the war. There were explosives all over the place, and they had other priorities. Later, I think they found that the bombs had become unstable – the risk of moving them was going to be higher than just leaving them there and letting them rot. Mind you, rumour has it that there will be a time when the chemicals become extremely unstable. At that point, the whole thing will either go up, or the critical point will pass and they'll become inert.'

'What if the whole lot goes up?'

'Nobody knows, really. Presumably windows broken,

162

nearby shipping damaged. You wouldn't want to be there at the time.'

'Are you allowed near it?'

'No. I used to sail out there as a teenager. There's buoys all around, warning you to keep off. Nobody wants to get too close, anyhow. Quite apart from the risk of the whole thing going up, the remains of the hull are pretty dangerous. I've heard that divers used to go exploring there on the quiet, years back, but that there's nothing to be found any more.'

The librarian went over to a shelf and flicked through a book.

'Here's a picture.'

Marcus looked at the black and white photograph. It showed three masts sticking out of a lumpy-looking sea. Marcus gave an involuntary shiver.

'Can I photocopy this?'

'Sure – over there.'

He thanked the librarian and took a copy of the photo and the accompanying text. He'd show it to Abby next time they met. If she was still speaking to him.

Perhaps he ought to make peace with her. He'd drop her a line when he had a moment. But for now, he had work to do.

Abby spent the duration of Mr Davies' evidence trying not to grimace. Give nothing away, they said. Don't show that you know your client is going down the pan. Have confidence in him.

But the man was a moron. Worse than that, a mean, libidinous moron. He saw nothing wrong with failing to pay the mortgage, moving in with his new partner and buying her a new Porsche (even though he had forgotten to mention that one to his own solicitors). The discarded wife could get a job, re-house herself in a miserable flat somewhere in the Fens and work her fingers to the bone until she was eighty-five. She'd get a pension from the state and be just fine. Sure, he was going to get rather more from his pension, and of course there would be the business to sell one day, but that's life, you know.

The worst thing was, he seemed to have no idea just how awful he was. He continued, blithely confident that the deputy district judge would understand his predicament and agree totally with him.

He was wrong about that. The judge gave a crisp and succinct judgment, expressing his concern that Mr Davies appeared to fail to understand the contributions made by his wife over thirty years of marriage to his current standing. The Order he would make would have to be that the wife kept the house. Was there anything else?

There was, of course. Mrs Davies' barrister made his application with the inevitability of the first light of dawn every morning.

'Sir, we've made our position quite clear from the first affidavit. You've ordered what we sought, so I must ask for an Order for costs.'

The judge looked at Abby. Defeat, she knew, was oozing from every pore. By now, she just wanted to get out of the door, on to the train and away from Northby as soon as possible. She murmured a few things about how tough it all was for Mr Davies, which sounded hopeless even to her, and ground to a halt. The judge didn't pause for a moment.

'Mr Davies to pay the costs.'

They trailed out in defeat. Now for the fun bit. Another hour incarcerated in the interview room with her client.

He was unhappy. Very unhappy indeed.

'I'm going to sue.'

'Sue who?' Things were so bad that she almost wanted to laugh.

'You and your bloody Chambers. That Miss Dengie knew what was what. If you'd argued it better, we'd have got it, no trouble.'

It was then that the injustice of it all hit Abby. No question of suing Rita, who'd got it crushingly wrong in the

164

first place. No, *she* was wrong for failing to hypnotise a judge into a state in which he would unquestioningly order whatever nonsense she suggested.

Still, remain polite at all costs. Family clients were often very disappointed after the hearing and needed time to calm down. That's what they had said at Bar school.

'Well, mull it over for a while. My goodness . . . is that the time?'

Chapter Nineteen

Abby ran all the way to the station, only to see the train pulling out from platform one. She spent the next hour wandering around the small concourse, lugging the papers with her. Damn Mr Davies. Damn Rita and her hopeless Advice. A complaint letter in her first week was going to be a unique start to her career. Would presumably finish it, too.

When she was finally allowed to board the next train, she stomped on to it and sagged into a seat. Thankfully, it was quiet and nobody sat anywhere near her. She stared out at the countryside, gazing at the vast fields stretching to the horizon.

It was all so bloody unfair. If she'd been asked to advise in the first place, she would have told Mr Davies to forget the house and hang on to his pension. Rita must want her head examining. But now, the fault was going to lie with Abby.

Success at the Bar wasn't going to be handed out just on ability, she knew. Other things counted. Staying power, for one – having the money to hang around whilst a practice was built. And with her overdraft, she didn't have that. Contacts helped, too. With his godfather in Chambers, James Dorton certainly had those. But she didn't. That just left luck. She'd hoped she stood equal with everyone on that front, but maybe it wasn't to be.

166

Still, she mused later as the tube rattled its way to Chancery Lane, there could well be a note of apology from Marcus at Chambers. Maybe even some flowers. Perhaps they could have a night out this weekend. It was rather an appealing prospect. Get out, forget the law for a bit.

Ron looked up as she entered the clerks' room.

'Ah, Miss Penhaligon. Miss Dengie asked if you could pop up to her room when you got back.'

Damn. Abby peered into her pigeon hole to use up thirty seconds. It was depressingly empty of notes from Marcus, imploring phone messages, or even a cheque or two.

She knocked tentatively on Rita's door.

'Come.'

She entered and was ignored for ten seconds whilst Rita finished typing something into her laptop. She had a small room to herself at the rear of the first floor. It had been decorated in a style which managed to appear expensive and tasteless at the same time – overwhelmingly pink, with full pelmets, swags and tails on the curtains. Suddenly Abby realised who'd arranged the decorations for the waiting room downstairs. The air was heavily scented and wilted roses had been left carelessly in a vase over the fireplace. In all, it had the air of an Edwardian brothel.

Rita looked up at last. Her scarlet lips stretched in an approximation of a smile. It could have curdled blood, so far as Abby was concerned.

'Ah, Abby. I thought it was time we met, see how you're settling into Chambers.'

'Fine thank you.'

'Ron tells me that you were doing a return of mine in Northby today.'

'Yes.'

Rita continued to smile horribly.

'And how did it go? As I seem to recall, the wife wanted everything.'

'She got the house.'

Rita paused for a moment.

167

'But surely the house was all there was?'

'Apart from his pension, which was worth more than the house.'

'But it's not payable for ten years yet. You aren't seriously saying that you let the judge treat it as a realisable asset?'

Abby winced. 'I argued it as you suggested in your Advice. But the judge was quite clear that the wife should get the house.'

Rita's smiled had disappeared.

'But that's ridiculous. You can't have been forceful enough. Let your opponent trample all over you, I suppose . . .'

Abby was having none of that.

'No, I did not. I stuck to your line of argument, with which I disagreed. The judge disagreed with it, too.'

By now Rita was snarling. All of a sudden, Abby realised how terrifying the older woman must be in court.

'Your own feelings should be irrelevant. Yet you quite clearly allowed them to intrude. I must say I'm very disappointed.'

'With respect, I did nothing of the sort. I was stuck with your Advice, which was wrong. It was as clear as a bell that the wife was going to get the house. So clear that the judge even commented to that effect when he dealt with . . .'

Too late. Oh dear. This was really going to piss her off, thought Abby.

'When he dealt with costs?' asked Rita, quietly.

'Yes. Mr Davies was ordered to pay the costs. The wife had set out her stall in her first affidavit and the judge said that he had caused the costs to be incurred by his attitude to settlement.'

'What?'

'Just as I said.'

Rita stood up and walked over to the window. She may have been disappointed before, but she was mad now. With a ruling like that, there was no way on earth the client was going to pay her. She turned to Abby.

'I was prepared to give you a chance, a fair chance. I've already heard a few negative things about you – about your attitude. I know how difficult it can be for a woman at the Bar, but this is unacceptable. It is a most unfortunate start . . .'

The phone rang.

'Yes?' snapped Rita.

In an instant her tone changed to saccharine.

'Of course, darling. That sounds amazing. Eight o'clock? I'll be waiting.'

As she cooed into the phone, Abby was dismissed with a regal wave of the hand. Taking the cue, she escaped gratefully.

Abby stumbled back to her room and sagged into her chair. Suddenly, all the frustrations of the day crowded in on her and she started to cry. Little sobs at first, with delicate sniffs in between. Then the tears really began to flow and the sniffs became noisier. Abby searched in her pockets for a hanky. Alex was against her. And now Rita. It was all so bloody unfair.

A tissue appeared in front of her.

'Here, have mine.'

'Seb!'

'Just popped in on my way home to see how it was going. Not too well by the look of it. What happened?'

Through her sniffs, she told him.

'What was Rita wearing today?'

Strange question, thought Abby.

'Red jumper, flowery skirt.'

Seb grinned. 'You're in the clear.'

'What?'

He perched on the edge of her desk.

'This has happened many a time before. Rita's out of touch on the family law side now, she's trying to develop this niche crime thing. She's completely out of date on pensions, and she knows it. She had no intention of going up to Northby to lose horribly, so she took a day out of court and told Ron to send you instead. If she'd been in another court, she wouldn't have been wearing a jumper and skirt, would she?'

Abby was flabbergasted. 'You mean, she thought she might lose, so she dumped it on me?'

'Yes, essentially. Gets her out of a hole, and gives her some ammunition against you.'

'But what about the client … it's unprofessional, surely?'

'Of course. But that doesn't bother her. She doesn't need the ancillary relief work, anyhow. She doesn't care if the solicitors never use her again.'

Abby breathed out. 'What a cow!'

Seb grinned. 'Yes. But don't worry. If there's any complaint, her Advice will materialise pretty quickly. You were put in an impossible position.' He looked at her closely.

'Now, can I ask a strange question?'

'Sure.'

'What was your mother's name?'

Abby looked at him hard. 'Why?'

'Just something I heard – it may be that I knew her once.'

'Harriet.'

He looked startled. 'Middle name?'

'Harriet Kate – did you know her?'

Seb had gone a little red, she noticed.

'No, no. I knew an Ellie Penhaligon.'

'Must be someone else.'

He looked puzzled, and was just about to say something more when the phone rang. It was Ron.

'Miss Penhaligon, there's a man downstairs asking for you.'

Marcus! It had to be. Not just a written apology, he'd come in person. Should she agree to go out tonight or would that make her lack of social life too obvious? Still, after a day like this, who cared.

170

'Great . . . Ron, can you tell him to wait, I'm just with Mr Waters at the moment.'

Seb shook his head. He needed to find out more. It had to be her . . . but this was clearly not the moment. He'd try again later.

'I'll leave you to it,' said Seb.

Abby grinned at him as she shook her hair free.

'Thanks – honestly, you've just made my day so much better!'

She flew down the stairs, hair streaming behind her, and raced into the waiting room.

'Marcus, I'm sorry too—'

She stopped in her tracks. The waiting room was empty save for a main in his mid-thirties, dressed in a dark grey Armani suit and red silk tie. He was tall, gorgeously so. Her gaze moved up his body: broad shoulders, strong, tough-looking hands with perfect nails. He had a tanned face, firm jaw and dark, dark eyes. His high, intelligent-looking forehead was crowned with dark brown hair which fell like silk over his shoulders and was tied back with a single band.

'Miss Penhaligon, I'm so sorry to surprise you. My name is Antoine Rousseau.'

Abby thought she'd died and gone to heaven. She became aware that her mouth was hanging open. Control yourself, for goodness sake, she told herself.

'How can I help?' she asked.

'I was given your name. I understand you're working on a case in which you need to know about a shipwreck – the *Richard Montgomery*. There was an advert placed in a paper by a colleague of yours who suggested I contact you . . .'

Abby sat down, trying not to stare. He spoke with the lightest French accent, a cadence which sent a shiver down her spine.

'Yes, well, that is, I'm about to. I'm not formally instructed yet.'

171

'My mother, she lives in Paris now. She was in Essex when the ship sank and often told me about it. She may be able to help, but I would need to know exactly what information you seek, so that I can visit her. She's not well enough to travel at the moment.'

'No, I see.'

Abby smiled at this paragon. He really was, she mused, the most attractive man she had ever seen in her life. He smiled back, his eyes locking on to hers.

'I'm so sorry . . . I really must tell you that as a barrister, I'm not allowed to communicate with witnesses about a case. That is left to the solicitors. But it really is very helpful of you to come and see me like this. Can I take your details and pass them on to the solicitors?'

Antoine's face fell.

'Oh, I'm so sorry. Of course I will speak to them. I hope I haven't embarrassed you at all?'

Abby replied much too quickly, 'No, not at all. It was a pleasure, really . . .'

'Let me give you my details over dinner.'

'Well, that's very kind, but . . .'

He held up his hand in a gesture of disappointment.

'Is it really not possible? I would so love to spend an evening in your company . . . and I have travelled some way to talk to you today.'

He was quite irresistible. And she wasn't actually instructed on the case. Not yet.

'Then I'd love to, Antoine. Just give me a moment to organise my things.'

He waited as she raced upstairs. She grabbed Alex's neglected papers and bundled them up. On her way back, she popped her head around the door to the clerks' room.

'I must say, your social life seems a bit of a whirl, Miss Penhaligon. A vicar and a Frenchman in as many days.'

Abby tried to smile graciously. Ignore them. Mind you, she didn't care too much what they thought. And as for Marcus, well, he could stew. If he couldn't even be bothered

172

to contact her after yesterday, he wasn't worth wasting time on. Yeah, let him rot. She'd never liked him that much, anyhow.

'I have some good news for you, ma'am. I had a phone call from Dinkwater & Co. They're a blue chip firm, want to instruct you and Mr Waters on a very old appeal. Something to do with that vicar, I understand.'

Abby grinned. At least they'd know now he was genuine.

'Great. What happens next on it?'

'They're sending the papers tonight. Should be with us on Monday, so you'll be able to start going through them then. We've put in a consultation with you and Mr Waters together with that vicar on Tuesday at four. Privately funded, apparently. Rather a nice little earner for you, ma'am.'

Brilliant. It was really happening. Abby smiled.

'And I've just taken a booking for you next Tuesday. A trial in the Magistrates' Court. Mr Singerhof again – he was very pleased with your performance in the Winter case. That's a solicitor worth having on your side – he's got a lot of good quality work to give out.'

The day had gone from misery to near bliss in the course of an hour.

'Have a good weekend, Ron.'

'And you, ma'am.'

As she left, Ron sighed. James Dorton was presenting lists for the Crown Prosecution Service quite regularly now. With a bit of wrangling, he could probably arrange for him to deal with the trial next Tuesday – see how the pair of them fared against one another. They were going to have to make a decision on Dorton very soon. It would be a tragedy if he was taken on and the way was blocked for Miss Penhaligon. If he could just swing it for them to be against each other, it could be a useful way of proving a point . . . Maybe she wasn't up to the challenge, though.

Well, better find that out sooner rather than later.

'Kevin, get the CPS for me, would you?'

Marcus's Saab had been nice, but this was even better, thought Abby, as she reclined into the leather upholstery of Antoine's BMW. He drove quickly through the Friday evening traffic, making towards South Kensington. He was welcomed like an old friend at a small restaurant, a white stuccoed building with a terrace. Gently, he ushered her up the steps. She felt as though she was the only woman in the entire world.

'Champagne before we start to think about ordering? Or would you prefer Pimms?' He looked at her seriously as they took up their corner seats.

'Champagne would be wonderful, thank you.'

As the waiter brought their drinks, Antoine smiled at her again.

'Since we can't talk about the case, I would like so much to hear about you.'

'What would you like to know?'

'Start at the beginning.'

'OK. I was born in Basildon, Essex. It's about forty miles from here. I was brought up by my mother, who's dead now. I went to university, then Bar School. Now I'm trying to join Chambers permanently.'

'Is that difficult?'

'Yes. Only about half of those who set out actually succeed. The odds are against me at the moment.'

'But it's something you've always wanted to do, no?'

'Yes. I've never wanted to be anything else. Bit sad really.'

She grinned at him. He looked back at her and smiled gently.

'No. I think if you really want it, you'll succeed.'

He took a sip of the champagne and she followed suit. Then he summoned a waiter and the two men had an animated discussion in French, so fast and colloquial that Abby couldn't follow it.

174

'He suggests the lobster, it's fresh and good, apparently.'

'OK.'

'And for the main course, they do a very good sole *veronique*.'

Abby grinned. 'Then that's what I'll have.'

Over the starter, Abby tried to quiz Antoine a little about himself. Each time, he deflected the questions, turning them back to her own life. Before long, she had told him all about Cambridge, Bar School and the trials of being the pupil of Alexander Golightly.

As the main course appeared, together with a bottle of Pouilly Fumé, Antoine seemed thoughtful.

'This case could help you a lot in getting into Chambers.'

Abby nodded. 'Yes. It's likely to be high profile. If we win it, it will certainly help. But if it goes pear-shaped . . .'

'What do you mean?'

'Sorry, your English is so good, I forget . . . It means, if it goes wrong, then things will be even harder.'

'Is it likely to go wrong?'

Abby took a gulp of the wine. It was a warm evening and she was thirsty. It was delicious, light, fresh on the tongue.

'I don't know yet.'

The sole was superb. During the meal they chatted on, Antoine listening intently to every word Abby spoke. She'd always had a theory that the more good-looking the man, the more inclined he was to want to spend an evening talking about himself. Yet Antoine seemed completely unaware that all the women in the room (and quite a few men) were watching him. Instead, he looked only at Abby, and insisted she tell him everything about herself. He listened so intently as she spoke that she found it difficult to stop.

'Can you manage a dessert?'

He pronounced it properly, the long vowels stretching out languorously. Abby noticed how the skin under his eyes puckered up very slightly as he smiled.

'Please don't be offended, but you of all people need not fear for your figure.'

175

Abby laughed. 'I can't agree with that, but perhaps I could go for the *mille-feuille.*'

'I love the way you say that with your English accent. Again?'

'*Mille-feuille.*' She started to giggle. '*Mille-feuille, mille-feuille, mille-feuille.*'

Now he was laughing too, and filling up her wine glass again.

'I hope you win your case, Abby, and get your place in Chambers.'

'We should. The person who carried out the murder has admitted it to a priest who will give evidence. The wrong man was convicted, years ago. It needs to be put right.'

His tone was casual. 'Was this murder on the ship – the one you want to know about? I could ask my mother if she'd heard anything.'

She'd drunk too much, she knew. There was that feeling of dissociation between herself and her immediate surroundings. This wasn't reality. No way. Sitting in an elegant French restaurant with the best-looking man she had ever seen – it was just not happening.

But somehow, against all her impulses, discretion took over.

'I'm sorry, I can't tell you anything more. But I do need to know what was on that boat – I think it may be the key to everything.'

Even that might be too much, she thought. But he had a right to know, after going to all this trouble to find her and take her out to dinner. It would be rude to tell him nothing, to send him back to France with a flea in his ear. He'd probably never bother to contact her again. And she wanted to see him again, very much.

'If you could speak to your mother soon, it would be incredibly kind, Antoine. We're having a meeting next Tuesday, and I'd like to have as much information as possible in time for that. I'll be there, along with a senior barrister called Seb Waters. We'll be seeing the client –

176

he's an old man, now and the vicar – he's the one that's paying for the appeal. I think he knows more, but he's not telling me – especially not where the money's coming from.'

Antoine nodded quickly. 'Shall we leave the coffee?' he asked.

'Oh, OK.'

'Let me drive you home.'

He seemed sober, could obviously hold his drink rather better than she could. She climbed into the BMW and directed him to her flat. Perhaps they could have coffee there . . . perhaps that was why he had stopped the meal so suddenly.

He drew to a halt outside her front door. Abby cleared her throat, but he spoke first.

'Thank you for eating with me this evening. May I contact you again?'

Abby scribbled down her telephone number on some paper and handed it to him. Her fingers touched his and suddenly she understood all those teenagers who swore they'd never wash again after touching some forgettable teenybop idol. It was like electricity.

'Would you like coffee at my place?'

Her voice was husky. God, any more obvious and he'd think she was on heat or something.

He leant over and kissed her lightly on the cheek. His lips were firm and cool and she caught the most delightful hint of his aftershave, a deep, slightly tangy lemon. Then he withdrew a little, and placed his hands around her cheeks.

'You are so beautiful. But I have to go home straight away, and I know once I am with you I can never leave. But I will ring – it will not be long, I promise.'

Abby nodded as he took his hands away. She climbed out of the car.

'Adieu,' he called, as the engine purred into life once again.

Abby floated into her flat and found the nearest chair. So this was it. Her mind was reeling, a confusion of images flitting through it, all of them aided by the heady mix of alcohol, lust and exhaustion. Antoine, standing in the waiting room, looking so elegant and at home. That smile. The way he spoke. The hair, tumbling over his back. Those strong hands, bulky shoulders. The way he walked, the way he drove, his hands on the steering wheel as he caressed the car through the traffic . . .

He could have been here now. They would both have been naked within minutes, she knew. It would have been impossible to be alone with him without it happening. She'd never felt like this before. Not this heady desire. She wanted to touch him, look at him, hear his voice. It was purely physical – it couldn't be anything else. But the need to capture him, make him hers, was all encompassing.

She had to have him. It was as simple as that.

Once Pascal reached the end of the street, he accelerated sharply, almost re-tracing his route. He drove quickly back to Brompton Road and took the turning to the anonymous flat around the back of Harrods. He drove past the barrier into the underground car park, hidden from all except those who lived in the flats above.

In front of his parking space was the lift. Each flat had its own elevator to the car park – he wouldn't have rented the place otherwise. He did not propose to spend his time waiting for some filthy communal machine to work its way down.

A moment later, he was in the flat and Thierry was pouring him a glass of Chablis. He needed a drink. The girl hadn't noticed how little he was taking. In fact, she hadn't noticed very much at all. He grinned. It was rather useful at times to be French, and handsome as hell.

He looked at the other two men. They'd been waiting since he'd gone out earlier. He took a sip of his wine and spoke slowly.

178

'We're going to have to kill them. Option three.'

Sam looked at him quizzically.

'It's too risky. I was told this girl, Penhaligon, was working on the case as a lawyer. So I took her out and she talked. There was some murder way back which may have involved something on the wreck. They want information about the cargo.'

Thierry frowned. 'Shit. That means they'll search it. And search it well.'

'I'm not going to run that risk. Even if they don't, the case will attract publicity. Some joker will start doing trips out to the boat, the press will be interested. We won't be able to get to it without the risk of someone else turning up.'

The other two men nodded in agreement.

Pascal continued. 'The old man who's bringing the appeal – we need to kill him to stop the whole thing in its tracks. And she said there was a vicar who had got involved, was paying the legal costs. I think he ought to go too, or else he might get some funny ideas.'

'So we kill the vicar and the old guy. How?' asked Thierry.

Pascal smiled. 'Very easily, in fact. The girl told me that they're meeting in her Chambers next Tuesday. The vicar, the old man and the barristers. All of them in one room – it's too good an opportunity to miss.'

Thierry rubbed his hands. 'A bomb?'

'Yes. I'll need a simple timer from you – in fact, leave two just in case there's a problem. I'll set it and take care of the Semtex.'

'OK.'

Thierry had picked up some useful skills during his time in the Ordnance Corps. Over the years he'd passed them on to Pascal, a quick learner. This was a dirty business, Pascal knew. He'd blown up a competitor's stock more than once.

'How are you going to get it in?'

'Simple. There's no security, I watched it a while from

179

outside when I went to see the girl. The door's open until late, no one watching who goes in. I can get something in there pretty easily on Monday evening. I'll need to get the time of the meeting from the girl. I could have got it if I'd stayed a little longer with her – believe me, it would have been no ordeal.'

Sam grinned as Pascal continued. 'But I'll find out and set the timer once I know.'

Sam looked at Pascal. 'What do I do?'

'You go back to your place immediately and lay low until you hear from me. Don't go out, but keep your boat ready in case we need it.'

He carried on, 'Thierry, stay long enough to get the timers made. Then get yourself to Sam's place and wait there for me to contact you.'

He paused a moment.

'I'll stay in London to check it all goes to plan. Then I'll go straight to Paris and ring you for a drink, Thierry. That's your cue to get on the train to France.'

'What if it goes wrong? What's the fallback position?' asked Sam.

Pascal nodded. 'Then we just have to get the drugs off quickly. If the fuss dies down, we can always delay the deal with George until they can be put back on. So if we hit trouble, I'll call you, Sam, and suggest a sail. That means you get out to the wreck and collect the drugs. Don't wait for me, just get out there. It'll be one hell of a night, but it's the safest option. And then we'll just have to hide the stuff anywhere we can until things look better.'

'But there's no way I can lift nearly two hundred bags in one night . . .' protested Thierry.

'You'll find a way. There's twelve million pounds down there – every bag you bring up is more money for you.'

Sam was already on his feet. As he went to leave, he turned to Pascal.

'That girl – she'll be in the meeting, too, won't she? If there's a bomb . . .'

180

Pascal nodded. He stood up to face the others, looking Sam in the eye. When he spoke, his voice had a chill in it.

'She'll have to die, too.'

Chapter Twenty

Carefully, Marcus took the violin from its case. It was a quiet Saturday afternoon and the Vicarage was empty. He hadn't played for far too long. Without the discipline of daily lessons, he had let things slip badly.

He'd lied to Abby when he said he no longer played. But he didn't think of it as really playing any more. For too long, it had held no meaning for him.

He'd stopped playing seriously when Jennifer died, although he'd had to wait a while for the opportunity to cease completely without losing face. After he'd given her the money that first time, she would often show up. He'd keep a look out for her, moving into some Brahms the minute he saw her walking up the subway. She'd smile and stop a while. Sometimes, they'd go for a coffee in a nearby fast-food shop.

She'd filled him in on the detail of her life. About her expensive boarding school in the south-east; about her music scholarship; about her parents divorcing and her mother re-marrying; about the money running out when her new step-father started to drink; about leaving the school she loved and going back home; about her step-father trying to grope her and her mother not believing her when she said something.

Each time he saw her, she was thinner, sadder – something had always changed for the worse. She could never get up to date with her pimp's rent. And she needed his drugs badly. The last few times she saw Marcus, she knew what awaited her. She was at the top end of a cul de sac, she said. There was no way out. He'd listened, but done nothing. And he'd paid the price for that ever since.

The last time he met her, she appeared quietly and sat down by his open case. She often did that, hated it if he stopped. So he carried on for a while. He was playing at South Kensington, his violin echoing along the subway under Exhibition Road. It was a quiet Sunday evening and there were few people about.

He took a break at the end of the piece. She seemed tired, was fighting to keep her eyes open.

'Are you all right?'

'I'm dying.'

'What?'

'There's no way out, Marcus. I can't take it any more. I've just taken enough to see me out. I thought I'd come and listen to you playing as I drifted away.'

She seemed so calm, bizarrely happy. He couldn't believe for a moment what she was saying. Then, suddenly, he realised what she meant.

'Come with me.'

He took her hand and pulled her to her feet.

'No Marcus, just play to me.'

'No I fucking won't.'

She started to scream. Quickly, Marcus picked her up. She was tiny and he could sling her over his shoulder, caveman style. Roughly, he shoved his violin into a case and made for the road. There, he summoned a taxi and made it to a hospital. She was already unconscious by the time they got there.

'What drug has she taken?' they'd asked.

'I don't know. Heroin, probably.'

They'd whisked her away, doing all they could, but she was in a coma by that stage. Then she started fitting. When there was nothing more they could do, they let him sit with

183

her through one long night, praying to a God he didn't believe in for her to wake up and say she was sorry and hadn't wanted to die.

But she didn't. He'd drifted off to sleep and found her white and cold at five in the morning. Nobody had noticed in the chaos of the hospital.

He'd stayed with her body for a few hours until her mother could be found. She shouldn't be alone. Emaciated, covered in needle marks, she was a victim of far too much evil. Used, abused, rejected.

Her mother had finally arrived, ashen faced. She'd looked at him as though it had all been his fault, somehow. He'd left, picking up his violin case as he went. Suddenly, Marcus had realised that the whole thing was utterly pointless. Who gave a toss about perfect arpeggios in C sharp minor when Jennifers were around? Music made no difference, it was unimportant. It was no more than a sop to the middle classes, an opportunity for them to show off to each other. It solved nothing. It was an emollient for society, nothing more. He despised it.

He never went back to the Royal College of Music. He'd gone home to Cornwall for a while. Then he'd drifted back to London. He'd bought a motorbike and started despatch riding to earn some money. It was just a stop gap whilst he thought hard about what he wanted to do for the rest of his life. But before long, he was doing well, getting the longer distance runs which paid the most. It suited him. He was free, could work when he chose, was his own boss out on the road.

After a year or so, though, he'd crashed at Oxford Circus. A stupid accident, really, just an idiotic Volvo driver pulling out in front of him. But it was enough to break his right wrist badly. They'd done a good job in the hospital, but some of the flexibility was gone. It was his bowing arm, and no longer could he get that clear fluidity of tone that had been his hallmark. Perhaps, with more physio, he could have achieved it, but it was a good excuse.

He gave up the violin completely, left London and joined the navy. It was the only escape he could think of.

And there he found God. Or as he always said, God found him. Not at a service, or a rally, or anything dramatic; he had been working on the bridge, when he'd looked out over the Atlantic to see the sea and the horizon merge together in a rippling haze. Suddenly, he became aware that he was part of a greater thing – a world that was a living organism in itself. In that moment, he moved from a cynical battle-scarred atheist to a believer.

He was woefully ignorant, of course. He'd gone to see the chaplain on board, felt compelled to do so, expecting to see laughter in his eyes. But the chaplain had listened to him carefully, and gave him some books to read. Marcus sat up all night reading them, then went back for more. By the end of his seven years in the navy, he knew where his future lay. His place at theological college beckoned. His parents were proud but bemused. Every now and then, they'd come and visit, and were tactful enough to keep any doubts firmly to themselves.

Still, though, he hated himself. There was so much more he could have done for Jennifer. Got to know her before things became so bad. Got her away from her pimp, taken her in maybe. Anything would have been better than nothing. If he'd acted earlier, she'd still be alive. Every day, that thought occurred to him. Many nights, too. He knew, had known for some time, that he was going to have to do something about it. Prove to himself, if to nobody else, that he did have a purpose. That he could change events, rather than just give succour to those afflicted by them.

Gradually, he'd started to play the violin again. He'd kidded himself that he was just filling the time,but his need for music had never gone away completely. His wrist played him up terribly. At first, it was so stiff that the sound from the instrument was like that of a screeching cat. But he was getting better, and his wrist had stopped aching so much. The music was starting to mean something again. He took out the Paganini caprices. These were good for his bowing. He had to dig hard into the string, stop, push on to the tip, draw it back – all in an instant, getting the angle of the bow utterly right. On through the triplets, the arpeggios flowing fluently, quietly first time round, then full fortissimo to the end. It *was* getting better, he knew it.

As he put the violin away and loosened the hair of the bow, he thought of Abby. She'd seemed a bit quiet on the way back on Thursday – perhaps she'd taken offence at his refusal to tell her where the money was coming from. Still, she'd understand in time. Give her a while to cool down a bit.

Dinkwaters had phoned him about the consultation. He was looking forward to Tuesday. Maybe he could take her out afterwards, have a drink and put things right. He was hopeless at dealing with women, he'd been told. Just put yourself in their shoes had been the words of wisdom. He'd always ignored the advice. They'd have to take him as they found him. No point in pretending to be someone he wasn't.

But maybe he would have to try a bit harder this time.

Seb buried his father on the Saturday. It was a quiet affair, but many of Dad's old friends had turned up. They'd stood in the sun in the country churchyard, listening to the age-old words of the parish priest. Then they'd returned to the house. He'd prepared the food himself, shopping in the morning. It had been something to do, had stopped him thinking about it all too much. It had helped.

But now, as the darkness grew, he sat nursing a whisky. *If only I'd known.*

Abigail Penhaligon – it was an unusual name. And she looked so like Ellie. It had to be her.

Maybe Ellie had changed her name. Maybe her real name was Harriet and for some reason she'd not been using it when he knew her.

He'd need time to talk to Abby about it. She might not believe him at first, think he'd taken leave of his senses. He couldn't just breeze in and announce that he was her father.

She might not be too pleased about it, anyhow. He tried to think it through from her perspective. Abandoned by a father with no apparent interest in her. Brought up in poverty as a result. Perhaps he had no right to simply come along and claim her as his daughter. Perhaps he'd not earned the right to be regarded as her father.

Thank goodness he hadn't been able to blurt it out when he'd seen her. The more he thought about it, the more he realised it would need careful handling. He'd better have his explanation ready. And the evidence. She'd need convincing. He'd take the photo of her and her mother, along with the letter. Then she'd see – and he hoped like hell that she would understand.

He'd tell her on Tuesday. He was seeing her for the consultation then. They could go out somewhere quiet, he could take his time over it. He had to get it right. He could blow it horribly, estrange himself from his only child. That, he knew, would finally break his heart.

This was going to be the most important meeting of his life.

By Sunday evening, Alexander Golightly was exhausted. He'd had more sex, over three days and nights, he worked out, than he had had in the past six months with the Hon. Lucinda. And it had been better, too. Rita was surprisingly attractive when she took all that panstick off. And the things she whispered in his ear didn't bear thinking about.

He hadn't performed too badly himself, now he thought about it. Rita hadn't complained, anyhow. Of course, the first time had been a little hurried. But then he'd got into his stride. Now he was relaxing with a whisky. He wasn't in court tomorrow, so for once there was no evening work to do. Rita, though, had a hearing in Brighton, so she was in her study, reading her notes.

187

All in all, things looked pretty good. He had another night with Rita, then back home to Surrey tomorrow to recover. With a bit of luck, this could become a regular event. Best of both worlds. Wonderful. Absolutely bloody marvellous.

Chapter Twenty-One

Alexander was early into Chambers for once. He'd got up with Rita, so he thought he might as well leave when she did. More to the point, he felt like getting up and getting out. She was taking years off him, that woman.

'Bright and early this Monday morning, sir,' said Ron.

'Lots to do today,' he replied. 'Anything interesting in for me?'

His eyes fell upon a large-looking brief made up of several lever arch files. It had just been opened by Ron.

'Dinkwater & Co.? Very respectable firm. Didn't know they instructed us.'

Ron nodded. 'They rang up on Friday, asked for Miss Penhaligon. They weren't interested in anyone else. She's having Mr Waters in as a leader, so we're keeping it in the family.'

Ron watched the barrister's jaw hit the floor.

'But they act for the Church of England. Lots of high-quality work there. How do they know Miss Penhaligon?'

Ron looked heavenwards and dropped his voice respectfully.

'The Lord has his ways, Mr Golightly.'

Alex walked over to his pigeon hole. No cheques.

Ron seized his advantage.

'Of course, it's particularly good to attract this work

189

into Chambers at the present time, if you get my drift, sir.'

Alex quite clearly didn't. He looked at his clerk blankly.

Trying not to sigh too obviously, Ron continued.

'It's the political climate, you see. A few years ago, you needed to be in with the Tories, or so they said. Not sure about that one myself. But today, it's all God and football, isn't it?'

Alex thought it through.

'That's true, I suppose. Plenty of Christians in the Cabinet; a good few football fans as well. Yes, I can see the argument. Perhaps we ought to be developing an expertise in ecclesiastical law.'

'Good idea, sir.' Ron modestly ignored the fact that it was actually his idea. 'Don't forget the tenancy meeting at ten-thirty – it's been brought forward.'

'I want a fantastic bouquet. Your very best, please. And quick'

'Of course, sir.'

The girl serving Pascal was only too happy to oblige. What a lucky woman this Frenchman's girlfriend had to be. Carefully, she drew out the best roses, lilies, gypsophila.

'And would you like us to deliver?'

'Yes, straightaway, please. 29 Pump Court, Temple.'

'Certainly. Would you like to write a note?'

Pascal took the proferred card and paused before he wrote: *Abby, thank you for a wonderful evening. I can't wait to see you again – perhaps Tuesday? I'll call this afternoon. Adieu!*

He left the card with the assistant, paid in cash and left quickly.

Alexander Golightly hurried up to Seb's room.

'Abby Penhaligon's getting work from Dinkwater & Co. I can't believe it.'

'Why the surprise?'

190

'They're top notch. Blue chip firm. Did you know they do lots of church work? I just didn't have Miss Penhaligon down as their type.'

'She's a very bright woman, Alex.'

Golightly nodded. 'Yes, perhaps it was some Cambridge connection.'

Seb threw out another thought, dropping his voice conspiratorially.

'Perhaps it's more than that, Alex. You know she's a Labour party member. And you know how big the Church is in the party these days . . .'

It was comical watching him take the bait. He took it surprisingly quickly, too. Maybe Ron had dropped the hint as requested.

'Of course! That must be it. Well, fancy Abby having those connections.'

Seb waited for the inevitable final links to work their way through Alex's brain.

'You know, if we took her on, it mightn't be so bad for these Chambers, Seb.'

Seb assumed a confused expression.

'I mean, having a contact with the powers that be could help us at the top end as well – get us noticed a little more.'

Seb couldn't resist it. 'I'm sure you're right, Alex. But maybe we ought to join the party too?'

Alex went red. 'Do you think it would help? I'm in the Tories at the moment, of course, but it did cross my mind after the election that perhaps I ought to change allegiance . . . But I'd have to tell Lucinda. Oh no, it would be awful.'

Seb grinned. 'Maybe we should just let Abby's connections work their way through then. You can always think about joining up if that doesn't work. Lucinda will know which side her bread's buttered.'

Alex nodded sagely. He'd never understood irony.

Abby had spent the weekend sighing over Antoine and

191

getting to grips with the papers Alex had left for her. She'd finally got to the bottom of them and had typed out her researches.

The door opened and Alex breezed in.

'Good morning, Abby.'

'Morning, got those papers done for you.'

He beamed at her.

'Thank you. I must say I'm impressed at you dealing with these over the weekend.' He ran an eye over the typescript. 'Excellent. Yes. Good point.' Carefully, he placed the papers on his desk. 'Thank you Abby. This is going to be very useful.'

Abby was aware that she was staring. Presumably he hadn't spoken with Rita about the Friday case yet.

'And Abby, I just popped in to say that something's arrived for you in the clerks' room. Ron suggested I tell you quickly. A case. Dinkwater & Co.'

'Thanks . . .'

'Do call me Alex.'

'Thanks, Alex.'

Abby escaped from the room. Prozac. It had to be a Prozac overdoze, if such a thing was possible. He'd misread the instructions and was on a happy cloud, fifty feet up. She opened the door to the clerk's room.

'Mr Golightly said there was something for me – is it the James papers?'

'Here you are, ma'am. And here's your trial for the morning, too.'

'Is Mr Waters in?'

'He's in a meeting with the other tenants – it's just about to start. Then as soon as he's through, he's off to Pentonville for a conference.'

'Oh, well. I was hoping to have a chat with him about the James case.'

Ron nodded. 'With a bit of luck, you might be able to have some time before the consultation tomorrow – you'll have to get your skates on in the Magistrates' though.'

Just then the door opened and a vast bouquet of roses walked in. The clerks and Abby stood in silence as it gracefully walked across and settled itself on to the floor, closing the door behind it.

After a few moments, a diminutive figure appeared from behind it.

'Lord God Almighty, that weighed a ton. Couldn't see a thing behind it, like moving a bleeding tree.'

The man took a notebook from his pocket.

'Twenty-nine Pump Court. Abby Penhaligon.'

'That's me.' She was stunned.

'Your lucky day, then. Sign here, love.'

As he left, Abby stared at the arrangement.

'How the hell am I going to get it home? It won't go on the bus.'

'We'll sort something out, ma'am. Must be some admirer. Is it the vicar or the Frenchman?'

Abby blushed dark red as she rooted around for a card. Eventually, she found it. Please God, let it be Antoine. Quickly, she opened the envelope and read the message.

'Oh, good Lord . . .'

'Something wrong ma'am?'

Abby read the words a second time. All weekend, she'd been wondering if she'd made it too obvious. But now she knew he cared just as much. He was probably thinking of her now, just as she'd been incapable of getting him out of her mind.

She beamed stupidly at Ron.

'No, nothing wrong at all.'

Seb was chairing the meeting as usual. Initially, it had been planned for the early evening, but by mutual consent it had been brought forward, since most of the combatants were in Chambers that morning.

'Thank you all for coming in. Only item on the agenda, as you all know, is the tenancy question. I take the view that we ought to prioritise our two working pupils and offer

193

a guaranteed place to at least one, with the possibility of another tenancy to the other.'

There were nods all round.

'Have any of you been against James Dorton or Abby Penhaligon?'

Seb looked round the table. Nobody had. As ever, all they had to rely upon was feedback from the clerk, and that nebulous idea of whether the face fitted.

'I know who I'd prefer,' said Joe.

Seb nodded. 'I've had a letter from Rita. Written in vitriol, by the look of it. She prefers Dorton, but I think one would expect that.' He smiled as he spoke.

Nigel Monroving cleared his throat.

'As the senior family practitioner, I'd have to say I'm worried by what Rita has to say. And I agree with Alexander – Miss Penhaligon does seem a touch . . . well, not quite what one would expect from a member of these Chambers.'

Alexander went a little pink. 'In fact, having seen some of Miss Penhaligon's work, I have to say that I may have softened a little in my views – she's certainly very bright.'

Nigel looked quite horrified. Seb took the cue quickly.

'Starred first from Cambridge. Certainly brighter than me.' He paused and looked at Nigel, whom he knew had got a third back in the middle ages. 'And rather more impressive than Mr Dorton's two-two from Wolverhampton.'

Nigel was unimpressed. 'You can't judge a barrister on his degree grade. Many of our best advocates got thirds. The skills are totally different. It's not just academic ability – it's more difficult than that.'

'Maybe,' said Joe, 'but Abby's done very well in court – got a good result in Chippington last week. This family thing on Friday – Rita doesn't mention in her letter that she'd already advised and Abby was simply running her argument.'

Seb looked round the table.

'We've got a vote against Abby from Rita, one for from Joe. Nigel?'

'Against.'

'I'm for,' replied Seb. 'That leaves you, Alexander.'

Alex's plump features contorted themselves this way and that. If this girl was getting work in from good firms, it could raise the profile of Chambers. More importantly, it could do him the world of good in his next application for silk. Maybe even get him on to the High Court bench.

But there was the Rita factor. Once Rita found out he'd voted for Abby, she'd be livid. No more weekends like the last one. He'd be out of favour immediately.

He was realistic, however. She'd tire of him before long, move on to a younger man. He was on a time limit on this one. But why end it before that point? It would be bloody good fun while it lasted. But he could always seek out another woman. There were probably hundreds of Ritas out there, awaiting him. And his career did need a shove.

'James is my godson, although I have to say that I'm impressed with Abby.'

Seb tried again.

'Forget family loyalties. Who is the better barrister?'

Alexander played for time.

'I don't know, I've never seen them in court.'

'What are you doing tomorrow?'

'Paperwork day.'

'Ron's arranged for them to be against each other in the Magistrates' Court. Why don't you go and watch? Form a view then?'

A day's grace. It would give him time to think it through, maybe float the idea with Rita. He spoke thoughtfully.

'Yes. I'll go and watch. I'll let you know afterwards.'

Pascal heard the weather forecast just before he rang Abby. Thames, Dover, Wight, possible gale within forty-eight hours. *Merde*. They were going to have to get this just right. He'd sounded confident when he set up the fallback position, but the weather could cause problems.

195

Real problems. He had a bad feeling about it. That bomb was going to have to do the job.

'Twenty-nine Pump Court.'

'May I speak to Miss Penhaligon?'

Abby was in her room as the call was put through. She sounded breathy, dreamy. Good. Safely on the hook.

'Antoine, thank you. The flowers – what can I say, they're magnificent.'

'I've missed you, Abby. And tomorrow – can we meet? What time do you finish?'

'The meeting's at four. Should be finished by six.'

'Shall I pick you up from work?'

'Wonderful. See you then.'

Abby put down the phone. She couldn't admit it to herself, but she was a little disappointed. He'd seemed distracted, a little short. She'd expected some extravagant declarations after those flowers. Still, he must be shy. Some men were hopeless at expressing themselves, after all.

She looked at the James brief. The church solicitors had certainly been busy. They'd drafted a statement from Abraham, and one from Marcus. Seb wanted Marcus at the meeting, even though he was a witness. Exceptions could be made to the rule. This was, in effect, a dying declaration which was of vital significance to the case. He wanted to make sure that Marcus had no doubts.

Marcus. She no longer cared about his refusal to tell her what he knew. She'd overreacted, she knew. There was nothing he could do. Without him, she wouldn't have this case, and she should be a bit more grateful. She'd better say sorry after the consultation. Try and make amends.

She couldn't stop wondering about the source of the money, though. It must relate to the boat in some way. Carefully, she went through what she knew. The ship had come from America loaded with bombs, Marcus had said.

Maybe it carried something more. The Manhattan Project had been in full swing for some time by 1945. Maybe

196

Abraham was right. Perhaps the ship was transporting the raw material for nuclear weapons and Marcus had been bribed to keep quiet. The legal fees would be paid if he didn't tell.

The more she thought about it, the more likely it seemed. It explained why he was so touchy about it. It also explained why money seemed to be no problem in bringing the appeal.

With a sigh, she bundled up the papers and opened the trial set for the next day. Ron had handed it over to her with a broad grin.

'What you might call a regular customer, Danny Frenkel.'

'Trial or plea?'

'Your first trial. Magistrates' Court, tomorrow morning. Good luck. Oh, by the way, you're against Mr Dorton.'

Abby looked at the backsheet R v Frenkel. Theft. More to the point, shoplifting from a superstore. There was a long list of previous convictions, all for shoplifting. Oh damn. Still, the magistrates wouldn't be told that.

She read through the prosecution evidence. He'd been followed by a store detective for twenty minutes. He'd taken a trolleyload of goods and had then turned back to the entrance, where the toilets were. He'd gone in there for a few moments, and had then left the store, complete with trolley. At no time had he actually gone through a checkout and paid for what he'd taken. He'd been stopped immediately and returned to the store. The total value of the goods came to £157.60.

Looked pretty difficult to challenge. Still, let's see what he has to say.

Abby looked at Danny Frenkel's proof of evidence. This was for her eyes only. It was his case, which she would have to bring out of him as he stood in the witness box in two days' time. She read it through carefully, sighing as she came to the end.

Oh dear. He'd forgotten. Gone straight out through the

197

door with a loaded trolley and clean forgotten to pay.

Come on Danny, you can do better than that, surely?

Nobody would believe him. How on earth can you forget that you haven't paid for your shopping? She read his statement again.

'*The store detective was watching me. She always does. She's caught me several times before, always keeps an eye on me when I'm there. I wouldn't have tried to steal with her right there.*'

Abby turned to the end.

'*I really didn't intend to take the shopping. It's just so easy to forget, once you're past the checkouts in the entrance area. I had a lot on my mind. I just didn't think. I don't think that's theft.*'

Certainly isn't, thought Abby to herself. But winning this one was going to present a few difficulties. Her best point was the fact that Danny knew he was being followed by the store detective. But once she ran that one, the magistrates would want to know how he knew. And the only answer was that he recognised her because he'd been caught shoplifting there before.

The great mantra of English criminal justice was that whoever was appointed to decide whether someone was guilty – a jury or magistrates – would not normally be told of the accused's previous convictions. Every now and then this caused a storm, of course, but the idea was one which Abby believed in – the court had to look at the evidence for the particular case alone. They couldn't be prejudiced with information from old cases.

There were limits to the rule, however. If the accused embarked on a character assassination of one of the prosecution witnesses, his form was revealed, for a start. But in this case, Abby would have to tell the court all about those convictions. Danny Frenkel would be casting aside one of the most sacred rights of an accused. She sat back in her chair and thought hard. He could just say that he forgot and not mention the precons. But that would be a half way house. She'd not be able to explain the fact that he knew the store detective without explaining his history.

And, she thought, this was in the Magistrates' Court. They were experienced, hearing dozens of shoplifting cases over the course of a year's sitting. They'd work it out for themselves – he knew the store detective because he had form. Chances were one or two of them would even have dealt with him before.

Abby sat back and thought tactics. She was going to have to go out on a limb, break one of the first rules.

His form would go in. That would get the attention of the Bench, if nothing else.

Pascal put down the phone and left immediately, a briefcase in his hand, for King's Cross. He had a contact there. Bernie would never let him down – for a price, obviously.

He found the lock-up with no problem. He hadn't visited for a while, but he remembered the tortuous route well.

'Pascal, it's been too long.'

Bernie kissed him on both cheeks, French style. As the son of a French mother and an Irish father he moved easily between the cultures. Handy, in his business.

'And what can I be doing for you? Ringing me up out of the blue like that . . .'

'I've got a bit of a problem. Could do with some of your yellow plasticine.'

Bernie nodded. 'Well, it just so happens that I've got a little put by. How much do you need?'

Pascal showed him with his hands. A small amount would do for the Chambers bomb, but he'd keep some spare just in case it was needed.

'Where and when?'

'Leave it in my lift, five o'clock exactly. Tonight.'

'It'll cost you.'

Pascal opened his briefcase. 'Take it. There's ten thousand in there.'

Bernie grinned. 'That'll do nicely, sir, as they say.'

Pascal left King's Cross and took a taxi to Chancery Lane. He'd thought carefully about how to get the bomb into the room where they were meeting, nice and close to the occupants. He'd seen the sign to the conference room when he'd gone to see Abby. But getting the bomb there would need some planning.

The safest route for him would be for Abby to carry it in. He had mulled it over carefully. A present, maybe, with the bomb inside? No. She might open it and find the Semtex. And even if she didn't, there would be no guarantee she'd take it into the meeting with her.

No, he'd have to plant the bomb himself. There would be a risk, he knew, but he could minimise it. Visit tonight, when the place was quiet. But it would have to stay safely in the conference room until the meeting started. The last thing he needed would be some clown moving it.

It would have to be hidden in something which wouldn't be moved. Something so normal in a barristers' Chambers that nobody would notice it. And that was why he was in Chancery Lane.

He walked down the narrow road, looking through the windows. He used the reflections to watch passers by. If he saw Abby, he was going to dive into the nearest entrance.

He found a cookshop at the bottom end of the road and went in. There, he found what he needed. Archbold, it was called. A big, several-volume textbook, used by most criminal lawyers and housed in a large cardboard case. Ideal for what he had in mind. And chances were it would go unnoticed at the side of the conference room for a day or so.

He took a copy to the desk and paid cash. If the assistant was surprised at this, she didn't show it. Then, quickly, he left the shop and caught another cab in Fleet Street. This time, he was heading back to the flat.

There, he waited for an hour. He passed the time by getting out a Stanley knife and carefully cutting the pages from one of the volumes of the Archbold. He slid the book back into the cardboard case with the other volumes. Excellent. Satisfied, he took the dummy volume out again.

Thierry had left already. He'd been up all night, working on the timers. As ordered, he'd made two, just in case Pascal needed a second attempt. It paid to be prepared.

Thierry had picked up his skills a long time ago and had had plenty of practice since. He'd done well with these two. They were identical, simple devices, both running off a minuscule sports watch. Tiny and slim.

Four-fifty. He was ready for the delivery now.

Pascal sat on the floor and waited. God, he loved this feeling. That gnawing at the base of his stomach, the fact that he would be living on his wits now. It tested him, he could prove himself. It was as if he knew he existed only by succeeding in the tasks he set himself.

At five o'clock precisely, he heard the grind of his lift, called to the basement. He smiled. It was all coming together. The noise stopped for a moment. Then the lift started to return upwards. He pressed the 'open' button and the door drew back. There, right in front of him, was a small plastic bag.

Carefully, he lifted it out.

Semtex. His favourite explosive. All the way from the Czech republic. Yellow, discreet, pliable. Just the thing for the job.

Deftly, Pascal moulded the Semtex into the empty volume. He checked his watch and took the timer. Twenty-three and a half hours would do it very nicely indeed. That would take him to 5.06. Time enough to make sure the conference had started, even if they were running late. Not too late, though, in case they finished and left before it went off.

This was feeling good.

The next challenge was going to be getting into Chambers. Pascal looked at his watch. Five forty-five. He could leave it until night-time and break in. But that would involve the police, and a search. The bomb might still pass unnoticed but he couldn't take the chance. No, it would have to be a social visit. Just calling by to see if Abby was there. Hopefully, she had gone home and he'd be able to find an excuse to get into the conference room. And if she was there, he'd bluff it out somehow.

It would be a farewell visit, but she'd never know.

Chapter Twenty-Two

Abby took a bite from the cheese sandwich she'd made the previous night. Going out for one took time, and cost money. It was geriatric by now, though, the bread tasteless and chewy, but she was starving.

She was going through the store detective's statement, planning her cross-examination. Alex had already left for the evening, muttering something about the opera. The building seemed quiet as Abby sat back in her chair.

Cross-examination was something which she found difficult. She had to work out a strategy, a line of attack. But at the same time, everything depended on the answers to her questions. She had to be prepared to change tack suddenly if the need arose. Some students at Bar School used to try to cover every eventuality. They'd prepare a list of questions, with follow-ups from every conceivable answer. The whole thing ended up looking like a flow diagram and Abby knew she'd spend all her time tracing down her list of questions rather than actually listening to the answers. There came a point, she knew, where she just had to trust herself, know that she would be ready with the right question at the right time.

This store detective would be a good witness. She would have given evidence before, and have an understanding of what to expect. She would be calm and collected. Abby was going to have to rattle her cage a little.

*

Pascal arrived at 29 Pump Court at six-fifteen precisely. The clerks were still there, sorting out the lists for the next day. He paused outside for a few moments, assessing the building. He looked like a tourist, dressed in forgettable clothes and with a rucksack on his back. He moved up the steps to the main door. It was open, as always in working hours, with a sign inviting callers to ring on the bell to summon a clerk.

The door to their room was closed. Excellent, he thought, I don't even need to tell them I'm here.

He saw the sign to the conference room – an arrow, leading down the stairs to a basement. It was a potential trap, he knew. But it would take no more than a minute. Carefully, he crept past the clerks' room and waited at the top of the stairs. He listened carefully. Nothing but the beat of his own heart.

He loved this. The adrenalin surge. He felt it physically, the tingling of every nerve in his body.

Quietly, slowly, he took the steps one at a time. It was dark. His eyes were becoming accustomed to the gloom, though. The door at the bottom was open. He peered around it carefully. Definitely empty. On the other side was a door to a toilet. Good, if anyone came downstairs, he could hide in there for a moment.

The conference room was large, with a low ceiling, painted white. It felt a little damp and musty. There was a long maple table running down the centre, with a carafe of water in the middle. Twelve chairs were arranged around the table. Down the near side of the room ran a white cupboard with shelving in the middle and doors at either end.

Pascal thought hard. Two barristers, the client, the vicar, a solicitor. They wouldn't need all those chairs. They'd congregate near the door. The barristers would sit at the end, probably, the others around them. They'd leave the chairs at the far end empty.

Silently, he opened the nearest door of the cupboard. It

smelt musty inside. He knelt down to take a better look. A bundle of old receipts, a ledger from 1954. Behind that, a book, burgundy in colour: *Halsbury's Laws of England*, volume 12. On its own, years old by the look of it.

Excellent. This cupboard was clearly used only rarely. No one was going to notice a book slipped into it. It would just be left to gather dust with the rest of the cupboard contents.

Silently, he removed the rucksack and took the Archbold from it. In a moment, it had been slipped into the corner of the cupboard. Then, carefully, he closed the door.

He paused a moment at the entrance to the room. The adrenalin was still pumping. He was on a high. He was also aroused. Abby was probably a few floors away from him. It would be so easy now to call in at the clerks' room, find out if she was there. And if she was, he'd meet with little resistance, he knew.

Merde, it was tempting. It would be her last time, too. And he'd know it, every step of the way. That was one hell of a turn on. It would be total power. He would have decided her destiny and she wouldn't have a clue.

He peered up the stairs, wrestling with the decision.

No. This was a God-given opportunity. He'd got in without being seen. There would be nothing to link him with the Chambers tonight. And that was better than a few minutes fumbling with the English beauty. It would be giving in, a weakness.

He was up the basement stairs and out of the door within forty-five seconds.

205

Chapter Twenty-Three

The Magistrates' Court was close to the tube and just under an hour's journey for Abby. She was there in good time on the Tuesday morning. It was already busy. There were four courts on the go, and the central lobby was heaving with people – defendants, lawyers, press, supporters, probation officers. The air was thick with cigarette smoke.

Abby looked around for someone who might fit the description of Danny Frenkel. He was in his twenties, she knew. Apart from that, she had few clues.

'Abby, looking for your man?' It was James, looming up out of the smoke. 'If he turns up, just get him to plead. We'll be here all day otherwise. And you've got to admit, the evidence is overwhelming.'

'Don't you believe it, James. This is a fight.'

He smiled patronisingly. 'How idealistic. Oh well, just hoped you'd see sense. Come and see me if you change your mind.'

Abby decided to shout. 'Danny Frenkel?'

She tried again, this time yelling as loud as she could.

'Danny Frenkel!'

The room went silent for a moment and she blushed. Then the buzz of communication started again and she saw a thin, bird-like man appear out of the throng.

'You my brief?' he asked.

'Are you Danny?'

'Yes. Do you think I've got a chance?'

She grinned. For a man with his record, he looked surprisingly honest.

'There's always a chance. Just not a very big one in your case.'

He smiled. 'It was actually true, you know. I do want to fight the case.'

Abby nodded. 'Then we'll make a fight of it. And I will need to tell the beak all about your previous convictions – that way we can show how you knew all about their security arrangements.'

'Yeah, I'd worked that out. Still, in for a penny . . .'

He had a certain charm about him, and Abby could see him being rather refreshing in the witness box. All she needed was a sour old prune of a store detective, and who knew what might happen?

She made her way to the court lists. They were in Court Three. The paper showed the names of the magistrates, but they meant nothing to her. It was 9.45 and she pushed open the swing door into the court. The clerk was sitting at the front, between the magistrates' empty chairs and the lawyers' stalls.

'Can I help you?' she asked, in a tone which implied that this would be completely out of the question.

'Yes.' Abby's voice was firm. The clerk was there to give legal advice to the magistrates. She would be either a barrister or a solicitor, and an expert in procedure in her court. Abby needed her respect. 'I'm in the case of Frenkel.'

'Danny Frenkel again? Oh Lord.'

Damn, already known. Actually, though, given the line of defence, this was rather a good sign.

The clerk looked up from her papers. 'Plea, is it?'

'No, it's listed for trial.'

The clerk put down her pen. She spoke very slowly, as though she were addressing an imbecile.

'Yes, but so are twenty other cases. They won't all fight

207

and what I need to know from you at this moment is whether yours is going to.'

'He's not pleading guilty, if that's what you mean.'

The clerk rolled her eyes.

'OK. But the trials go after the pleas. We'll get through the quick stuff first. Don't bank on getting on before noon – if at all, today.'

Abby smiled. 'Somehow, I'd expected that. See you later.'

The clerk looked down at her papers again. Abby was clearly dismissed.

All the interview rooms were in use. Abby found Danny Frenkel again and they stood in the corner of the entrance hall. There was little to talk about. Abby knew his defence inside out. He was nervous now, smoking, unwilling to talk much. James had commandeered a room, and had holed himself up there.

It was 11 o'clock. A steady stream of cases were going in and out of court. They were clearly processing the list. The pressure to plead, she was learning, was huge. It started from the moment the defendant was arrested. Tell us you did it, it's so much easier – that was the unspoken message throughout. You might just get a caution. If it has to go to court, you'll be dealt with quicker, get a lighter sentence for being so sensible. If you hold out to the point of trial, you could still plead guilty on the day and not have to wait around in a boring smoke-filled room for hours. And if you didn't feel the pressure to plead guilty, your barrister might well experience it for you.

Abby watched the second hand travelling around the clock face. The conference was at four. She could get back to Chambers in forty minutes from here, she knew. The trial would take two hours, minimum. What it added up to was that she had to get on before lunch. Otherwise, she wouldn't get back in time.

Come on, come on. She cursed the listing officer for putting so many cases in.

Abby suddenly realised she was starving. Danny had wandered off, promising to keep an ear open for the tannoy if his case was called on. There was a WRVS stall open. She bought a coffee and a Mars bar. Gratefully, she sank into a free seat, slashed blue plastic on some yellow foam rubber.

'Come on, Abby. We'll be here all day if you don't plead. Look, if you get him to cave, I'll open it low. Just say it was clearly spur of the moment, he's done very well keeping out of trouble lately, you know the score.'

James was standing in front of her.

'No.'

'For heaven's sake, it's not the trial of the century, you know. Who do you think you are, Perry Mason?'

'No.'

'Look, you're going to have to be a bit more professional about this. Part of your job is to advise as well as represent. He's got a hopeless case. Save us all the hassle of proving it. Tell him he's got to plead.'

God, he was pompous. Who the hell was he, with a 2:2 from Wolverhampton and acne still on his chin, to be telling her what to bloody well do?

Abby stood up. 'James, he tells me he didn't do it. Don't tell me I'm being unprofessional in sticking to his instructions.'

'Well, I do think it is unprofessional, actually. You're just going to string out a hopeless case. Surely you can tell him to plead guilty?'

Abby glared at him. 'If I was going to be unprofessional, I would at this minute be giving in to the temptation to tell you to fuck off.'

He stepped back. 'I say, Abby . . .'

'But don't worry, I won't,' she said sweetly, and stalked off.

A familiar figure was hurrying in through the swing doors. She walked over quickly.

'Alex.'

209

He was very red in the face.

'Ah, not on yet. I . . . well, let's just say I got delayed . . . I thought I'd come and see you in court.'

Abby blushed. 'Some form of assessment?'

'My dear girl, not as formal as that. But we do have to see you on your feet.'

She grinned. 'Of course. And it just so happens that I'm against James Dorton. Can I assume that some comparisons are going to be made?'

Alex held his hands up. 'I plead guilty. You've seen straight through us.'

'Alex, great to see you. How's my favourite godfather?'

James had pushed straight past Abby. Even Alex looked slightly sheepish at how obvious his godson was being. James was unabashed.

'We've been released until two. Abby's insisting on her day in court. How about lunch? There's a place two minutes away . . . Sorry Abby, see you later . . .'

The two men disappeared, leaving Abby quietly fuming. Bugger. She was going to be late for the con. Might even miss it completely. And then Antoine was picking her up afterwards. She shouldn't have agreed to see him straight from work. There'd be no opportunity to change, freshen up a little. He was going to see her tired, ratty, with the city grime still on her clothes and skin.

Antoine. She closed her eyes momentarily. He was thinking about her, she knew. She could see him, standing, watching her, his eyes serious, listening to her so carefully, so attentively. Just thinking about him made her respond, a tingle starting somewhere at the base of her spine.

Funny, she thought, no men for six months, then suddenly I have two dates in a week. Marcus, with his clear blue eyes, sitting in shock that night they'd met. Marcus, the first man she'd ever met whom she knew was brighter than herself. And as full of ideals, beliefs, energy. Attractive, too. Very attractive.

210

But compared with Antoine ... well, it was just different, that was all. Antoine, she knew next to nothing about. She hadn't a clue what he believed in, where he was coming from. But it didn't seem to matter. What she did know was that every time she looked at him, every moment she even thought of him, she wanted him to take her to bed. She was shocked by this, but there it was.

It was just a simple, overwhelming fact of life.

Back in Chambers, Seb Waters stood up and pushed his chair under his desk. The papers were neatly tied up, ready for the consultation. He'd spent the morning going through them. This was going to be one hell of a case. A whole life ruined in seconds. Just for being in the wrong place at the wrong time.

Chance governed everything, he knew. You could plan a life, work hard, think you knew your destiny. Yet, in a moment, everything could change.

He looked out of the window at the Temple. Lawyers had worked here for hundreds of years, settled in these squares and lanes just off Fleet Street. It was a quiet, composed world, full of reflection and stillness. He got the same thrill coming to work even now. He'd first felt it as a student, fresh from Cambridge. The moment he stepped through the old arched door which led from the bustle of Fleet Street, with its taxis, motorbikes and pedestrians leaping out before the traffic lights had changed, it was a different world. He'd walked down the quiet lane, Temple Church on his right, past the Georgian façades of the buildings.

The names, as always, were painted on boards outside the sets. Great long lists, starting with the head and ending with the most junior tenant. The thrill when his name had finally been painted on to the end of the board was still with him.

Looking out of the window, he'd had to abandon his earlier plan of a sandwich in Temple gardens today. The rain had started an hour ago. By now it was drumming steadily against the window pane. The wind had got up a bit, too. No, it was going to be lunch indoors along the great tables of Inner Temple Hall. He hadn't been there for a while, it would be good to catch up with the gossip.

On the way downstairs, he popped his head around the clerks' room door.

'Just going out for lunch.'

'Ready for your con, sir?'

Seb nodded at Ron.

'Are you going to want the conference room?'

Seb thought for a few moments.

'We could just meet in my room, it's so damp down there . . .'

Ron shook his head. 'Not the tidiest of rooms, if I may say so, sir. And they're important solicitors . . .'

Seb nodded. 'I suppose you're right. Can you send someone down to open the windows and air it a bit, then?'

Seb paused a moment.

'Miss Penhaligon back yet?'

'No. Neither is Mr Dorton. I suppose if they're at the back of the list, she might get caught.'

Damn. He had the photo in his pocket. He'd rather hoped to have his chat before the con. Maybe it was just as well. Leave it until afterwards. It would be wrong to rush it, after all.

'Oh well, that's just how it goes. We can start without her if necessary, I suppose. She can always join us when she gets here.'

'Parties in R v Frenkel into court please.'

At last! Abby looked at her watch. It was ten past two. She was going to be late for the con. There was no way she could get through the trial in time.

With an encouraging grin, she led Danny into court. He sat behind her, ready to whisper comments if she needed

212

more information as the hearing progressed.

James marched in with a CPS clerk. His witness, the store detective, would be waiting outside.

The magistrates came in, everyone stood, and then relaxed back into their chairs.

'May it please you, madam . . .'

James was off, telling the magistrates all about the case. He got first bite at the cherry, telling them about the evidence, what it was the accused had been doing. Abby turned round slightly in her seat. The public gallery was empty apart from Alexander, who was already looking bored.

With reason, thought Abby. Opening speeches, she knew, were important. A good speech would be almost like a map for the court – setting out where the case would go, what the evidence would be, how it would add up to a conviction. It had to be interesting, something that would grab the attention of the magistrates, who were looking a little jaded after a long morning.

But this was boring. James's voice, she thought, was part of the problem. Deep, slow and rhythmic – in terms of elocution and diction, beautiful, but in terms of interest, bloody awful. It was a voice which made her want to nod off to sleep rather than sit up and take notice. And the content could have been better too. There was no succinct summary of the evidence. He was just ploughing through every detail of what was in the store detective's statement. It didn't matter, for the sake of the opening address, that the store detective first noticed Mr Frenkel at 2.04 pm, or that he was walking in the general direction of fruit and veg. He was fair, though, made no hint at the previous convictions.

Still, he got to the end eventually, and called his witness. The magistrates looked as though they were going to sleep soundly that afternoon.

'Are you Dolores Tirana?'

She was a lady in her early forties – short and slim,

213

her greying hair bleached a rather curious orange colour. Thin, mean features gave her the appearance of an outraged mole.

Dolores began to reel off the contents of her statement. She wasn't allowed to prompt herself from it, but she'd clearly memorised most of it. James hardly had to ask any questions.

'And that is your evidence?'

'Yes.'

'Stay there one moment.'

Abby rose to her feet. Dolores peered at her over the edge of the witness box. The lady Chairman of the Bench waited expectantly.

'Ms Tirana, Mr Frenkel has a lot of previous convictions for shoplifting, hasn't he?'

It was as though she'd taken all her clothes off and streaked around the courtroom. There was a gasp and James stood up.

'Madam, of course this is something which is not usually mentioned. You may recall . . .'

Abby waved him down.

'Madam, I have asked a question and would like the witness to answer it.'

The chairman gave a small smile. 'Very well, Miss Penhaligon.'

Dolores looked a little put out by all this. She looked down from the witness box, her face a picture of confusion.

'I'll put the question again, Ms Tirana. Danny Frenkel has previous convictions for shoplifting, doesn't he? Lots of them.'

'Er, yes.'

James was grinning now from ear to ear. This just wasn't done. What a cock up! Didn't that silly woman know that you didn't mention precons? And with Alexander watching. Wonderful! The tenancy was looking pretty good.

'No need to be diffident, Ms Tirana. You've stopped

him yourself on four occasions, haven't you?'

Dolores nodded.

'And presumably, knowing him as you do, you watch out for him.'

Dolores was recovering a little now. Clearly not too happy with the unexpected questions, thought Abby. Good.

'Well, yes, I do keep an eye open.'

'And when you see him, you watch him carefully.'

Dolores hadn't worked out yet where this was going. Abby was starting to feel like a puppetmaster.

'Yes, of course.'

'Why?'

'Well, because of . . . what we were talking about a moment ago . . . I just want to make sure he doesn't try anything again.'

Abby smiled. 'For his own good, no doubt.'

Dolores didn't smile. 'Yes.'

'He's a regular visitor to the shop, isn't he?'

'He comes in now and then, once a week, I suppose.'

'And each time he comes in, you follow him.'

'Watch him.'

Oh for God's sake, Dolores.

'Watch him by following him.' Abby's voice had become sarcastic.

'OK. Watch him by following him.'

Abby lowered her tone a little. 'He knows who you are, doesn't he?'

'I suppose so.'

'So he knows why you follow him.'

'Yes.'

'He's not taken anything for a while, has he?'

'Not been caught.'

Ha ha, very funny. Abby let it ride.

'Because he knows that every time he sets foot in the shop, you're behind him.'

Good, James hadn't the sense to object. Obviously, Dolores couldn't know what was going through Danny's

215

mind and Dorton should have been protesting loudly. More fool him for keeping quiet.

The witness paused.

'I suppose so.'

'Remind us of the layout of the store. The toilets are by the entrance, aren't they?'

'Yes.'

'And there's a big lobby area outside them, with no checkouts.'

'Yes, but you can see the checkouts from the area.'

Abby nodded. 'And you stayed there whilst Mr Frenkel visited the toilet?'

'Yes. I was a few feet away from the entrance.'

Brilliant. Thank you Dolores, that will do nicely.

'It would be quite remarkable if he tried to steal things with you standing right in front of him, wouldn't it?'

Abby took a moment to look at the witness. In an obvious sort of way. The sort of way that would make the magistrates wonder what she was doing and look at the witness too.

There was silence. Dolores's face grew redder and her lower jaw edged its way forward. Never be afraid of silence, Daniel Ditchcombe had told her. It often says more than words. Dolores clearly had a bit of a mean streak in her. You could see it writ large on her thin features. James had his head down, writing every word in his notebook. He hadn't seen that look. Abby had. And so had the magistrates. The lady Chairman was looking very thoughtful indeed.

'Has it ever occurred to you that he might simply have forgotten to pay for the goods?'

'No, we know exactly which customers forget and which are stealing.'

Abby paused a moment. Why the hell was Dolores talking about 'we' all of a sudden? Time for some stage management. Daniel had taught her a trick, once.

Abby picked up a blank piece of paper from the table in

216

front of her. She looked at it as though it was important.

'Other people have gone to the toilet and left, forgetting to go through the checkout, haven't they?'

This was a leap into the dark. Abby had no idea if what she had said was true. But she liked the way Dolores was looking at the blank sheet of paper.

'What do you mean?'

Eyes still on the paper. Dolores evidently thought there was something significant on it.

'It's a problem which all the staff are aware of, isn't it?'

'Possibly.'

Another glance at the paper. Take your time Abby. Let her worry.

'It's something that has been brought up at meetings, isn't it?'

And meetings, she thought to herself, are recorded. And what I'm holding in my hand could just be a copy of the minutes. Bluff it out Abby. It's worth a try.

Dolores grimaced. She nodded slowly. 'Yes, it was mentioned in a staff meeting.'

Yippee!

'And when it's happened in the past – when other people have left the store with a loaded trolley forgetting to pay – what have you done?'

'We've stopped the person in the car park, asked them if they realised they hadn't paid.'

'And each time, presumably, the person has apologised and returned immediately to go through the checkout.'

'Yes.'

'Did you invite Mr Frenkel to go back into the store and pay?'

The witness looked abashed.

'Not as such, no.'

'You just called the police and had him arrested.'

'Yes.'

Oh this was wonderful. Let's drive the point home.

'And what about the others who have left the store like

217

this – were any of them charged with shoplifting?'

Pause.

'Well?'

Dolores looked to the floor.

'No.'

Leave it there. Know when to stop. Don't take it any further or she'll start backtracking.

'Thank you, Ms Tirana.'

Abby sat down.

Ron was having a tough afternoon. The phones had been going mad. He didn't have enough barristers to cover the next day. Again. The only option was to point solicitors in the direction of other Chambers. That was happening too much these days.

He sighed and reached for his cigarettes. God, he was getting through the packets at a rate these days. He needed a holiday. Time to get out of this hothouse. But he knew that he wouldn't take time off. Even if he did he'd spend it worrying all the time, anyhow.

'Kevin, pop down to the conference room would you? Open the windows, make sure it's OK for the con later.'

Kevin, momentarily off the phone, nodded and rose. He was glad of the break. He'd been sitting at his desk all morning. It was good to stretch the muscles a bit.

He negotiated the stairs carefully. The door to the conference room was ajar and he pushed it open. The room was stuffy, as ever. Stuck in the basement, it got damp in wet weather, and it was pouring with rain outside now. There was the slightest tinge of stale aftershave. Possibly lemon. One of the tenants must have been down here recently.

There were a couple of windows which opened out at foot level onto the lane outside. Kevin opened one using the pole left in the corner. The room would get even damper, of course, but at least it would air a little. Then he turned to face the door, leaning on the chair at the far end. Things looked reasonable enough. The table was clean and polished, the chairs lined up carefully, each placed with its seat under the table.

Coffee. Mr Waters always like to have a pot of coffee on the boil. Kevin opened the far door of the cupboard which ran along the length of the room. There was an old percolator there.

He took the water container into the washroom and filled it from the tap. Then he took it back into the conference room and measured out some coffee for the machine. He'd pop down later and get it going, ready for the con. At least it would get rid of the lemony smell.

'And I just forgot. I went out to the car park with the trolley – it had just slipped my mind that I hadn't actually gone through the checkout.'

Danny had played a blinder. He had answered Abby's questions sensibly and politely. The magistrates were beaming at him.

Abby sat down and considered the situation. Being so open about his convictions had presented another bonus. The magistrates were obviously desperate to show that although they knew all about them, they were not going to be influenced by that information. So they were bending over backwards to be fair to the defendant, listening to everything he had to say. The whole thing was going like a dream.

James got to his feet.

'This is a load of rubbish, Mr Frenkel.'

Subtle, thought Abby. She turned her head to the back of the court, where Alexander Golightly was sitting. He smiled at her and nodded slowly.

Danny took a step back in the box.

'Sorry, but I've told the truth.'

'Why should the court believe you, you've not told the truth before?'

'Sorry?'

219

Abby had deliberately avoided asking Danny about this one. She'd rather hoped James would walk into the trap. And he had, wonderfully. It was his own fault. Inattention to detail. She suppressed a grin. Never let the court know what you are thinking. Whether your case is sinking like a stone or swimming sleekly along, keep your face neutral.

James was pressing the point. Unwise, really.

'All those convictions, Mr Frenkel. Have you forgotten?'

Danny looked at the magistrates.

'I pleaded guilty to every single one. This is the first time I've ever pleaded not guilty. I've never lied to a court in my life.'

James looked crestfallen.

'Are you seriously expecting the court to believe that you just forgot?'

'I don't expect anything, sir. I was stupid, but I really hadn't intended to take those things. Not one bit.'

Abby looked at the clock behind the magistrates. They'd actually got through the evidence fairly quickly. It was just after 3.30. She was still going to be late for the con, though.

James sagged down in his chair, over-acting like hell on the incredulity front.

Abby made a very quick closing speech. The defence spoke for itself and there was no point running through it again.

'. . . And most important of all, this man has been completely frank with the court. He's told you all about his previous convictions. With that great long list, it is quite remarkable that he has always pleaded guilty. Not today though, because he comes to court an innocent man.'

She sat down. All three magistrates beamed at her as they left the court.

It was 3.40. Abby dashed outside and found a public phone.

220

'Ron? I'm going to be late for the con. We only got on this afternoon, but the Bench have just gone out . . .'

'Don't worry, miss. I'll tell Mr Waters to start without you . . . you can just come into it as soon as you get back. Hurry if you can, though.'

Marcus arrived early for the con. He'd left plenty of time to allow for a journey to Colchester to pick up Abraham. The two men were taken into the waiting room. Marcus had been hoping to have a quick word with Abby, invite her out afterwards. Hopefully she'd have got over her sulks by now. But the clerk had told him that she was still in court and would be late. Oh well, maybe later.

He sat himself down in the waiting room with Abraham and flicked through some old editions of *Tatler*. Quite a few familiar faces there, smiling out from the glossy pages. He wondered if they ever thought about him. Probably not.

Just before four, Duncan Dinkwater arrived. They all shook hands and exchanged small talk for a while.

'This way please, gentlemen.'

Ron was wearing his jacket. The moment he was back in his room, he'd be back in shirtsleeves. But escorting clients to a con – even if it was just down the stairs – demanded a jacket.

Seb was already at the table, seated at the end nearest the door. He stood as they entered and introduced himself.

'Seb Waters. Pleased to meet you. Miss Penhaligon has sent a message – she's stuck in court but will get here as soon as she can. In the meantime, I thought we'd make a start. Perhaps if you'd all like to take a seat with me?'

Ron looked around the room. Everything seemed in order. Kevin had opened the window. He'd forgotten the coffee, though. Silly sod. Got the percolator out but hadn't set it going. Ron moved over to the machine and flicked the switch. Nothing happened. Not working again. Probably the damp. Oh well, they'd just have to pop upstairs if they needed anything.

After twenty minutes, the magistrates returned to court. Everyone avoided eye contact with them. It was bad form, Abby knew. She looked down at the desk in front of her, held her breath and prayed.

'We find the defendant not guilty. Mr Frenkel, you are free to go.'

It was as though an elastic band had stretched and stretched and finally broken. Abby wanted to bellow, 'Yeeeees!'

James gathered up his papers and stalked out of court.

Danny reached out and patted her lightly on the back.

'Thanks love. That was amazing.'

She said her goodbyes to him. Alex had already gone. She hoped he'd heard the verdict.

Abby placed the papers in her bag and slung it over her shoulder. She should make it back just before five.

It was 4.50. Seb's voice was soft.

'So, Mr James, I will be drafting the appeal papers with my junior barrister this week. I think that there has been a terrible miscarriage of justice. But with the Reverend Kirkwall's evidence, there is a good chance that we will be able to set the record straight.'

Abraham looked past him for a few minutes, biting his lip.

'Nearly half a century. So much time.'

'I know. But at least it's something.'

'I wouldn't have wanted you to bother. It won't make any difference now. I've lived my life waiting to die, really. But, I don't know, sometimes I just wonder if she's still around.'

Seb raised an eyebrow.

Marcus spoke this time.

'Isobel – the wife?'

222

Abraham nodded and looked towards the floor.

'I'd just like her to know it wasn't me. She's spent her life probably hating me, telling her child I killed its father. That's the hardest thing to bear. I really did love her, you know.'

Seb touched his hand. 'Do you want to stop for a few moments – have some coffee maybe? The machine here doesn't seem to be on, but I can get some sent down.'

Abraham nodded.

Seb reached for the phone. Quickly, he punched in some numbers.

'Engaged, I'm afraid . . .'

Marcus stood up. 'Don't worry. I'll go and ask your clerk myself. Could do with stretching my legs – I'll get him to try and contact Miss Penhaligon as well.'

Abby was soaking wet. She'd run down Chancery Lane as quickly as she could, but it was no good. The rain was sweeping along, falling almost horizontally with the strength of the wind. She was bent double, fighting her way against the elements. Her old mac wasn't up to the task and the rain had found its way through in no time. There was an unpleasant trickle around her collar and she could feel water running in rivulets down her back. Her tights were sopping and her feet were slipping in her shoes. Her long hair had escaped from its chignon and was hanging in rats' tails.

She was sweating, too. She was so hot in her coat, in such a hurry to get to the con. Her makeup, she knew, would be a dark smudge across her face by now. Oh God, she longed to be able to climb into a bath, apply perfume, refresh her makeup and emerge perfect for her conference. And for Antoine. What on earth was he going to think of this smelly, English bag lady he was taking out for the evening?

Bugger! She tripped on a paving slab sticking up like an ill-fitting tooth. In a moment, she was flat on her face on the ground. Her arm started to hurt. Badly.

'Are you all right?'

It was an elderly man, also bent double against the weather. He offered her a hand.

'I'm so sorry, I was in such a hurry . . .' Abby stood up. There were huge holes in the knees of her tights and blood was already emerging from behind a layer of grime.

The man shook his head. 'I'll get you a cab . . .'

'No . . . thank you, but I need to get to Chambers. I'm late.'

It was her wrist that hurt the most, she decided. She'd landed on it. Please don't let it be broken. Please.

Abby thanked the man and limped off, aware that he was watching her in case she fell again. She got to the bottom of Chancery Lane, crossed the road and went in through the gate.

She glanced at her watch. One minute to five.

'Is there anywhere I can get some coffee for Mr James?'

Marcus had knocked on the clerks' door. Ron was up in a moment.

'Of course, sir, shall I make it?'

'No, I'll do it, if you just show me where the kettle is . . .'

Suddenly, the inner entrance door swung open violently. Marcus stepped back quickly before it hit him.

'Abby!'

She was in a terrible state. Sopping wet, looking a real mess. Great big holes in her tights. And she was holding her right wrist.

She looked up at him and opened her mouth to speak.

Then it happened.

A deafening bang, followed by a low rumble. The floor shook beneath their feet. There was the sound of glass shattering. Then, a terrible silence.

Marcus knew immediately what had happened. They'd had controlled explosions in the navy.

'Shit.'

He turned and ran down the stairs into the darkness. Abby followed him, almost falling down the final steps.

She couldn't see. The air was so thick with dust that she couldn't make anything out. The lights had gone, too.

It was bad, she knew. She could smell the blood already. She shouted up the stairs.

'Get a torch, for God's sake.'

She felt her way into the room. There was a dreadful silence. She was aware of Marcus in front of her.

Suddenly, there was a thin beam of light. It was Ron with the torch. He shone it into the room and they followed its path. He must be shaking – the beam was wavering. Finally, it pointed towards the floor. Abby followed the weak stream of light.

Someone was there, someone she didn't know. Head at a strange angle, limbs hanging uselessly. Very, very still. There was another body beside him . . . Abraham James.

My God.

Abby followed the beam as it moved up the table, shimmering against the dust in the air. It was getting thicker and she was starting to cough. The more she coughed, the less she could breathe. Calm down, Abby. Focus.

'Shine the torch at the top end of the table,' shouted Marcus.

The beam shook and swept across. The chair was empty.

'Down!'

A male form was huddled on the floor, lying on its back. The torch steadied. His face . . . good grief, it was Seb. Eyes open, staring. Not of this world. Abby looked down and caught her breath.

Where his chest should have been, there was a gaping hole. His shirt was gone, a few remnants of fabric hanging down into the blood-soaked cavity. Tissue, muscle . . . in the gloom it was difficult to make it all out, but it was bad, she knew. Very bad.

Abby screamed. 'Seb!'

225

She fell to her knees. Marcus was already beside him, feeling a limp arm, searching desperately for a pulse.

'There's something. Get an ambulance, for Christ's sake.'

Chapter Twenty-Four

Pascal de Montchavin paused by the radio. Five-fifteen. It should have happened by now.

He pressed the switch. Local radio would be the first to report it, surely. He found a commercial station, blasting out third-rate pop.

He sat in the mezzanine, overlooking the living room. He'd set up a den there, his favourite part of the rather anonymous flat. There was a desk, small sofa, a light. And some photos – the only ones there. An ancient one of his mother: dark, fine features, olive-shaped eyes. His father had been fifty when they'd married. She'd been eighteen.

She'd disappeared when he was twelve. Gone on holiday, they'd said. Only she never came back. Whenever he'd asked, his father looked pained and changed the subject.

At boarding school, of course, there was no such restraint. One of the boys showed him a society magazine. Mother had moved in with a racing car driver.

It was the only time he'd been abandoned by a woman. He was her only child, she'd loved him, he'd loved her. But she hadn't taken him with her. The one picture he'd had of her had been flung into an old cupboard.

Much, much later, after she'd died, he'd found out about Father's legal battle with her. He'd hired the most expensive lawyers to prove she was nothing more than a gold-digging whore. She and her racing driver would

227

corrupt the young Count. They should on no account be allowed near him.

At that point, he'd retrieved the photo and left home for ever. Both his parents had failed him so he'd manage without them. He'd trust no one. He too had taken to the sea. Unlike Marcus, though, Pascal had got a series of jobs on charter boats in the West Indies. It suited him well for a while – no ties, hot weather, a succession of over-sexed and beautiful women who could be loved and left.

George had shown him what a ready market there was for drugs. When he left, Pascal moved neatly into his niche. It was so easy to do. Cocaine attracted rich clients and brought big profits.

There was another benefit from working the boats. He was building up some rather good connections with large-scale clients. He'd tapped in to the new European aristocracy – the monied classes who needed what he could supply. When the time came for him to leave the Caribbean, he had a long list of clients, all of them happy to pay top money for his wares. Back in Europe, though, everyone wanted ecstasy.

Again, there was big money in it, and he was in pretty much at the beginning. But you could only run that sort of operation for a while. And it was getting boring. The real money, he knew, was in wholesale – selling to other dealers, vying with each other to dominate the market. George was doing well, he knew, but had sourcing problems.

The problem with the supply of E though, was always going to be storage. To make big profits, you had to supply serious quantities. And that required space. He had to have a place which the police would never visit.

The idea of the *Richard Montgomery* had been a break-through. Pascal had bought a boat when he returned to Europe. He'd wanted some time away, so he'd set off and quietly sailed around Britain. It was partly for the hell of it, partly to lie low for a while, but mainly to take a look at some isolated islands.

He'd seen the wreck as he'd been sailing from Essex to Kent. His pilotage book mentioned it, and told a little of its story. It had been wrecked towards the end of the war, stranded on a sandbank, loaded with thousands of tons of explosive.

He'd never forget his first sighting. It had been a slightly misty evening and he'd been fussing over his boat's lights, making sure they were shining as brightly as possible. He'd looked up over the bow to see the masts looming eerily out of the water. The night was so still, the water strangely quiet. He'd sailed well away. Few things frightened him, but this certainly had.

It had also set him thinking. Thousands of tons of explosive was a powerful disincentive for anyone thinking of getting too close to the wreck. And it was accessible, a few miles down the river from London. There was no need to use some godforsaken Scottish island a week's sail from anywhere. With the right men, it could work.

'We're getting reports of an explosion in the Temple. Police are not saying whether it is a bomb . . .'

Pascal sat up. A smile worked its way across his features. Right on time. He moved over to the radio.

'There are casualties, the number unconfirmed. Peter Ivor is at the scene now . . .'

There was a crackling as the outside broadcast cut in.

'Yes, Sue, I'm outside Pump Court in London. It seems that several people have been injured and at least two killed. I've just arrived and it's a terrible scene . . . yes, two killed, that has just been confirmed to me now. There's another casualty who is being taken to University College Hospital.'

Pascal's eyes widened. He thought hard. Two dead, one injured. And at least one person who should have been at the meeting had not been hurt at all.

Shit. His mind was racing.

Drugs off the boat now? He looked out of the window, but the storm was just as strong, the rain lashing against

229

the front windows. He needed to find out more before he gave an order. He didn't want Thierry and Sam to be removing twelve million pounds worth of assets from the wreck in this sort of weather. Not unless there was no other way.

He looked at his watch. Six o'clock. The girl might be dead. But if she was alive, she'd be expecting him. He'd better get there now.

The rescue services had given Abby a blanket. She sat outside the building, not trusting her legs to hold her up. Beside her, white-faced, was Marcus. Their hair felt stiff and crackled when it was touched. Abby thought it was dust. Marcus knew better. It would be human skin.

He stared in front him, his voice low.

'Another two bodies, three maybe. How many more will it take?'

Abby was silent, her face chalk white, her hands shaking. They were with Seb now, the paramedics. He could be alive or dead. How could you survive with those injuries? It looked impossible to her.

'Righty-ho, into the ambulance with you two.'

'I want to stay,' Marcus insisted.

'No point in that. You need sorting out, both of you.'

Marcus just stared ahead.

'Come on, sir. Your friend is going to the same place. We'll let you know how he is.'

Abby allowed herself to be shuffled towards the ambulance. Then she heard a shout.

'Abby!'

She looked up. He was running towards her, horror on his face. A policeman tried to stop him, but he sprinted past.

'Antoine!'

'What has happened? Are you all right?'

The date. She'd completely forgotten.

Suddenly she started to cry, great uncontrollable sobs.

230

Then his arms were around her and she was smelling that comforting familiar scent.

'Who has died? Tell me?'

Abby couldn't talk.

He held her at arm's length. His tone changed suddenly. It was forceful, abrupt.

'Who has died?'

Abby looked up at him. 'The solicitor in my appeal. Perhaps Seb . . .'

'What about the vicar?'

'I'll survive.'

Marcus was suddenly behind Abby. He's seen the whole encounter. Most important of all, he'd seen a momentary look of pure terror flit across the Frenchman's features as he appeared.

Pascal pulled Abby back to him and cursed to himself. This man should be dead. So should she. Christ, she smelt awful. Filthy, too. He forced himself to think as he held her.

The drugs had to come off the boat tonight. But it felt like a good force seven. Sam's fishing boat could take it, he had no doubts. But diving in those conditions would be difficult. In the meantime, he had to act the concerned suitor. He could hardly disappear into the night, not the way that vicar was looking at him. And he was going to have to keep an eye on the girl until he decided his next move.

'Abby, you go in the ambulance. I'll follow. I'll stay with you . . .' Mutely, she allowed herself to be lifted in the ambulance. Marcus followed her, tight lipped. Pascal went to climb in, but his way was barred politely by the ambulanceman.

'Maybe you'd like to follow separately, sir? We're going to University College Hospital.'

Pascal frowned and nodded briefly.

In a moment, the ambulance was moving, leaving the Temple behind it. Abby looked at Marcus. He had a nasty gash to his head. She'd no idea when it had happened; presumably he'd hit something whilst crawling in the wreckage.

'This had something to do with the case,' muttered Abby.

'Perhaps.'

'And I can't stop thinking that it's something to do with what you wouldn't tell me last week.'

'What do you mean?'

'Come on Marcus, you're keeping something from me about this case. For God's sake, someone's been killed . . .'

'I can't tell you.'

'For fuck's sake, Marcus . . .'

He shook his head.

Abby's voice rose. 'Then leave me out. I've had enough.'

Marcus turned his head. He looked in pain.

'Don't you think I have as well? One man comes in, rants and raves, jumps under a train . . . I take up the case, find myself crawling through the aftermath of a bomb looking for more bodies.' He turned to her. 'It could have been us, too.'

Abby nodded. 'If I hadn't tripped and fallen, I would have been in that room five minutes earlier.' She started to tremble. 'I want no more of this, Marcus.'

His jaw was clenched. 'Neither do I. But I've got to see it through.'

She looked at him and shook her head. 'Then see it through without me.'

Pascal followed the ambulance to UCH. He went to park in Gower Street and sat in the car for a few moments.

It was no good. Whatever the weather, they'd just have to salvage what they could. Even if they only got half the drugs off, there would be six million pounds worth. It was worth taking a risk for that.

He took out his mobile phone and punched in the sequence of numbers. It was answered immediately.

'How about a sail?'

As arranged, there was no reply. Merely a click.

And now, the girl. For the moment, he needed her.

Inside the hospital, Marcus was taken off to have his head stitched. Abby emerged a little more cheerful from the X-ray department – no fractures, just a sprain. As she came out of the room, she saw him.

'Antoine!'

His back was turned. He spun around and opened his arms. Quickly, she fell into them.

'Thank you for coming here, I'm so terrified.'

His voice was soft, soothing balm.

'Come with me.'

She was startled.

'I have to stay here . . .'

Pascal reached out towards Abby, taking her hands into his. Slowly, he shook his head.

'I have some bad news, Abby.'

She pulled her hands away.

'Seb?'

'Yes. Abby, he didn't make it.'

She sat down suddenly. All at once, she started to tremble, violently, uncontrollably.

'My God. Two hours ago, I was rushing back from Court . . . now this.'

'You need comfort, a drink. Come with me.'

She looked at him. She'd follow anyone who gave her orders at the moment. Numb, shell shocked, she had no idea any more. All she knew was that she needed someone to be with through the night.

Mutely, she let him lead her from the ante-room. Behind her, he smiled slowly. Maybe this other barrister was still alive – he had no idea. But if there was hope, she'd have stayed at the hospital. And for the time being, he wanted her with him.

Gently, Pascal steered Abby into the flat. For the moment, he'd let her be. If the drugs were lifted off the wreck, he'd wave goodbye to her in the morning. If it went wrong – pear-shaped would be her term – then things would not look too good for her.

She'd work it out fairly soon, he knew. She had too many pieces of this particular jigsaw. And even if she didn't work it out for herself, soon the police would speak to her, start to put it all together. So for the moment, he'd keep her with him, away from the police.

He settled Abby onto the large blue sofa and mixed her a drink – a strong brandy. She gulped it down.

'May I have a bath?'

He smiled at her. 'You are my guest.'

She followed him through to the bathroom. It was enormous, done out in white tiles. There was a double size bath and he ran the water for her, pouring in some bubbles.

She soaked in there for a long time, getting the smell out of her body, out of her hair. However much she scrubbed, though, she could still smell blood. When she closed her eyes and tried to relax, she saw Seb. She saw him as she'd seen him in the torchlight, the thick smoke obscuring him. She'd looked without registering for a moment, then her brain had assembled the dreadful vision into reality – the blood and tissues, the crushed bones . . . it had been Seb.

Seb's dead. Someone tried to kill me.

She couldn't believe it. Couldn't understand it. It made no sense. Yet everything had an explanation in the end, she knew. Maybe in the morning she could start thinking about it properly, work out what the hell was going on.

Pascal had made up a bed for her in the spare room. It was at the back of the flat, quiet. The bed was enormous.

'Let me tuck you into it.' His voice was gentle.

She lay down.

'Will you be all right? There are some clothes of mine in the wardrobe. In the morning, just take what you need.'

He was looking down at her. Abby trembled.

'I'm frightened. Someone tried to kill me.'

'Nothing will happen here.'

'Hold me.'

His arm was around her again. She'd climbed into an old shirt of his, and he had to admit, it looked good on her now she'd cleaned up a bit. Her hair was slightly damp, hanging down over the collar. Her nipples were showing through the linen.

In a moment, his hand was over her breast, moving in slow, lazy circles. She made a low moan and turned her body towards him. He felt himself respond. He'd had the hots for her at Chambers last night, hadn't really gone off the boil. And since the opportunity was clearly presenting itself . . .

'Stay with me all night, Antoine.'

Chapter Twenty-Five

The ambulancemen had worked hard, pooling their expertise. As a result, Seb Waters was still alive when he got to UCH. That in itself was an achievement.

They'd rushed him into Accident and Emergency, with a slight pulse, but massive blood loss. And horrendous chest injuries. It was going to be one hell of a job to pull him back.

The senior registrar watched him carefully. The blood loss was becoming uncontrollable. There was clearly all sorts of debris in the chest wall, which was going to have to come out immediately.

'I need theatre quickly. And I'm going to need help. This is one for the Professor, I think.'

He watched her as she drifted into sleep. She'd wanted him to hold her afterwards, snuggled into his arms. Women always did, at least the first time. He'd always thought it ridiculous – uncomfortable, hot, sweaty. But at least it had kept him awake for a while. He needed her to sleep for the moment. He had work to do.

Her hair was spread over his chest, shining in the moonlight which permeated the thin muslin drapes. Gradually, her breathing slowed and her body relaxed.

It had been a good diversion. She'd lived up to his expectations, this English girl. Naïve, inexperienced. But promising. In a different world, maybe it would have lasted for a while.

But that just wasn't going to be possible.

She was asleep now. Carefully, he extracted his arms. She stirred a moment, then snuggled into the soft pillow. Good. Softly, he climbed out of the bed and padded silently across the room. There, he took the key and placed it just above the light switch on the opposite side of the wall. Then he crept into the living room. He peered out onto the quiet street below. The street lights gave off an orange glow and he could see the rain still lashing down. The wind had eased a little. The worst of the gale was over.

They'd be there now. Thierry would be diving, retrieving the drugs, bringing them back up.

He needed to be there, he knew. Sam was competent, knew the waters as only a fisherman could. But Thierry was used to Pascal. It was a personal thing, the relationship between diver and skipper. He knew how to position the boat, how long his diver should be taking.

Still, there was nothing else for it. He'd just have to sit it out.

Sam and Thierry had been at Sam's council house in Leigh on Sea when the call came through. They were watching the news. The bomb had been the lead item. Two dead, not yet identified.

Sam watched the screen blankly. Shit. It was a mess. Someone had survived. It would just be a case of waiting for Pascal's phone call now.

The two men started to ready themselves. Thierry checked his diving gear and packed it neatly into a waterproof holdall. Sam changed into his fishing gear.

Half an hour later, the call came. Sam nodded at Thierry.

'Looks like we're going for a sail.'

Thierry grimaced.

They drove down to the harbour. It was an easy walk from the house, but with Thierry's gear, they needed to drive. The white van, reeking of fish, moved slowly towards the quay. There was nobody out. They would all be sheltering from the weather, snug around their TV sets.

The trawler was at its mooring, its tender kept by the sea wall. Carefully, they climbed into it and started the engine. Once out of the lee of the wall, the storm hit them full force. The tender struggled to climb the waves, lurching up and crashing down. They could see white water at the crests, the spume flying across the surface of the tender.

It was a short journey to the trawler, rolling at its mooring. Both men were relieved when it was over and they could climb up the ladder and onto the decks. Sam opened the door and they were into the warmth of the companionway.

He switched on the power whilst Thierry went below to climb into his diving gear. Quietly, Sam slipped the mooring and motored off. Within five minutes they were moving towards the wreck.

The gale was past its worst but the seas were choppy, the wind at odds with the tide. It would take an hour and a half, at least, to get there. Thierry was checking his air supply.

'Two loads of three hours.'

Sam looked at him. 'There's no way you'll get the drugs off bag by bag in that time. If each round trip is twenty minutes, it's going to be impossible.'

'Then we'll just have to do what we can, leave the rest on.'

'But we might never get a chance to come back.'

Thierry looked over the bow.

'Better than nothing.'

Sam thought of the twelve million pounds. He wanted his share.

'What if I put the boat closer to the hold and put a net down on the other side so it doesn't snag? That will reduce your distance quite a bit – and save you carrying each bag up.'

Thierry nodded slowly. 'Yes. If I take a net down with

me I can weight it down on the sea bed near the hold and just put the bags into it.'

Sam grinned. 'And then we can use the winch to get the stuff on board in one go. Yes, that makes sense. We'll get a whole lot more off, that way. It's going to be a different route for you, from the boat to the wreck – is that going to be a problem?'

Thierry shrugged. 'I know my way around there pretty well by now. It's taking a chance, but it's worth a try.'

They sat in silence as the boat eased its way into the main shipping channel. They could see very little through the spume. The trawler lurched up and down the waves, crashing through them. Sam stood impassively, knees bent, taking the impact of the pounding.

Thierry felt the beginnings of nausea in his stomach. He rarely suffered from sea sickness, but the smell of diesel and the stink of old fish combined to make life pretty unpleasant. He couldn't go out onto the deck, though. He'd be swept off within minutes.

Sam was watching the GPS. Using satellites far above the earth, the tiny machine would tell him where he was, direct him safely to the wreck. Eventually, he nodded.

'We're just approaching it now.'

He peered out of the engine house. Over the top of a rolling wave, he could just make out a mast, black against the violet night sky. Sam steered slowly towards it whilst Thierry busied himself with the nets.

'This will be the one. Small mesh, not too big a net. If we secure the end to the winch, I'll take the rest with me.'

They were approaching the bow now. Sam rolled back as Thierry prepared to go over the side.

'Just hold her against the tide. Keep her steady. I've got to know where I'm coming back to.'

Sam heard nothing as Thierry went over; the sound of the confused seas masked the splash. Then he sat back to wait. He was headed into the tide, matching the speed of the boat to the strength of the current so that it would stay

239

still. At least the tide was predictable here. He knew these seas as well as anyone and was used to holding the trawler steady. He looked at his watch: 10.30.

He watched the lines to the net, secured onto the winch. They tightened. Good. That would be Thierry down below, fastening the net to some stones on the sea bed.

Ten minutes gone. Sam scanned the surface of the water. Still choppy. There was no way he'd ever want to go in there. He hated water, couldn't even swim. He made his living from the stuff, relied totally upon it, but he loathed it. His was a life dominated by the cold, by the wet, by having to get up in the middle of the night to catch the tide. It was filthy, hard work which paid little. He wanted out, desperately. He needed his place in the sun, somewhere warm and relaxed. Somewhere that he could look at the ocean secure in the knowledge that he had enough money never to have to work in it again.

Quickly, he looked towards the horizon. They were very vulnerable. If the port authority wanted to come and take a look, they'd be in deep trouble.

God, make it quick, Thierry.

Thierry had made good progress, feeling his way along the hull. The trawler had got in close and he'd found a lovely spot for the net, on a patch of sand right by the entrance to the hold. He weighted it down with six large stones, just to the side of the boat. Sam would be able to winch it straight up when he had finished.

Now he could pick up the bags and deposit them straight into the net. It was much quicker, and after an hour he had emptied the first hole and was halfway through the second. This was going well. He had two more hours of air on this tank. He might even finish without needing to change over.

He swam back to the second hole. It was under an enormous old bomb case, rotten and almost empty, but still very heavy. He'd tried moving it to the side, but it was too much for him. Each time he took a bag out, he had to lift it a few inches with his left hand and hold it steady whilst he felt for the next plastic sack.

He was tiring a little. The bags were heavy and it was difficult to get them out of the hole. His arm was starting to ache, holding the bomb case up. He looked around for a prop. If he could just hold the case with something, he'd be so much quicker.

It was difficult to see in the murk. Thierry had a light in his helmet, but it was feeble, casting out a wavering glow. He scanned the hold and moved towards the other side. There was something lying across the bottom of it that might just do. He felt downwards with his right hand. Yes . . . metal for sure. He went lower, feeling all the time, dipping his head to shine the light onto it.

Good. It was a length of old piping. That would do just fine for what he had in mind.

Slowly, he dragged it across to the second hole. God, it was heavy. He was using up extra air with the effort, he knew. Still, it would save time in the end. Nearly there now.

With a grunt, he pulled the piping upright, digging it into the sand by the box.

Good. Now for the box itself. He lifted it up, holding it steady with one hand whilst he slipped the prop under it with the other. It held steady. Brilliant. Now he could really get on. With the piping and the net just outside the hold, he'd get all the drugs off easily. Twelve million pounds after all, thanks to an old piece of metal and some fishing net. Wonderful.

He reached down and grabbed another two bags. He could take two at a time now he didn't have to hold the case up.

He worked steadily, clearing the hole, leaving the bags in the net ready to be winched up. Twenty minutes later, there were just two bags left in the hole. He'd get these out and then move on to the final cache. That was the smallest: just thirty-three bags. He had to stretch right down now, to the

241

very bottom of the hole. There were definitely two more to go, he'd counted carefully. He felt around with his right hand. Nothing. Perhaps they'd been pushed to the side of the hole when he'd lifted out the other bags.

Thierry positioned his head so that he helmet light could shine into the hole, trying to work out where the hell those two bags had got to. He moved closer supporting his body on his left arm, suspended over the hole so that his light would shine into the depths. With his right arm, he scrabbled around in the hole, feeling for those bloody bags.

He never saw the piping wobble and start to move. Nor did he see the bomb case topple and fall. Right back into place over the hole.

It hit him on the head, hard. He never knew a thing . . . just blackness.

Chapter Twenty-Six

1.45 am. The gale had blown right through now.

Sam watched the clock. Thierry had had three hours of air. He'd gone over at 10.30.

Something had gone terribly wrong.

Did diving cannisters have a reserve? Sam had no idea. Thierry was an experienced diver, though. He'd be sensible.

Maybe he was lost. It was a new route to the wreck, even though it was closer. Perhaps he was confused. The water would be muddy, filthy after the storm.

Come on Thierry. Come on.

Sam walked around the deck of the boat, looking at the water, praying for Thierry to surface. He paused at the winch. The rope was on, ready to lift the net up from the sea bed. Better not try it. If Thierry was fine, just loading the last few bags, the whole lot could spill out.

He'd give it another half an hour.

Thierry came round after a few minutes. He was groggy, his head hurting like hell. Something was on his shoulders. He tried to lift them, raise his neck and take a look around.

The weight was too big. He couldn't move.

This wasn't happening. It was a nightmare.

He struggled again, trying to work out what the hell was going on. He was pinned into a hole at the bottom of the sea. Something was on top of him. Something which he was never going to move. Not in a million years.

The bomb case. He'd propped it up whilst he'd felt for the bags. It must have fallen onto him.

There was no way out.

Damn that piping! It must have given way whilst he was over the hole. He should never have used it. He'd risked his life on a fifty-six-year-old piece of rotten piping. God, he was stupid.

He cursed himself.

His right arm was in front of him, down the hole. The other, the one he'd been using to support himself as he searched, was twisted behind him, on the other side of the case.

He couldn't see his watch. He'd no idea how long he'd been unconscious for. But he had set out with only three hours of air.

At some point soon, unless he could get out, he was going to die, suffocate slowly, trapped on the floor of the sea.

He kicked out hard, wriggling his lower body. He tried to roll from side to side, anything at all to try to move that awful weight.

Stop, think. There has to be a way out.

He tried an enormous heave, starting the movement at his hips and flipping himself up, his powerful shoulders thrusting forward.

Nothing. Not the tiniest movement from the bomb case.

Don't panic. If he started to panic, he'd use his air up more quickly. He had to think. If he could just move his arms, one on either side of the box, maybe he could dig at the sand, make enough of a hole to weasel his way out.

It was tricky. With his shoulders pinned, he couldn't move his hands very far. But his fingers could scrabble at the sand. He could feel it, the grains moving about. If he stayed calm, he could make it. There was a little indentation already, he just needed to carry on . . .

244

Was the air starting to run out? It was becoming difficult to think straight. It felt hot, sweat in his mask. His hands didn't seem to want to move any more, however much he tried.

So this was death. Sneaking up on him, cheating him of everything. Throwing its dark cloak around him, spiriting him away from this world. Bastard death. Bastard . . .

Sam checked his watch. Two o'clock.

It had gone wrong. It was all his bloody fault, his greed over those bags. They should have taken what they could and made a run for it. All this bloody nonsense with a new route, using a net – it had just increased the risk.

Grimly, he reached for the winch mechanism and started turning. God, it was heavy. There was something in the net.

Pull, man, pull.

With a lurch, the stones weighting it down shifted and the net rose up the side of the trawler. Sam moved quicker, taking the lift up high until the net could be emptied onto the deck.

Quickly, Sam counted. 164 bags.

But no Thierry.

Pascal waited in his den. There had been no sound from the girl. He wouldn't sleep, though. Not with Thierry and Sam out there.

He looked at his watch: 2.15 am. They should be finished by now. He padded around the den, waiting for news.

'Just keep the blood running. We can save him yet.'

The Professor had rushed in from his North London home as soon as he'd been called. This one was going to be difficult. Multiple trauma to face and upper body, caused by an explosion. A barrister, apparently.

The patient was already in theatre when the Professor arrived. Quickly, he gowned and scrubbed up.

245

Blood and gore no longer bothered him. It was just meat. It didn't help anyone to be shocked at the sight of it. He had to get right in to each injury, stem the blood flow, get the debris out. One by one, he could get there, he knew it.

Deftly, he started to lift the tissue, searching out the damage.

As Pascal sat at his desk, there was one short ring from his mobile phone.

He answered it immediately, his voice low.

'Yes?'

'It's Sam. I'm ringing from the boat. Thierry went down at ten-thirty. Something's happened. He hasn't come back.'

Merde. He glanced at the clock. Two-thirty.

Pascal gripped the phone tightly. He should have been there, helping, not finding an excuse to screw the English girl.

'How much air did he have?'

'Three hours, he said.'

Pascal looked out of the window. There would only be another hour of darkness at this time of year.

'What about the bags?'

'I've got one hundred and sixty-four on board.'

Pascal grimaced. 'Leave now. Get back to port, do a little fishing on the way. Keep the bags on the boat. Just act normally. Come straight to the flat.'

'But he's down there. In the wreck . . .'

'There's nothing you can do. Once it's light, you'll be seen. Just go. Now.'

Sam shrugged.

Abby had always been a light sleeper. She'd stirred briefly at the sound of the phone. It was enough. Her body registered the strangeness of her surroundings: a different bed, linen sheets, an odd smell. She opened her eyes and look around, confused. It was dark, but a light shone from the hallway.

246

She was frightened.

She sat up in the bed. Suddenly, she remembered. Yesterday. The bomb. Seb. The hospital. Antoine appearing out of nowhere to take her away.

Going to bed with him. He'd promised to stay, but the bed was cold.

She padded silently to the door of her room. She could hear him on the phone, muttering quietly into it. Then he hung up and paced over to the window. He was on some sort of mezzanine, raised up from her on the other side of the living area. She had a clear view of his face in the gloom of a light.

Appalled, she watched him. This was not the Antoine of last night. His face was set, his lips pursed.

What the hell have I done, thought Abby. I went home with somebody I hardly knew and stayed the night. I must have been deranged.

Patterns were starting to form in her mind. Links were being forged, circumstances were unravelling. She didn't know yet what it all added up to, but she knew that she shouldn't be here. Not alone in this flat with a stranger.

I need to go. This is a mistake. I want to go home.

She coughed lightly, watched him jump from where she stood.

'What?'

'Antoine, I want to go home.'

Chapter Twenty-Seven

She knew something. She was no longer giving him that doe-eyed look. She must have heard him on the phone, put two and two together.

'I want to go home.'

He tried to laugh. 'But it's the middle of the night, *cherie*, wait until morning . . . was it so awful?'

'No. I'm going. Antoine, this is a mistake. I should never have left the hospital with you . . . my friends will wonder where I am.'

She moved back towards the bedroom. She had to dress. He'd said she could take something from the wardrobe. Before she went to take off his shirt, some vestige of decency made her shut the bedroom door.

There was a metallic scrape. Quickly, she turned around. The door had been locked from the outside.

'Antoine . . .'

She pulled at the handle. It stayed put.

'Antoine, for God's sake, what is this? I have to go home. We can see each other again, but I'm not feeling very well and I want to go home. Now.'

Silence.

Abby moved over to the window and looked out. Three floors up, with a sheer drop to the garden, and no drainpipes even if she was feeling daring. No phone. Maybe she could lean out and scream when there were people

248

around in the morning. But for the moment, she was a prisoner.

The Professor had been working for two hours when the cardiac arrest happened. The monitors suddenly started screaming. It made him jump; he'd been concentrating so hard on extracting debris from the patient's chest wall. Damn.

The rest of the team rushed into action. Defibrillators were applied and they all stood back whilst an electric current was passed through the heart.

The line stayed flat, the machine note constant.

They tried again.

The Professor shook his head. There was only so much trauma that the body could withstand. The injuries were terrible, he knew. Somebody less fit would have died hours ago. But even this barrister could only take so much. It was just not possible to survive these wounds.

The Professor was a deeply religious man. As his team got ready to disconnect the monitors he stood quietly beside the body of Seb Waters. Life was leaving him now. Soon, there would be the stillness after the storm, a moment like none other for those left behind.

As always, he made a silent prayer. There, at the point of death, it always seemed right, somehow.

'One more go, sir?'

The registrar was looking at him earnestly. Some superstition about third time lucky, no doubt. They all grew out of it in the end. The Professor gave a wry smile.

'OK. Stand back.'

The defibrillators were applied one last time, a pad on each side of the chest. One more go and then you can rest in peace, Mr Waters, whoever you are.

In an instant the sound had gone; the awful, flat tone from the monitor, that harbinger of death. In its place was a series of random beeps, settling gradually into a pattern which they all recognised.

249

Quickly, the Professor looked up, seeking confirmation. This shouldn't be happening. In thirty-five years of practice, he'd never brought anyone back this far.

The grins around the table told him what he couldn't quite believe.

'OK. We're in business folks. Let's see what we can do.'

Marcus woke up at seven in the morning, brought round by the clatter of the breakfast trolley. A large male nurse was peering at him.

'All right are we?'

Marcus nodded. His head hurt, but it would heal. The stitches felt strange and were beginning to itch.

'How's Abby – the girl I came in with?'

The nurse smiled. 'Not on this ward, I'm afraid. I'll try and find out.'

'And Seb Waters?'

The nurse turned back. 'He's in ITU. Nearly died on the operating table, but he's still with us. We'll know more when they assess him at the end of the day.'

Marcus shook his head. It all seemed impossible to take in, somehow. The nurse looked at him carefully.

'I'll try and find the girl for you . . .'

A few minutes later, he re-appeared, looking worried.

'She's gone. Came out of X-ray, was left alone for a moment, then she went. Do you have a home number for her?'

Marcus could remember it.

'I'll try her from the ward phone.'

The nurse was back in five minutes.

'No answer. Probably went home, though. She was in reasonable shape. No fracture, apparently, just severe shock.'

Marcus climbed out of bed.

'Where are you going?'

'To find her.'

'But you need a check-up – the doctor needs to take a look at your stitches.'

'I've got to go.'

'But you're on painkillers – you'll need topping up soon.'

'Bugger that. I'm discharging myself.'

And him a vicar too, thought the charge nurse. The times they certainly are a-changing.

The bomb squad had moved in overnight. The area was cordoned off. No one would come near the place now without a pass.

DC Peters knew what he was doing, had done this many times before. Ten years in the bomb squad, and he'd seen it all.

Semtex, had to be. It was the favourite explosive of all the terror groups. But they needed every last scrap of material from the room, just to confirm it. They'd keep an open mind about who did it. So far, there had been four calls from extremist organisations, all claiming responsibility. Well, they'd find out in the end. In the meantime, every last thing in that room had to be collected, noted, bagged and subjected to forensic examination.

Peters started at the top end of the room. It was one hell of a mess. The strong basement walls had contained the blast, but concentrated it. No one would have stood a chance. Still, better get on with it. Item no. 1. He logged it on the scale plan: one photograph, woman and baby. Probably a wife and child. Some writing on the back, covered in dirt and indecipherable in this light.

He took the tweezers and placed it carefully into a plastic bag. Everything in the room would be treated in the same way. It was slow, painstaking work. But it had to be done.

It was also a pretty unpleasant task. The stench of death was everywhere. All the surfaces of the room were covered with a layer of dust, blood and tissue. People had died here, in this room, and he moved silently, respectfully.

He could see the photograph through the plastic. It

looked old, in black and white, the woman dressed in clothes twenty years out of date.

Many men carried photos of their family, of course. It just seemed odd that this was clearly so old. The child was just a baby – usually, the photos were more recent. It could mean something. Probably didn't, but forensics might be able to make something of the writing on the back.

Marcus had put on his clothes at the hospital. They were filthy. He had to get home.

Quickly, he found his way through the back streets to Tottenham Court Road. There, he got a cab back to Archway.

Once at the Vicarage, he threw on some clean clothes . . . including his dog collar. It could be useful. Then he took another cab to Sadlers Wells. First thing had to be her home. Check it out. She might be there, although somehow he doubted it.

She was out.

He banged on the door of the house above the basement flat. No answer. He tried again, pushing the buzzer for a full thirty seconds.

'All right, all right, I'm coming.'

A woman of indeterminate age appeared at the door, still in her dressing gown, a cigarette in her mouth. She recoiled at the sight of him. Must be the cut on his head. Then she noticed the dog collar and looked puzzled.

'I'm sorry to wake you . . .' He went into his most upper class accent. He had to convince her that he was not some maniac. 'Abby had an accident yesterday – you may have heard of the bomb at her work. She seems to have disappeared. Have you any idea where she might be?'

The lady looked at him quizzically, working out if he was OK or not. Eventually, she relented with a shrug.

'I'm her landlady. Give me a moment and I'll get the key to her flat.'

The door shut in his face. Marcus turned around and

looked onto the street. Thursday morning, things were quiet. The storm of yesterday had given way to a balmy stillness. It was going to be a hot day.

Ten minutes later, the door opened and the woman emerged. She was dressed in some old jeans and a sweat-shirt. He followed her down the steps.

They went into Abby's flat. Marcus noted the tidiness, the gleaming sink. He went past the kitchen into the living area. The bed was neatly made up. There were flowers everywhere, old vases bulging with them. Even cups had been pressed into service. Marcus looked at the largest vase.

There was a note. No name. The writing looked French, somehow. He'd gone out with a French girl for a while at music college. She'd told him how they were taught to form their letters identically at school.

The Frenchman who had appeared after the bomb. She'd called him Antoine, he was sure.

Marcus hadn't liked him one bit. He'd heard the exchange after the bomb. Why the hell had the Frenchman wanted to know if he was alive? But he'd said he was coming to the hospital. Perhaps he'd turned up and spirited her away.

Marcus thought quickly. Could be nothing. But it was the only lead he had. He needed to find him.

He turned back to the flowers, taking the message from the leaves. There was a stamp on the back: Sunshine Flowers. And an address in Kensington.

He found the shop easily. It was clearly an expensive establishment, bursting with extravagant arrangements. Busy, too. He waited in the queue for twenty minutes whilst some moronic woman asked if she could have the gypsophila in blue. It just had to be blue to match Chloe's Alice band. No madam, it doesn't come in blue . . .

The assistant was far too polite, allowing the silly cow to drone on endlessly.

Finally, he was at the front of the queue. He smiled

hopefully at the assistant and showed her the card from the Frenchman.

'Yes, I remember. Couldn't forget a man like that. Yes, paid cash. No name, didn't need to know. Sorry. Lucky girl, though. Cost a packet, that arrangement. He was desperate for it to be done quick, as well.'

Marcus left the shop and walked back to the tube. Someone in a rush who paid large sums in cash. Maybe it was nothing, but something felt very wrong. Very wrong indeed.

Abby woke up to an empty stomach and a terrible thirst. God, she had had the weirdest dream. Terrifying, too. She felt a wave of comfort as she realised that she was awake now.

She opened her eyes. Everything seemed wrong, somehow. She wasn't even in bed. She'd somehow fallen asleep on top of it, at a strange angle.

Then she realised. This was Antoine's flat. It hadn't been a dream at all. This was for real.

She leant out of the window and shouted at the top of her voice: 'Help!'

She was at the back of the building, though. If she leant right out, she could just see around the edge of the block onto the street. But no one noticed her, not even when she leaned out so far she felt dizzy.

She was hungry – starving in fact. There had been no communication from Antoine since he'd locked her in last night.

She sat on the bed. She'd been so stupid, out of her head with lust. And for what? Some bloody Frenchman, lucky enough to have a good-looking head on his shoulders. Now he had gone pervy on her, locking her up in his bedroom.

Or was there more to it? She lay back, resting her head against the wall.

Think Abby. Get a grip. There is an answer somewhere and knowing it might help you get out of this.

He'd wanted to know about the case. She'd told him too

much. Yet she knew nothing about him. He'd come into her life because of the advert Marcus had placed.

Everything came back to the case, somehow. He was part of it all. He had to be.

I don't want the bloody case any more. I just want out. I want to go home, sit in my room and close my eyes. And then I want Marcus to come round and make me feel better. Please Marcus, I need you.

'One hundred and sixty-four bags. Thirty-five still on it.'

Sam had driven straight to Pascal's flat. They were talking in low voices in the kitchen, away from the girl's room, taking stock. Pascal was sitting, listening to Sam's account of what had happened. The fisherman had driven straight up as ordered. He was plainly exhausted, kept awake only by strong French coffee.

'Thirty-five bags on the wreck. And one body.'

'Yes, one body.'

'If Thierry is found, he'll be identified.'

'Nothing on the wreck to link him with us, is there?'

Pascal raised an eyebrow. 'They'll put out an award. Once they start asking around, someone will cough, link him to us.'

'It won't be enough for them to charge us.'

'Maybe not. But they'll follow us, search everything. They'll find the drugs in the end.'

Pascal paused a moment.

'We've got to get rid of his body. Once they find him, we've had it.'

Sam nodded. 'But that's going to be impossible. We'd need a diver to find him, and there's no way we could get someone—'

Pascal interrupted. 'No. We don't find his body.' He stood up. 'We're going to have to destroy the wreck. Blow it up to kingdom come. Such a big bang that Thierry's body is destroyed, too. And the rest of the drugs. There'll be no evidence.'

255

Sam breathed in sharply.'

'But Thierry . . . his body.'

Pascal shrugged. 'We can't afford to be sentimental about this. What do you suggest? Retrieval of the body and burial with full military honours? Whilst he's there, he's the biggest risk to us, Sam.'

Sam nodded. 'OK. It's just, he was . . .'

'He was a friend to us both. But he's gone now. He wouldn't want us to put the whole plan in jeopardy.'

Sam stood up. 'What about the girl?'

Pascal looked at him hard.

'She knows too much now. It's only a matter of time before she works it all out. We're going to kill her.'

'How? I've never . . .'

Pascal grinned. 'Leave it to me. The problem isn't so much the killing, but what we do with the body. We can hardly leave it here – they'd be on to us in no time. No, we need to get her down to the water – she can meet a natural death there. What you English call death by misadventure.'

Abby was thirsty. Terribly so. The room was hot and stuffy.

She banged on the door.

'Please, let me eat and drink. For God's sake, Antoine, I'm desperate.'

No answer. She must be alone. What was going on?

Very little woke Sam. He could sleep anywhere, anytime. It was a vital skill at sea. Pascal had left him to sleep off the night's work whilst he went out for the afternoon. He snored as Abby screamed.

Marcus paced outside the phone box in South Kensington. Every box seemed to take phone cards these days. The tiny minority that still took coins always had a huge queue outside. God, it would be quicker to go and buy his own mobile phone at this rate.

He finally reached the front of the queue.

Chambers. They might know something. He dialled the

256

number. Please let there be a contact number. Please God, I don't pray about trivialities.

'Chambers is closed but in the event of an emergency, please call the duty clerk.'

An outer London number. Quickly, Marcus pressed another pound into the slot.

'Hello?'

'Is that the clerk to twenty-nine Pump Court?'

'Yes, it's Ron. Who is this?'

Thank you God.

'It's Marcus Kirkwall, the vicar in the James case.'

'Thank goodness you rang. Are you with Miss Penhaligon? The hospital said you'd discharged yourself.'

Marcus's tone was gentle. 'No, I've not found her yet. Any news on Mr Waters?'

'I don't know. They won't tell me as I'm not a relative. I'm just on my way there now, to try and get some sense out of them . . . I just don't know what to think, whether to dare hope . . .'

'He made it through the night, Ron. That's the most crucial time, just after it all . . . He's got a chance . . .'

There was the sound of a breath being drawn down the line.

'Thank God. He's . . . well, he's one of the oldest friends I've got. But Miss Penhaligon, where is she?'

'I've been trying to find her. She's not at her flat . . . I've got a feeling she may be with a Frenchman called Antoine. Have you heard of him?'

There was a pause at the other end of the line.

'He took her out last week. Sent flowers.'

'What do you know about him?'

'Nothing at all. He appeared out of the blue. Said he had some evidence for your case. She'd only just met him, he took her out after she'd finished one day . . . Look, this may not be tactful, but I think there was something between them . . . she went a bit funny when she got the flowers the other day.'

257

A muscle was clenched in Marcus's jaw. Calm down. Think rationally, for heaven's sake.

His mind was racing. The Frenchman who'd phoned him about the advert ... Marcus had boasted about Abby and Seb's involvement. He'd even told the man where Abby worked.

It had to be the same man. He must have got in touch with her. She'd not told Marcus, he'd had no idea.

Oh Abby, what the hell is going on?

'Think hard, Ron. Did he say anything about where he was living?'

A further pause. Hurry up for God's sake.

'No. Nothing.'

Shit.

It was a dead end. There was nothing at the flower shop, nothing the clerks knew.

He should have found her by now. She'd been gone more than half a day, in the company of a man who was starting to feel rather too professional.

She was in danger. He knew it.

Chapter Twenty-Eight

She must have fallen asleep once more. She was on the bed, her head hurting like hell. Her lips were so dry . . .

'Abby . . .'

She sat upright. It was Antoine, talking from the other side of the locked door.

'For fuck's sake, what's happening? I need to go home.'

'Do you want something to drink?'

'Just open the door.'

She heard the key turning. Thank God. Bugger the drink, she was off the moment it opened. She moved over to the entrance, ready to slip past as the door was unlocked.

It crashed open. Abby lurched towards the gap. It was filled by Antoine, who felt roughly for her wrists. There was another man behind him.

'Not so fast, Abby.'

'Let me go!'

'Not for the moment. I have a little present for you before you leave us.'

He held her tight whilst the other man moved behind her.

Shit! The man she didn't know was pushing at her sleeve, shoving it over her elbow and up her arm. Instinctively, she pulled away, but Pascal's grip was like a vice.

Then she saw the needle. Three inches of metal at the end of a plastic vial. He was ready with it.

Abby screamed. 'Get off, just fucking get off . . .' She shook her arms hard, twisted her upper body until she felt the muscles strain.

It was no good. The needle was right beside her skin. Pascal smiled grimly.

'Farewell. It was fun while it lasted . . .'

There was searing pain as the needle broke the skin. Appalled, she turned to watch the vial empty.

'What is it?'

Everything felt the same. She wasn't falling asleep. She was OK. In fact, she felt pretty good. Rising up above it all.

Antoine was changing. His body was elongating, growing scales. He was turning into a long, green serpent. His eyes were really becoming very peculiar indeed, changing colour from violet to green to orange. Then Seb appeared in them with a gun which he fired at her.

She fell to the carpet.

Marcus was going round in circles; round and round with no way out.

Abby had disappeared, presumably with this Frenchman. Nobody knew a thing about him. And until he heard anything to the contrary, she had to be at risk. Perhaps they'd just sloped off for a weekend in Paris. But she'd have told someone – her landlady, Ron, *someone* would know.

So she was at risk. Possibly dead.

Bloody hell.

It was three o'clock now. His head was throbbing. Every time he tried to think, it got worse.

He had walked to the tube station after ringing Ron. Now he was in the underpass at South Ken, right where he used to play. He'd been wandering the streets for some time, desperately trying to find a way out of the circle in his head.

260

His old spot was empty, the underpass silent for once.

Marcus sat on his haunches where he used to play. Passers by gave him a wide berth, this vicar, with his back to the wall. He looked at the grey cement, worn smooth with the passage of a million soles.

'Father, help me.'

He didn't usually pray like this. He'd never been one for calling on the Almighty to help him out. There was a lady in his parish who would pray that Tesco's had her favourite oranges on special offer that week. Another who told him that the Lord had lifted a traffic jam on the Kentish Town Road when she'd had to go in an ambulance. He'd nodded politely and thought what a load of rubbish. The Lord might be omnipotent but he would hardly be monitoring Tesco's or the traffic conditions in Kentish Town.

But it was the only thing he could think of.

'Father help me.'

He had never thought like this in his life, every iota of brain power fixed on one thing. Where was she?

'Tell me where she is, Father. Tell me.'

No bolt of thunder. No sepulchral choirs.

'Just tell me. I've got to find her. Give me a break.'

Suddenly, his mind stopped turning circles. He could think in a straight line again.

The Frenchman had come on the scene when they had taken the case on. He'd seen the advert in the local paper, had got in touch. He'd wanted to get involved in the case. He had some link with it.

And that link was the *Richard Montgomery*. He didn't know how, but it was the only connection, the only strand drawing everything together.

He had to get there.

Staff nurse Anna Simons waited for her patient to surface. She'd never spoken to him, but that was the lot of the ITU nurse. He should make it though. Internal injuries,

261

a heart attack, but he'd got through the first twenty-four hours.

The registrar and Professor stood behind her, waiting. The knock-out drugs were wearing off and any minute now he would re-emerge into the land of the living. Either that or he would stay where he was, in the never-never land between life and death. This was it, the moment of truth. Some never came back.

She listened as his breathing fastened. She spoke gently.

'Seb, wake up.'

The Professor leaned down to his patient.

'It's time to wake up now, Seb. You're safe, you're OK.'

Pascal grinned as Abby fell to the floor. He'd bought the heroin at King's Cross that afternoon. A purchase contracted in less than five minutes; so easy to do. He knew the dosage all too well. She'd gone under within three seconds and would be out of it now for hours. If by any chance he'd under-estimated it, he had a top-up vial in his jacket.

'Let's get going.'

He took her head, her hair tumbling over his hands as he lifted.

Sam had her feet and together they carried her to the lift.

There, Pascal let her lie for a moment. He took the package he'd picked up earlier and placed it carefully in a rucksack. The leftover Semtex. Thierry's spare timer.

Sam checked the garage as the door opened. There was nobody around. His white van was there, parked next to Pascal's hired BMW.

It took less than thirty seconds to get her into the van. Pascal watched her as they drove. They needed her alive. For this stage, at least.

The evening's rush hour was over and the roads were fast. Sam drove carefully though, sticking to the speed limit. The last thing he needed was to be stopped by the police.

Poplar, Canning Town, Aveley; Sam navigated as they drove out along the A13 into south Essex – the hinterland of the Thames, a once great area, now run down and neglected.

It was getting dark. They'd timed it beautifully.

Leigh on Sea. Pretty as a postcard. More importantly, quiet as the grave.

Sam's boat was tied up at its mooring, awaiting its new cargo. They'd go out at half tide, motor slowly over to the wreck. Then they'd make for Holland, find somewhere temporary to store the ecstasy they'd managed to salvage.

He left the van and took the tender from the sea wall. Then he motored out to the fishing boat. Quickly, he found what he was looking for – a long, shallow fish box. Just the thing. Nobody would look any closer in the dark.

Carefully, he motored back, leaving the tender at the mooring. He tied the boat up and hurried with the fish box to the van, where Pascal was waiting with the girl.

'OK, let's put her in here.'

In a moment, Abby was laid out in the box and the two men carried her on board the boat. Still nobody was around.

'Put her down below until we get out.'

Sam nodded. She was still out, although it was no surprise, not with that dosage. No doubt it was the first time she'd taken heroin. He grinned.

They carried the box down the steps and put it on the floor of the cabin.

Quietly, Sam started the engine and the boat chugged slowly out of the harbour. He looked back to make sure nobody was watching from the shore. It all looked pretty quiet to him. Carefully, he motored a course through the moorings. Pascal was silent, watching from the wheel-house.

Down below, Abby was deeply unconscious. Beneath her, under a layer of fish, was just over eight million pounds worth of ecstasy.

Chapter Twenty-Nine

Marcus raced up the subway steps and hailed a taxi on Exhibition Road.

'Archway, quick, please.'

'Right-oh.' The cabbie performed a startling U-turn and sped off north.

Marcus looked out of the window and thought hard. He needed to get to the wreck quickly. The roads would be quiet now. His car would get him to the shoreline within an hour. But what then?

Twenty-four hours in an English summer is an eternity; the storm had long gone, taking the rough seas and chop with it. Pascal stood at the bow of the fishing boat, watching the phosphorescence shimmer as they moved through the glass-like water. It was dark, very dark. Good.

Thierry was dead. The only person in the whole world who really knew him. His best friend. They'd met during the charter years. Thierry was working, teaching American tourists to dive. The only Frenchmen working in the town, they'd got together quickly, a formidable duo. God, they'd had some good times. They were from opposite ends of the spectrum, him from a long line of aristocrats, Thierry from a family of petty criminals. They couldn't have looked more different, either: Thierry with his brute strength, wide grin and tanned skin; Pascal with his fine bones and good looks. But they had been two of a kind. Both had walked away from their old lives, had rejected them for the unknown. Both needed risk, the joy of big winnings, the excitement of making the chance work for them.

But it had gone wrong this time. His only friend was dead, his body underneath an old wreck in the cold filthy waters of the Thames Estuary.

And now Pascal was going to have to blow that body into oblivion.

Marcus paid off the cabbie and raced into his study. He kept an old AA map of Britain by the side of the bookcase. The pages were crumpled, the edges folded down. The photocopied pages from the library about the wreck were still on the table.

Quickly, he found the Thames Estuary and scanned the towns nearby. He needed a pilot book, something which would tell him exactly where to go to find the wreck. But the most the library pages could tell him was that it was visible from the Isle of Grain. Wonderful. Not a lot of use in the middle of the bloody night.

Still, there was the Isle of Grain on the road map. But he needed to get to the wreck.

He closed his eyes and thought. In the morning, maybe, he could scrounge a ride on a fishing boat, hire a yacht perhaps. Anything. A good night's sleep was what he needed now. God, his head hurt. He needed to get to bed.

He started to climb the stairs. Never had his bed seemed more welcoming. He could get his head down, forget it all for a night. He'd feel better in the morning. He was too tired to undress. He just lay down on his bed and closed his eyes.

Oh, no. Not again.

The images were back. Henry Jenkins in the tube station, and then Seb. The two scenes intermingled, became one dreadful tableau. Marcus tried to shut his eyes tighter, squeeze out the pictures he was seeing.

266

But there was no escape. He couldn't bear it. However tired he was, he wouldn't sleep tonight. Not until he had done what he needed to. He had to get there tonight. Steal a boat, do whatever it took. He just had to go as soon as he could.

He raced down the stairs again and looked closely at the map. The Isle of Grain looked too quiet. He needed a place nearby, somewhere he'd be able to steal a dinghy. Sheerness? Possibly . . . He traced the road with his finger.

Queenborough. Almost as close, but with a yachting logo on the map. That had to be his best chance.

He hurried out to the garage, opened the door, and started up the Saab.

'Twenty minutes or so till we get there.'

Pascal nodded at Sam. He went down the steps and opened the box. Abby was still out cold. He grinned. It had been a short acquaintance, but rather a sweet one. And she'd never know a thing.

After this, they'd motor straight over to Holland. He'd never be able to use the wreck again, but that was the price he'd have to pay if he was to get rid of Thierry's body. And he'd just have to face it out with George. A re-negotiation, maybe. But they would be splitting the money only two ways, now.

Marcus raced through Hackney. The traffic was light and he found his way on to the A2 quickly. Key Street, look out for Key Street. There it was. He took a left and followed the signs.

Queenborough, Kent. He drove through the town, down towards the river. Looked pretty small, very quiet.

The road ran out near the river, but there was plenty of space to park his car. Marcus abandoned it and started walking. A jetty from a yacht club stretched out into the river. Several dinghies were floating quietly, tied to it.

It was a still, warm evening. There were lights on in the

yacht club and he could hear music: Slade, by the sound of it. With a bit of luck there was a party on and nobody would notice a dinghy being stolen.

Marcus walked silently down the jetty. It was long. There had to be a big tidal range here. He looked at a couple of inflatable tenders: reasonable, but not ideal. Then he saw it. A dory: square, fibreglass. He'd used them dozens of times in the navy. Good size, probably used as a rescue boat by the yacht club. It would do very nicely indeed.

He knelt on the jetty and tugged gently on the line. Once the dory was alongside, he leaned over to the outboard, unscrewed the petrol cap and dipped a finger in. Good, almost full.

He glanced back at the club. Someone was talking into the PA, prizes were being doled out by the sound of it. That would keep them all inside for a bit. He'd need to be able to make a quiet getaway. If anyone saw him, he'd be in the shit. Even with his dog collar on, it would take some explaining.

He clambered into the dory and pulled the cord to start the engine. It caught first time, spluttering into action. Someone obviously looked after it very well.

Quietly, he pointed the boat down river. The tide was ebbing. It carried him away from the jetty quickly, out into the black waters of the Thames Estuary.

Chapter Thirty

Pascal grinned as he prepared the Semtex.

This was going to go up with one hell of a bang. If it started off the explosives on the wreck, too, there would be over three thousand tons worth of explosion. Now that was power.

Beyond him, the girl was still out. She was attractive, even in sleep. Her hair spilled over her shoulders, her chest rose and fell rhythmically.

She'd been good, but that was dangerous. He could recognise the signs in himself. Never again would he be vulnerable to a woman. Everything depended on that – every iota of self-respect he possessed.

He'd always set himself little tests. It had started when he was a kid. The first one, when he was eight, had been to catch and kill a rat by midnight. He'd thought it up one evening in bed, bored and unable to sleep. He could still remember the thrill when he'd succeeded, watching the rat squirm and shriek as he drowned it. The thrill was addictive.

Every now and then, unbidden, his mind would throw up a new test. After the rat, they had been largely pointless – hitting a bigger boy; making a girl cry.

With adolescence, however, the tests had changed: screw one of the servants by lunchtime, get one of the village girls pregnant and then deny it; steal some money from Papa's wallet and go to Paris for an evening.

But, again with time, the tests changed. They were serious now, making demands which he just had to meet.

Sail to England alone.

Leave home.

Tell Papa he hated him.

Passing those latter tests had given him the greatest thrill of all. Once he achieved his goal, he would be on a high for days. It was as though he could measure his progress in life by the tests he set himself and the success he had in meeting them. He was very different, he knew, from that eight-year-old boy drowning a rat. Now he was grown, self-confident, independent. He could go anywhere in the world and look after himself once he got there. He had no need of anyone, any more.

But still, he had to be on his guard. Had to keep watch for chinks in his armour. He could backslide into need, into vulnerability. And then it would all have been for nothing. So he had to search out his weaknesses, make himself do what felt difficult.

He watched Abby again. He'd planned to throw her over the side once they were in the North Sea. She'd still be alive, if unconscious. Even if they found her body, they'd note the water in her lungs, the heroin in her body, and conclude that she had leapt off a cliff somewhere whilst out of her mind.

But she was very beautiful. And he was not invulnerable yet. He had to become so.

Then came the test.

'Blow her up with the boat.'

Somehow, it seemed very different to throwing her over the side. Blow that beautiful body into nothingness. It would be a violent, terrible end. But it was good enough for Thierry. If he felt nothing for the English girl, it had to be good enough for her, too.

Slowly, he grinned. He could do it. He could beat the weakness, after all.

Sam took the trawler right up to the buoy. It would have

270

to be the inflatable from here on. Carefully, Pascal climbed into the dinghy whilst Sam handed down the rucksack. The oars were ready and the Frenchman rowed gently towards the wreck. It was low water now and the masts stood proud of the water. He felt the dinghy scrape over some metal from the superstructure. They were very close now.

He looked behind. It was still, silent as the grave. Carefully, he tied the dinghy to a mast and clambered out.

Two explosions would do it, one either side of the central mast. It would be enough to finish off the wreck by itself. It might even set off the explosives in the hold.

He packed the Semtex around the mast and set up the timer. Nothing fancy; in this wet environment, he needed to keep it simple. Dead low water now. Two hours would do it. That would give them plenty of time to get away.

He rowed back to the fishing boat.

'And now the girl.'

Sam looked stunned.

'Come on, now.'

With a shrug, he pulled up the fish box and the two men manhandled it into the dinghy. Pascal was breathing heavily.

Rather neat, really. She'd be blown away. No body left. She'd just join that great long list of London's disappeared.

Merde, she was heavy as a dead weight. Roughly, he pushed her out onto the superstructure. Sit her up, arms together. He forced her around the mast, outside the Semtex, arms and legs arranged around the pole. Quickly, he tied her limbs together, then, for good measure, put some spectra rope around her body. No way she'd fall out of that lot.

There was no time to admire his handiwork now. It was midnight. One hour forty-five minutes to get out.

Adieu Thierry, *mon ami*. Rest in peace.

Quickly, he rowed towards the launch.

Marcus opened the throttle of the engine a little more,

hugging the edge of the river up to Sheerness. It narrowed just there, he knew from the map. Once he saw the lights, he made for the opposite bank.

God, it was dark. It was quiet, though, the water so still that the lights of the town reflected perfectly in it. On his left, he could see the start of the great chimneys of the power station, the tops disappearing into the darkness.

Right, onwards to the wreck now. It was here, somewhere, he knew.

He looked northwards. In the distance, there were the twinkling lights of another town. Southend, it had to be, up on the other side of the Estuary. All he needed to do was head along the river, south until he found it. It was a standard search technique, after all.

He looked at his watch. Midnight.

In the distance, he heard the low chugging of a motor. He was invisible, he knew. No lights, too low in the water to be picked up on radar. He looked around him. Nothing to see. He'd have to keep his wits about him or he'd be run over.

There were buoys flashing on the horizon. Must be the shipping lanes. The wreck was near the approaches to Sheerness, the book had said. He pointed the dory towards the flashing lights.

Too slow. He turned up the throttle and the engine note increased. The lights were coming no closer. The tide must have turned. He'd be fighting it all the way now.

Come on, dory, just get there.

12.15. He was a little closer, could count the seconds between flashes. Ten seconds. As the dory crept closer, he could see the next light. Five-second gaps for that one.

The fishing vessel must be going out to sea. There was no other engine to be heard. For the moment, he was alone. He wondered if the dory's owner had noticed it had gone yet.

12.30. Finally, he reached the flashing light. On to the next one.

It was too dark. Now he was away from the town lights, he could see nothing except the flashing light. He must be near to the wreck; he could be passing it for all he knew ... It was hopeless. He'd set out on this crazy voyage in the middle of the night. Why hadn't he waited for daybreak?

12.50. He was at the five-second buoy now. It was getting cold and there was a bit more of a swell out here.

I don't even have a bloody lifejacket. I must be going mad.

Abby was in a flood. It was raining, the house in Basildon was filling up with water and she was sitting on the sofa downstairs. Mum was in the armchair, smiling at her.

'What do we do, Mum?'

She said nothing, just smiled.

'Please Mum, how do we get out?'

Nothing.

'Mum, stay with me, I need you. Come with me ... we've got to get out ...'

Just that smile. Then, slowly, the older woman's arm lifted. She looked beautiful. The lines on her face had gone; she was young and pretty once again. Makeup perfect, hair neat.

'Mum ...'

Abby moved towards her. The water was around her legs, though, and it was difficult to walk. There was something stopping her.

'Please Mum, let's go ...'

Her mother lifted her arm again. This time, slowly, gracefully, she beckoned to her only child.

'Abby ...'

She tried to reach her, but something was pulling her back.

'Abby ...'

'I'm trying, Mum, I'm trying to get to you ...'

It was no good. She couldn't move.

273

'Abby . . .'

'Come to me instead, Mum, we've got to leave this place . . .'

The petrol would have to be running low by now. Marcus had reached another buoy, but the wreck was nowhere to be seen.

In desperation, he tried shouting.

'Abby, are you there?'

Nothing.

He bellowed. 'Abby . . .'

Silence.

He began to feel a little stupid. There was no logical reason to expect to find anything at all out here, let alone some girl who may or may not have been abducted. Maybe that blow to the head had made him stop thinking properly.

This is ridiculous, he decided. I'll get back, take the tide to Queenborough, face the music about taking the dinghy and get a lift out when it's dawn.

He pulled to the left to turn. More flashing lights. Better just check them out on the way back. No harm in trying.

'Abby!'

Nothing.

The water was up to her middle now. Still Mum was silent.

'Won't you come with me?'

Her mother shook her head.

Abby felt a tear roll down her cheek. 'Then I have to go.'

She turned away from her mother and opened her eyes.

It was dark. Cold, very cold. And wet. Her arms and legs hurt like hell. Abby looked down. There was water all around her, lapping at her. She tried to pull herself away, but couldn't move.

Quickly, she looked at her hands. They were tied together around some metal pole. Her legs, too. And there was something around her waist, holding her in place.

274

Jesus, it was cold out here.

The water was a bit higher already.

Abby started to cry.

The tide was beneath him now that he'd turned back, and Marcus knew that the boat would be moving much faster. Goodness knew how he was going to explain himself to the owner. Being a vicar could only help so much.

He could see the line of buoys in front of him. They were approaching much quicker now that he was moving with the tide, compared with the slog of getting to them. He was slightly out of channel, just in case any shipping came out. He'd passed one of the extra buoys. Nothing to see.

The dory juddered. A metallic scrape. Shit, I've hit a boat in the dark. He waited for it. A huge black hull would be next, pushing right through him and the little dory. That would be it. Curtains.

Silent again, no other motor to be heard. Thank God, must have been some floating debris rather than another boat.

He looked at his watch. 1.15. No wonder he felt so dog tired.

Another crunch. Marcus looked up.

In front of him was a mast. It was dead still, hung with seaweed, coming up out of the sea like his worst nightmare. His heart seemed to stop for a moment.

I've bloody well crashed into it! This has to be the wreck.

Then he heard a low sobbing to his left.

Quickly, he turned the boat towards the sound, following it.

'Abby?'

No response, but still the sobbing. He was so close now. She had to be there, in the dark.

'Abby! Answer me, for God's sake.'

'Marcus?'

He was close to the ship again, any minute now there would be another mast . . . Yes! And Abby was on it!

'I've got you . . . I'm coming . . .'

Quickly, he tied the dory to the mast and leapt off it. The water came up to his thighs.

There were ties around her wrists. Shit, he'd not brought a knife.

'Just let me untie you.'

'Marcus, thank God . . .'

He couldn't see the bloody knots. No idea what he was doing. Bugger, bugger. Stay calm, every knot can be undone in the end.

One slipped free.

'My waist.'

He felt down. It was harder, this rope, pulled tight as it would go. There was no slack to get his fingers under, to start untying it.

Shit, shit.

Don't panic. There's a good hour yet before the tide becomes a problem for her. Just keep trying.

He checked his watch: 1.35.

The worst thing you can do with a knot is hurry. Just work calmly. He forced himself to breathe steadily. Try this loop under, yes, now feels like there's a twist . . .

Suddenly, she was free, falling away from the mast. He caught her. She was cold as death, past shivering.

'Into the dory, let's move . . .'

She almost fell into the dinghy and he started up the motor. Get away now, get somewhere warm. as he held the tiller, he struggled out of his thick jumper.

'Put this on, Abby. You need to get warm quickly.'

Gratefully, she pulled it over herself.

'Where are we?'

'You were on the *Richard Montgomery*. God knows how you got there.'

'I was with him, Antoine . . . He locked me in his room, then I was here . . .'

They were back in the deepwater channel now, sweeping down with the tide. The lights of Sheerness were brighter, closer. Marcus made directly for them, cutting the corner to save time. The book had mentioned a sandbank just about here, but in a shallow boat on the rising tide, he should be OK.

There was a scraping sound and the dory came to a halt.

'Aground ... Shit ...'

'What do we do?'

'The tide's coming in now. If we get the boat back into the water, we'll try and bump our way round to Sheerness, I need to get you into—'

Suddenly, behind them the night sky erupted. Everything turned the most brilliant white, as though a strobe had momentarily flickered across the whole of the Estuary.

They both spun around. There was another blinding flash during which it was brighter than daylight for several seconds. Then, a low rumble, growing to a crescendo roar, so loud they had to cover their ears. On it carried, deafening. They could feel the noise as much as hear it.

Abby turned to Marcus. The sky lit up again, so bright that she could see every line on his face.

He grabbed her hand.

'It's the wreck. It's going up! It's full of explosives ...'

Abby could only stare back at the source of the light. Then there was a new sound, deep, very deep, something which they felt as much as heard. Constant, getting louder, louder ...

Marcus shouted, 'Lie down, quick. Hold on tight to the edge of the dory ... there will be a wave any moment, one hell of a wave ...'

Abby stood still, rooted to the spot.

Quickly, Marcus pushed her down onto the bottom of the dory. Then he lay on top of her, holding her still with his body.

She was about to protest, then she felt the boat lift. It was as though it had been picked up by a hand and turned around and around. It was moving forward now, floating on top of a wall of water. But Marcus was heavy on top of her, gripping hard, shouted at her to stay with it, it was just the pressure wave, it would go.

And it did. The dory had stopped, pushed a hundred metres up the shore. The sky was still light. In the distance she could see the outline of the wreck. It was burning, an orange haze enveloping it. Every now and then there was another explosion, smaller this time. She'd never seen anything like it. The scale was outside her powers of imagination. It was the only truly awesome thing she'd ever seen in her life.

She started to tremble.

'I should have been on that. My God, I should have been on that.'

Chapter Thirty-One

DC Peters looked carefully at the girl. Remarkably relaxed considering what she'd just been through. She'd been taken to hospital in Kent with mild hypothermia and had slept for twenty hours. Now, she was restless, champing at the bit. The resilience of youth, he thought to himself. The vicar had brought her in, as promised. That man was a hero. Without him, there would be another murder and not a shred of evidence.

'It's just that I haven't had a chance to speak to Mr Waters . . . I'd been told he was dead. I really need to see him . . .'

'I need to get a statement from you now, before anything gets forgotten.'

Abby sighed and settled back into the chair at the police station. She was shattered, wanted to see Seb, make sure for herself that he really was alive, that this wasn't some cruel joke fate had played. Marcus had explained it all in the ambulance, before her long, long sleep, but still, she had to get there.

DC Peters smiled. 'Tell you what. If you let me take the statement now, I'll drive you straight over to the hospital myself.'

Abby nodded. 'OK. What do you need to know?'

She took him through what had happened.

'This Frenchman, can you describe him?'

He took out his list of mug shots. Pages of them, a directory of England's most wanted criminals.

She scanned the pages quickly. Nothing.

Then she paused. Second line down, page seven.

'That's him.'

'Sure?'

'Completely.'

Peters nodded to himself. Brilliant: Pascal de Montchavin. They'd had some intelligence on his latest drug deals with George Ellsworth last year. They had ample now to pot him for kidnapping and attempted murder.

But they really wanted him for the bombing; for the murder of Duncan Dinkwater and Abraham James. If he'd been carrying around a photo of Abby Penhaligon, if she'd given it to him . . . it could just be enough to place him at the scene.

He could remember picking the photo out of the wreckage of the conference room. Then he'd not been able to read the writing on the back. But forensics had.

Abigail Elizabeth Penhaligon.

It could be the link he needed.

'I'm going to ask you to look at this.'

He passed the photograph to Abby. She looked at it, astonished.

'But . . . it's my mother . . . and me, as a baby.'

'Was it your photo?'

'I have a copy, but I keep it at home. Unless it was taken, but I haven't been burgled . . .' She looked at the officer. 'How did you get it?'

'It was found in the conference room after the explosion . . . I'd wondered if you'd given it to anyone?'

She shook her head.

'No. The one that I have is always kept at home. I'd never give it to anyone – it's too precious to me. I just don't understand . . .'

The officer sat back, disappointed.

'Well, have a check at home, just to make sure. It could mean something.'

Abby drummed her fingers as DC Peters drove to the hospital. Every light in London seemed to be on red. At least, every single one that they had to go through.

He took her up to the ward.

'If you could let me know when you've finished, I'd like a word with Mr Waters too, if he's up to it.'

Abby nodded and knocked on the door. A nurse appeared, smiling. 'Just a few minutes, mind.'

Seb was in a small bay off the main unit, sitting up, watching the entrance.

'Abby . . .'

She walked quickly over to the bed.

Suddenly, it was too much. She'd been fighting it ever since she'd got to the hospital. Tears started to prick at the back of her eyelids and her hands shook uncontrollably.

'Seb, he told me you'd died . . . it was just horrendous . . .'

He reached for her hand, grinning slightly.

'I'm fine. They can't get rid of me that easily, you know.'

Abby sniffed.

'It's OK. We've made it. Everything's going to be fine, Abby.'

She nodded. 'Yes. I'm just so . . . when he said you'd died, I really . . .'

He squeezed her hand and she continued.

'That French bastard – he must have been targetting me. Did you know that they even found a photo of me in the room after the bomb – he must have stolen it from my flat somehow, broken in when I wasn't there.'

Seb's voice was very quiet. 'Did you see the photograph?'

'Yes. The police showed it to me. I had it at home, it was my mother's.'

He looked at her and gently shook his head.

281

'It was my photograph, Abby.'

She paused for a moment, watching him carefully.

'Yours?'

'I found it a few days ago, clearing out my father's things.'

She tried to smile. 'Now I'm really starting to get confused.'

He waited a moment before speaking.

'Abby, I'd planned to tell you all this later ... Your mother sometimes used different names, didn't she?'

Abby frowned.

'Sometimes, I'd change my name for a while. It was a bit like dressing up, I could take on a whole new persona. I was Sophie one year, Ellie another ... it was a laugh, it really was.'

It was as though her mother was in the room with her at that moment.

'One name she used for a while was Ellie.' Seb's tone was low, controlled.

Abby could feel her pulse starting to race. Involuntarily, she nodded.

'She did say sometimes that when she was much younger, she used to pretend ... said it was a bit like dressing up. But I don't see why ...'

Seb took a deep breath and looked beyond Abby, his eyes focusing on the room behind her.

'Your mother and I were lovers for a while, back in the seventies.'

Abby could feel the colour drain from her face. Suddenly, she felt as though she was living outside her body, a visitor to the scene being played out in front of her. It would run to a predetermined script. She knew what the outcome would be, but she really wasn't a participant any more.

'Please, don't be shocked. I loved your mother more than anyone I've ever known since. She worked in my village for a summer, I was just about to leave for university, she was calling herself Ellie.'

282

He was looking directly at her again, frowning slightly. Abby tried to smile, but found, all of a sudden, that she had no control over her expression.

'Your mother moved on at the end of summer, and I went off to university. I didn't hear anything more. Then, last week, going through my father's things, I found a letter from her. From your mother. She'd had a baby. Didn't want anything from me, just wanted me to know.'

He paused, his eyes moist and red.

'My parents never told me, Abby. I never knew that she was pregnant, that she'd had a child. God, I was so angry . . .'

Abby spoke slowly and carefully. 'And that child was me.'

'Yes. That's why I had the photo. I wanted to talk to you after the conference, explain to you . . .'

'Explain what?'

She knew exactly what. But she had to hear it from him. Make him say it. Acknowledge her.

Seb looked at her hard. God, he'd wanted to tell her ever since he'd found out. Thought about this moment constantly. He'd come back from the brink to do this, he knew it. Somewhere deep inside his unconscious self, he had had to come back and tell her. Claim her. His only child. He took a deep breath before continuing.

'Explain to you, Abby, that I'm your father.'

Abby closed her eyes. She felt a torrent of emotions: turbulent, contradictory, violent. Anger, for sure. She'd hated this anonymous man for most of her life; this man who'd not lifted a finger to help her mother, who'd left her to live courtesy of state handouts in a rented house with a leaky roof and no central heating.

But at the same time she felt pride. This brilliant man was her father – it seemed unbelievable. And she felt secure, too. There was still a parent there for her, someone on her side through no matter what. God, it was all too much.

283

She opened her eyes slowly. He was watching her still, his eyes worried. He'd nearly died. If he had, she'd never have known. Her heart went out to him. Perhaps she hated him when he was just some anonymous figure, but now, here, in the flesh . . .

And Mum had loved him too. Yes. She had loved this man.

That decided it.

When she finally spoke, her voice was low, but clear.

'I can't quite believe it . . . It'll take some time – but thank God we've found each other.'

Marcus sat back in the comfortable chair at Dinkwater & Co. He read through the statement – the dying declaration of Henry Jenkins, his belief that the man had been of sound mind and was speaking the truth.

He signed his name at the end. Leave had been granted. The appeal would be listed in the early months of next year.

And then there was the little matter of payment. Twenty thousand to Abby and to Sebastian Waters, QC. She'd never know where it came from.

The *Richard Montgomery* had indeed been carrying some extra cargo: tobacco. Twenty thousand pounds worth, at black market prices. It was an easy way to make money in those days. Tobacco was plentiful in the States, but fetched silly money in wartime Britain.

Jenkins had got himself on to the boat the day after it was abandoned. He'd suspected there might be some goodies on board and didn't mind taking a risk or two.

And he'd struck gold. Or something just as profitable. So, under cover of a curfew he'd imposed to stop looting, he'd had a clear run. He had plenty of contacts and had sold the tobacco on at a vast profit. It had allowed him to retire early from the force and set up in the building business. He'd gone from strength to strength in the post war reconstruction boom. And all of it on contraband.

But a journalist had got on to him whilst he still had the

tobacco under the floorboards at his house. There had been a rumour, and the man wouldn't let go of it. He was getting too close to the truth; it was only a matter of time. If Henry Jenkins were to be discovered, it would have meant ruin. In a position of trust, looting a ship would have resulted in prison.

So, Jacobs had had to go. Henry had set things up, arranging to be the investigating officer that night. It had worked like a dream. He'd had a real stroke of luck when he'd found out that James had had the hots for his boss's wife. It had been so easy, in the end.

But it was a strange thing, guilt. He'd got on with his life, building the business for the next few decades. But with retirement and time came the images that plagued him so much: murdering another man, watching him die, dragging the corpse into the other man's room. The dreams started to come nightly. He'd started drinking to the point of unconsciousness every evening to stop them. But that had just made things worse. His wife went, the children avoided seeing him.

And still the images came. They started to torture him in the day, and there was nothing he could do about it. He'd lived on to a good age – it was a further punishment to him.

The only way out was to kill himself.

But he was a Catholic, and it was a mortal sin. He'd go to hell. Unless he could repent and try to make amends.

That was why he had gone to see Marcus. And why he'd given the vicar every penny he'd possessed. He'd got through rather a lot, mind you. But there was forty thousand left.

Marcus looked at his watch. Better make a move. Abby would be expecting him. The officer had said he'd take her home after the interview. Better catch up with her there.

Abby and Marcus sat in silence for some time after dinner. It had been perfect. He'd cooked for them both on the old Aga, and they'd eaten together slowly, talking, listening, watching.

The first chill of autumn had appeared from nowhere, swirling still green leaves from the trees in the London parks. Marcus had lit a fire in the Victorian grate and it cast cheerful shadows around the walls of the Vicarage.

'And where to, now?'

Abby was to wish she'd never asked that question. Marcus paused a moment.

'I've had a job offer. I want to take it.'

Lazily, Abby turned towards him.

'You've already got a job.'

'I know. This is different. A drug rehabilitation scheme.'

She nodded. 'Where?'

'Edinburgh.'

Her eyes opened wide.

'Marcus . . . why the hell . . .?'

He looked away from her, into the fire.

'Because I have to.'

'Why?'

He sighed and stood up. Silently, he padded towards the grate.

'It's a long time ago. I knew a girl, Jennifer. She was a junkie. I could have done something for her, got her out of the mess she was in, Abby . . . she died. It was an overdose.'

He picked up the poker and started to prod the logs. A flame burned suddenly and brightly around them. Abby waited a few moments.

'Why is going to Edinburgh going to help?'

'If I can just turn someone round . . . somehow, maybe, I'll be able to live with myself. I just can't at the moment. I should have done something earlier to help her.'

Abby stood up and walked over towards the fire. She knelt opposite him and took the poker from his hands.

'Marcus, it won't make you feel better at all. I don't know what you think you could have done, but what's happened can't be changed. You can't spend the rest of your life torturing yourself about it.'

He looked into the fire as she continued.

'Marcus, what about the rest of us? Isn't it a bit self-indulgent to swan off to Edinburgh to save the world when the rest of us would rather like you to stay?'

He looked up at her.

'Who, in particular?'

She sighed.

'Me, you stupid, daft man. How do you think I'll bloody well feel? Well hello Abby, let me give you this brilliant case, take you out, save your life—'

He stopped her quickly. 'Now you're sounding self-indulgent. You're not the only person in this world, you know . . .'

'So we're two of a kind. Takes one to know one.'

'Abby, it's no good . . .'

She glared at him.

'OK. Go and save the whole bloody world for all I care. Just remember, Saint Bloody Marcus, as you go around being a professional martyr that you've left a trail behind you now . . . I hope that helps you sleep at night.'

'Abby, I didn't mean . . .'

It was too late. The door had slammed. Marcus stared bleakly at it as he listened to her steps echoing across the hall. Moments later, he heard the front door open and then shut.

Chapter Thirty-Two

December 2000

'Abby, at last! Now the party can start properly!'

She grinned as she walked into the conference room. It was heaving with people. A glass of chilled champagne was thrust into her hand.

'Congratulations. Our new tenant – welcome on board.'

She grinned. 'Thanks Alex.'

He smiled back at her. 'You deserve it, Abby. Quite apart from the appeal, you've worked like a Trojan ever since you got here.'

He paused.

'I'm sorry, too, for being such a pain when you arrived . . . It was a difficult time for me . . .'

Abby laughed. 'I ought to disapprove, you know, Alex.'

'But you've met Lucinda . . .'

Abby thought back to the sherry party in the autumn. Thirty-five bloody minutes listening to the Hon. Lucinda drone on about her marvellous bloody gym and somebody's amazing curtains and wasn't it a shame how gels were never taught flower arranging any more. Maybe he had a point.

'Does she know? About Rita?'

Alex nodded. 'I admitted everything a few weeks ago. Couldn't take it any more.'

288

'What did she say?'

He paused.

'Well, funny thing was, she didn't say anything much. Just smiled, said she'd known for bloody ages, and Rita was at least saving her one domestic duty.'

Abby's hand went to her mouth. 'No!'

'Oh yes. So there seems to be the potential for accommodation, amazingly enough.'

'Well, Alex, what can I say? Other than where's Seb?'

'God only knows. I'm so glad he's back. Eight weeks as acting Head of Chambers has convinced me that I was mad to ever want the job myself. Can't wait for him to return full-time. Get on with my practice rather than all the crap we have to deal with now – Bar mark, advertising, equal bloody opportunities wherever you go. Thank God we've taken you on. Now there's two women, at least nobody can criticise us on that front.'

Abby grinned as he moved away. Some things would never change. Smiling at the faces around her, acknowledging the congratulations, she moved towards a sofa at the end of the room and sank gratefully into it.

It had been one hell of a six months. With Seb off sick, and too much work already in Chambers, she'd been run off her feet. She'd been in court every day bar two, and had drafted three hundred sets of pleadings. She'd developed a routine: up at five, do the paperwork. Then off to Court, usually somewhere in the Home Counties. There had been two days in Truro, though. That had been interesting: always the completely irrational hope that Marcus would be visiting his parents and she would just happen to bump into him outside the courthouse … a girl could dream, after all.

Then back to Chambers as soon as the court rose, and pick up the papers for the next day. Home for a bite to eat with Seb, then open the pink ribbon and get ready for tomorrow. She'd rarely finish her preparation before eleven at night. Off to bed for a few hours, and then the whole thing started all over again.

289

She was exhausted. But, as Ron said, either the solicitors wanted you or they didn't. It was a whole lot better to be wanted than rejected. Which brought her back to Marcus. There had been letters from him, dozens of them. Sorry for the row, just let me do my own thing for a bit. Blah blah blah.

She hadn't replied. She had no idea what to say, and in the blur of work it had been easier to keep putting things off for another week. In a way, she was glad she had kept quiet. If she'd written earlier, when her feelings were at their most raw, she would have been a complete cow. He didn't deserve that.

'You're not the only one in the world you know.'

She had replayed the row thousands of times since the end of the summer. She wanted to kick herself. There he was, desperate to do something to sort himself out, and she'd tried to insist he stayed. Just because she wanted him to. What sort of a monster had she become?

She'd agonised about it to Seb. He'd come to stay for a while after he'd been discharged from hospital. They'd both squeezed into her tiny flat and had had a great time. His Suffolk house was on the market now. A new start, he'd called it. Get rid of all those memories, do what he wanted for a bit. Crazy to spend hours on a train going into London each day, only to catch another train out to some distant court once he got there. Abby had helped him find the flat in the Barbican. World-class music on his doorstep, and he could walk to Chambers every day.

They'd talked long into the night, often both waking up cold in their armchairs. And gently, carefully, he had brought her round. Marcus had a need which had to be met. She must understand that, give him his chance. And maybe, just maybe, she was a little self-centred.

For this, he took the blame. And that made it easier for her to understand that, in fact, he was probably right. Just her and Mum, with no extended family, had worked. But it had created a little vacuum: an hermetically sealed environment with just two important occupants. And when one of them died, what else was there in the world of the one who was left?

Finding Seb was changing all that. She had another parent, knew about her grandparents, too. And finding her feet in Chambers had helped. Working those long hours, travelling up and down the country; at last she was fulfilling her own dreams. And with that new security came something else – an ability, finally, to examine the world through the eyes of others.

'Darling . . .'

She opened her eyes slowly and smiled at her father.

'Seb . . . I wondered where you were.'

'Just meeting someone at the airport . . .'

He stood aside, muttering something about getting a drink. And there was Marcus.

'Marcus!'

And he was grinning, grinning like she'd never seen before, holding out his arms to her. In a moment, she was in them.

'My God, I never thought I'd see you again!'

He laughed. 'Little chance of that. Why did you ignore my letters?'

She spoke into his left shoulder.

'I just don't know what to say.'

'Lucky your father did, then . . .'

'He did what? But you, why, how, I mean . . .'

'What am I doing here, you mean?'

'Yes.'

'Flying visit, literally, to congratulate you on getting your tenancy . . . I'm here tonight, going back tomorrow.'

She grinned at him.

'How's Edinburgh?'

'Cold. But Abby . . . I'm sorry I was so uptight about it, but I did have to go. And it's helped me. Something happened there – I'll tell you about it another time, but I was meant to go there. Really.'

291

He paused and looked at her.

Those eyes, she thought, not for the first time. God, I could lose myself in them. Sit and watch him all night. What the hell did I ever see in the Frenchman?

'But now I might be coming back. In the New Year. there's a new scheme at King's Cross they want me to run. I want to say yes . . . but . . .'

'But what?'

'I came to ask you wether you want me, really. I mean, it's your right to tell me where to get off, especially the way I just swanned off, as you so elegantly put it.'

'But I understand now – really.'

'I've got a lot off my chest. And I can come back in the New Year. But only if you want me.'

'How do you mean?'

'I want to come back, because being away for a bit has allowed me to think. And the one thing that you ought to know is that I'm in love with you.'

At that moment, Abby completely forgot where she was. Her arms encircled him, and she drew his face close to hers. The smell of him was quite delicious. All of a sudden, she was kissing him, and he was kissing her back, gently at first, then less so.

They stopped for a moment and looked at each other. He grinned at her.

'We're two of a kind, Abby, just like you said. Too long out on the limb, both of us. Dogmatic, egocentric, opinionated. But we both know it now. I've dealt with my demons; you've found your place, finally. We could be fantastic together if we took our chance.'

She nodded, unable to speak for a moment.

'I just wanted to give you the chance to say no, tell me to get lost. I will, still, if you really want me to.'

She grinned. 'Oh no. Never Marcus.'

Their eyes were still locked onto each other. It was at that moment that they realised the room was now silent. Thirty-two pairs of eyes were examining them quizzically.

But they didn't care any more. Their moment had come and they were both seizing it for all they were worth.

'I love you too, Marcus.'

And with that, they started kissing again.

Epilogue

January 2001

Isobel Jacobs always read her *Times*. She might be seventy-five years of age, but she was as fit as a flea, mentally as well as physically. It was delivered daily to the residential home on the Devon coast where she'd lived for the past three years.

Her eyes scanned the headlines: another European crisis; currency fluctuations. She turned to page three. Her eyes fell upon the headine.

Abraham James. Murder conviction overturned.

Her pulse started to quicken and she read the article. At the end, she breathed out slowly.

He hadn't done it. He was innocent.

All those years. They could have been together all this time.

Somewhere, deep down, she'd known it always. She'd had her child, a little girl, Louise. Brought her up well, worked in the City now, and visited when she could.

But Abraham . . . she still yearned for him. She knew now, he had been the love of her life. Tall, slim, intense – she'd fallen in love the first time she'd met him. Funny how these things seemed so much clearer in retrospect. But he was dead now, said the report. The years they could have spent together, the fun they could have enjoyed, the children they might have had . . .

She put down her paper, suddenly very tired. She was old, too old now. And alone, much too alone. The light was streaming in, reflecting off the sea outside, but inside, right in the depths of Isobel's soul, it was dark as pitch. It always would be now.

A life not lived as it should have been. Her only love, lost for ever. She should have believed him, stuck by him. It was preposterous. Abraham, the gentlest person she had ever met, could never have murdered a man in a million years. Why, then, had she believed them?

She should have trusted her own judgement, had faith in herself. He'd left jail years back, the report had said. They could have had some time together, at least. Even a few snatched weeks would have been better than a lifetime like this.

Isobel sighed. Slowly, a tear escaped from her eye. Too tired, now. Maybe they would be together some time soon.